The Price of Escape

The Price of Escape

BY DAVID UNGER

This is a work of fiction. Certain liberties have been taken regarding historical events and characters for the sake of the narrative. All other names, characters, places, and incidents are the product of the author's imagination.

Published by Akashic Books
©2011 David Unger

ISBN-13: 978-1-936070-92-3
Library of Congress Control Number: 2010939104
All rights reserved

First printing

Akashic Books
PO Box 1456
New York, NY 10009
info@akashicbooks.com
www.akashicbooks.com

To Anne: *whose love and devotion continues to nourish me.*
To Andrea: *for her critical eye, friendship, and support.*
In memory of Luis, my father (1898–1991).

He never forgets himself
In what he feels,
So that he never feels anything great.
—André Gide

PROLOGUE

Samuel Berkow could have sent one of the clerks to check on why the Martin belts hadn't been delivered to the store just yet, but he wanted to go out. The warehouse was in the St. Pauli district near the Elbe shipyards a short distance away. Despite the whorehouses and raucous bars, Samuel liked the docks. It was the only place where he could feel some resistance to the Nazis; at least the fed-up workers still had the guts to protest.

Though it was June, the sun was nowhere to be seen. In fact, it felt like a day in January. It wasn't raining, but there was smoke and fog everywhere and it seemed as if soot belched by the cargo ships and factories was drizzly dripping down the sides of the buildings. Samuel walked quickly, past the fish shops and restaurants, and more than a few beer joints and cheap hotels that lined the dreary streets to the river. When he was still a few blocks from the docks, he saw the tower of the Landungsbrücken building on the shores of the Elbe. The clock marked four o'clock. He would be seeing his Uncle Jacob at seven.

The port area, after sundown, was a dangerous place for anyone who didn't belong. It was full of sailors, spies, and agents, not to speak of thieves and muggers who preyed on the emigrants, many of whom were from Eastern Europe and paid exorbitant prices to live in the hotels. They hid gold and silver sewn inside their jackets, which they would give to dubious smugglers who promised to get them on ferries to London or Rotterdam.

It was here near the Überseebrücke jetty on the waterfront square where the radio had said trouble was brewing. It reported that one of the

munitions factories was running well short of its quota and some workers—
Communists and anarchists, the radio commentator had said—were claiming they had been working nonstop. They hadn't been paid for five weeks
or given a single day off—so they said—and felt that they had been unduly
asked to sacrifice for the soldiers on the front.

When Samuel reached the square, he saw trouble. A group of workers
in green overalls had gathered in front of the customs and shipping offices
near the Landungsbrücken building and erected a makeshift stage out of
pallets and plywood taken from the nearby warehouses. Speakers were hec-
toring the workers, stirring them up.

A dozen stevedores in blue outfits soon joined the factory workers from
the shipyards on the other end of the square. Samuel, wearing a raincoat
over his suit, looked out of place here, and so he decided to watch the
demonstration from under a wooden canopy by an empty loading dock. To
his right he saw two other men watching the demonstration; one of them
leisurely smoked a cigarette on the running board of a black car and looked
through binoculars, while the other spoke animatedly into a wireless radio—
he seemed to be reporting on what he saw.

Otherwise, the square was ominously empty.

From where he stood, Samuel could see that the demonstrators had
sticks, pipes, and wooden struts in their hands. A few were brave enough to
carry signs protesting the lack of pay or brandishing a gigantic clenched fist.

Mass gatherings had been prohibited by the authorities and on several
occasions strikers and protesters had been beaten and shot. They were pro-
voking the government. Nothing good would come of this.

Suddenly the wind blew hard and the voices grew quiet. Samuel heard
the creaking and jangling of wires from the cranes in the shipyard across
the river and one or two foghorns sounding in the distance. The snapping
of the flags that flew above and from the standards of many buildings could
also be heard.

Samuel felt his blood beating faster and then heard a rumbling behind
him. The noise grew increasingly louder until his eardrums vibrated. The

first thing he saw was the boots, almost in unison, pounding the cobblestones like the running of bulls. And then he saw a dozen men with Nazi armbands passing him with billy clubs and rifles in their hands.

If he had crossed their path, they would have trampled him.

A larger group of policemen appeared, rushing the protesters from across the square. They seemed to come out of nowhere, but clearly they had been hiding in the Altereb Tunnel connecting Hamburg to the other docks across the Elbe. They had been waiting for the signal to charge.

The stevedores suddenly moved back, pulled out their guns, and began firing at the workers as well. They were surrounded now, with nowhere to escape. Bullets and billy clubs started flying and the workers did all they could to protect themselves with their sticks and signs. One or two tried to scale the walls of the customs building and were shot down. Sirens sounded and five or six jeeps with soldiers pulled into the square.

But the soldiers weren't needed. The massacre was over. Samuel could see only shadows because of the blue smoke and fog, but he knew that thirty to forty men had been mowed down.

Just then a man and a boy came into the square holding hands, wearing dark suits, white shirts, and black hats. Samuel made a vague gesture to try to get them to turn back, but they were striding quickly and talking to each other. He saw the Nazi with the wireless radio wink to his colleague before pulling a gun out of his coat pocket. Without hesitating, he fired three or four shots point-blank and the Hasidic Jews staggered to the ground.

Samuel fell back against the wall. He heard laughter and clapping. His throat and tongue were dry, his chest ached. He couldn't believe what had just happened. Two people killed in a flash, like ashes flicked from a cigarette.

He felt disgust, but there was nothing he could do. If the Nazis had seen him, he too would've been killed.

When the car drove off, Samuel turned up his collar and hurried back to the store the way he had come. He would be seeing his Uncle Jacob in a few hours. What would he tell him? That he had come within an inch of being killed, or that the Martin belts had never made it from England?

* * *

"Come in, come in," Jacob welcomed his nephew into the foyer of his apartment hours later. His reading glasses were perched on his deeply lined forehead. He helped Samuel off with his raincoat and hung it on the metal rack behind the front door. "What's it like outside?"

Samuel knew that his uncle was not referring to the Hamburg weather. "You know that I wear it more for warmth than rain—"

"Stop it. You know what I'm talking about. What I heard on the radio."

Samuel sucked his teeth. "There was a big confrontation between factory workers and the S.S. Several men were killed near the docks; at least that's what I heard."

"Last week it was a Nazi rally claiming that no country in the world wanted to accept the Polish Jews that Hitler was only too happy to deport. You mix beer with stupidity and before you know it, ten Jews are dead."

Samuel shook his head, saying nothing of what he had seen.

"The only power we have left is to leave—and even that is quickly disappearing," his uncle went on. He led Samuel by the hand toward the den where he and his cousins were never allowed to play when they were kids. The room hadn't changed much: the old peeling upright, never played now; the bookcases filled with dusty tomes in gold and brown leather; and the two armchairs where his father and uncle sat when they needed to discuss things privately. On the wall were two Dürer etchings of a printing press seen from different angles.

His uncle called out as they passed the kitchen: "Lottie, bring the tea to the den. Two cups. My nephew's here. And any of those English toffee cookies we have left."

"Yes, Herr Berkow," she called back.

Samuel took the blue chair his father normally occupied. Jacob sat down across from him. He removed his glasses from his head and placed them on the table. "I've called you over, Samuel, because any day you'll be arrested. I want you to leave Germany now."

The curtains had been drawn back and pinned behind hooks. The cool

June air entered the room; his uncle always left the windows slightly open. Samuel could see the row of chestnut trees that lined Lutterothstrasse down below his Uncle Jacob's apartment. Across the street was a small park full of linden trees. Samuel had played with his cousins in the park, holding on to the iron bars laughing and squealing as the red carousel spun. It had been a more innocent time.

He wanted to tell his uncle what he had seen, but he couldn't. "I don't know if I'm ready to leave."

Jacob put his hand on Samuel's leg. "I've written to Heinrich to tell him you're coming. Guatemala City is obviously not Hamburg, but Heinrich seems to think it is a welcoming environment for Jews in general. One thing is certain: you can't stay here. I've already bought your ticket for the boat to Panama."

"Uncle Jacob, don't you think I have a say in this? I'm a grown man."

"I promised your father to keep an eye on you. There's no other choice."

"I could go stay with my mother and sister in Palma. Mallorca is quiet and Franco is ignoring Hitler's orders to arrest Jews."

His uncle shook his head. "You have to leave Europe, Samuel. Once Franco consolidates power, he will begin rounding Jews up." Jacob shifted in his armchair, trying to find a more comfortable position. "Besides, your mother's coming back to Hamburg this week. I've tried to dissuade her, but she and your sister, well, they are so much alike that they can't get along. Ha ha. Two years with your sister is enough. I'm sure you know what I mean," he said smiling.

Samuel nodded. He didn't understand his mother. Why had she refused to come back for her husband's funeral after thirty-five years of marriage?

"There's no future for you here."

"And what will you do, Uncle?" Samuel asked, trying to change the subject. "Will you join Erna and Greta in London?"

Jacob was dressed in the same three-piece herringbone suit he had worn to work two days earlier. The only change was that he now wore black slippers instead of shoes. "No, I want to stay and keep watch over the store.

The moment I leave, the Nazis will confiscate everything just like they did in Berlin. And you can forget about compensation—all the time and money your father, God rest his soul, invested will be gone."

"If I can leave, Uncle, so can you."

"I'm an old man. What's the point of moving to London now? The change alone would kill me. No, I am staying here. Besides, I need to get your mother out."

"That's my responsibility."

"No, no, no," his uncle replied. "You remind her too much of your father. I've already begun making plans for her to go to Cuba with her sister. I will get her out, I promise you, on the *St. Louis*."

Lottie came in carrying a tray with a covered teapot, two mismatched cups, and a small plate of toffee cookies. She had arrived from Leipzig thirty years ago—already thin and tired—and had grown only thinner and more tired over the years. When Jacob's wife Gertie died years ago, she became a family fixture, taking care of Jacob, along with his son and three daughters. Now that all the children were gone, Lottie was in charge of him.

Jacob stood up to take the tray from her hand. "You can go now, Lottie. It's late."

The maid looked down at Samuel and offered a faint smile, barely an acknowledgment. He couldn't understand how his uncle tolerated her all these years since she was always in a bad mood. She rarely talked and when she did, she snapped.

"Your dinner is on the stove—corned beef and cabbage. If you don't eat it by eight o'clock, it will be a soggy mess."

"Thank you," Jacob said, tapping her hand and putting the tray on the butler's table. "I will see you tomorrow at nine, as usual."

"As usual," she echoed, taking the cover off the pot and pouring the tea into their cups—it was mint tea, the family tradition.

The sweet aroma comforted Samuel.

As soon as the maid was out of earshot, his uncle said: "I've paid a lot to get you visas for Panama and Guatemala. At another time, this would be called a bribe. It may take a month, maybe more, to get them."

Samuel didn't know what to say. He had just witnessed murder. He had not foreseen the threat to the Jews of Germany till Kristallnacht. There had always been anti-Semitism—odd remarks, strange insinuations, even direct declarations—but the idea that hating or killing Jews could become state policy he could have not imagined. And there were rumors of camps where Jews were both starved and forced to work at hard labor. But he still didn't want to believe it—not in the Germany he had fought for, nearly died for, during the Great War.

"Himmler is just trying to impress Hitler."

Jacob raised an eyebrow. "Samuel, you yourself saw the bricks and crates being thrown through the windows of our Berlin store. The wives of our customers were there with their poodles, cheering and applauding . . . Himmler is the head of the S.S. He's the man behind it all. The architect of the Final Solution. Listen to me: you have to wake up, son. "

"I am awake, Uncle," Samuel said, bristling. He had half a mind to explain what he had just seen on the docks to both gauge his reaction and to convey that he knew exactly what was going on.

"I appreciate that you had a hard time of it during the war, your incarceration. Then the situation with Lena must have been very painful. May I be blunt?"

Samuel shrugged his shoulders.

"You're thirty-seven years old. When I was your age, I was already married with children. You walk around as if waiting for something to change your life and fill the big hole inside of you. We all love you, but this love will turn to pity unless you do something with your life. I know what I am telling you. You think your story is written, but it isn't. You'd be surprised at what you're capable of doing, if only you would stop being so cautious. I don't know, maybe those six months in the sanatorium after the war took the life out of you."

Samuel walked over to the window and looked out. The streetlights had been lit and he could see the tram stopping at the intersection of Lutterothstrasse and Hagenbeckstrasse. A few people clambered up the tram to head downtown. He had seen quite a bit—as a soldier, as a wounded veteran, as a buyer for his father's store after Hitler became president and chancellor. What his uncle said about him was true. He had seen too much unexpected suffering. What would another departure mean? If he left now, he would never return to Germany.

"I know your mother's angry your father left me the store, but after all, I was his partner. Your father knew I would look after you. Berta would give all the money to your sister or some stupid cause to save dachshunds or poodles."

"I've never understood my mother." Samuel knew this was a strange thing for a son to say, but his mother only showed emotion when she played Beethoven's *Appassionata* over and over again on the piano. She never touched human hands with as much feeling as she touched the piano keys. She was incapable of expressing affection, much less love. His father had deserved a hundred medals for putting up with her all those years.

Samuel sat back down and watched his uncle reach for the teapot. He missed the handle. Samuel had observed this at the store. His uncle's eyes were failing.

"Can I serve you more tea?"

His uncle waved him away. "I can take care of myself." He grabbed the teapot and poured the tea, hand shaking but hitting the target.

"Samuel, you should've been born with more guile."

"What do you mean, Uncle?"

Jacob smiled. "You're too trusting. You've always been. You're a good-hearted person, someone who believes there's a correct way to behave. You're what some people would call a straight arrow."

Samuel sipped the hot tea, then took a cookie and dipped it in the cup. His hand was shaking too, his scalp felt hot, but he would not contradict his uncle. "I will take that as a compliment."

Jacob smiled again. "Of course it is. Now take my son Heinrich. He's nothing like you—all guile and no heart."

"That's not fair, Uncle."

"Now, now, Samuel. I think I know my own son."

Though Samuel defended his cousin, Jacob was right. He was thinking now how he had contributed to Heinrich's suspicious nature. He had once left his cousin in the lurch, yet he had never owned up to it. In truth, Samuel had betrayed his cousin, and he knew that before Heinrich would lift a finger for him he would have to make amends for his betrayal—he would do it when they came together in Guatemala.

This is how it would have to be.

CHAPTER ONE

When the motorboat was flush against the tramp steamer's side, two dark-skinned deckhands dressed in filthy rags appeared. They held Samuel Berkow's leather suitcase, gray homburg, and umbrella as he climbed up the metal ladder to the top deck of the *Chicacao*.

"Thank you, thank you very much," he said to them nervously in English.

When Samuel extended his right hand, they stared at it floating in the air, bowed awkwardly, and moved off. When he called after them, they were already climbing down another ladder to still another lower level.

It was nighttime and Samuel was unsure of his next step. He placed his umbrella and hat on the suitcase and waited for the ship captain to greet him. Loose ropes, chains, spools of wire, rusting sprockets, wrenches, and half a dozen yellowing life preservers were piled around the central smoke-stack on the deck. It wasn't an old steamer, simply unkempt. It needed a good scrubbing, a new paint job, nothing like the ocean liner he had just left. Still, it was going to Puerto Barrios, Guatemala.

The 8,000-mile trip to the Panama coast on *Das Bauernbrot*, with its crystal chandeliers, Schubert waltzes, plush carpeted dining rooms, and stylish berths, had taken ten days, not enough time to leave Europe behind. The liner had allowed Samuel to continue remembering Hamburg at its best: its broad avenues; the Alster Pavilion teahouse where linzer torte and rote grütze were served on hand-painted china in the late afternoons; a boat trip on the Elbe; the Hagenbeck Zoo.

His wool suit was stifling. He loosened his tie, unbuttoned his coat and folded it across his forearm. He used the handkerchief he kept in his coat pocket to mop his forehead and the sweat pouring down his face.

Where the hell was he?

Suddenly, a short, greasy man appeared.

"I wasn't expecting any company on this trip," he began, grinning broadly, "but when my navigator mentioned on the radio broadcast that one of the passengers on the liner was in a rush to get to Guatemala, I said to myself, *Why not? I'm headed up the coast.* We'll anchor a bit north of here for the night. Say, you speak English?"

From the way the man talked, Samuel guessed he was from the United States. "I learned English when I was a prisoner of war in England—the Great War," Samuel said, raising a finger in the air. He wondered how this man would react if he picked up on the fact that he had fought on the German side against America.

"Before my time, I'm sure," the man chuckled. He had small, wet eyes and his cheeks hung from his face like little udders. The short sleeves of his shirt squeezed his upper arms. He looked like one of the typical brownshirts that shuffled drunk around the piers of Hamburg, sniffing the air for trouble, ready to brawl.

"The name's Alfred Lewis, but my friends call me Alf. That's quite an outfit you have on there, mister—were you on your way to the opera?" He let out another string of chuckles and stuck out his arm.

"Samuel Berkow. Pleased to meet you." Samuel shook his hand. Normally he would've had no business even talking to someone like Lewis—they clearly had nothing in common. "I should thank you for taking me on. I don't know what I would've done in Panama."

Lewis scrunched his face. "What everyone else does . . ."

"And what would that be?"

"Get fucked and get the fuck out of there!" he said laughing. "What the hell can you do in a place full of niggers and heat? Yeah, very well if you've got a plum job with the Canal Company, but shit, even the damn mosquitoes flee the place. Say, where you from? You have that funny kind of European accent."

"I'm from Germany."

"Not a yid, eh?"

"Yes," Samuel admitted. The last few years, with Hitler as chancellor, had conditioned him to hide the truth until there was no point in lying. But here in the New World he felt differently.

"Well, your people are all shipping out from Germany, Poland, and Russia. Guess they don't like the party in Europe—"

"I'd hardly call it a party," Samuel said.

"Ah, it won't come to nothing. I can't imagine that all that goose-step marching around and saluting will add up to much. Wait till *we* enter the war!"

"I hope you are right."

Lewis nodded. "Well, welcome aboard, Sammy. I'm from Pittsburgh, or was so originally, and now I'm a kind of glorified errand boy, if you will. For the last ten years I've been skirting up and down this coast, doing odd jobs for the Fruit Company." He stopped talking and wrapped his left arm around Samuel's waist. "Well, we can gab downstairs. I'll bet you're starved."

"I'm not really hungry."

"Well, you're just in time for chow. Come on down to the dining room. If you're not hungry, you can watch me eat!"

"What about my valise?" Samuel asked.

Lewis glanced down at the scuffed leather bag. "That's a what? A valise? Just leave it here. One of my boys'll bring it down."

"But—"

"Relax, Berkow," Lewis said, giving him a light tug. "I told you my boys will handle it. They have their instructions." He dropped his hand, waddled over toward the center of the deck, and hopped down the mid-ship stairs.

Eight steps down they entered a mahogany-paneled dining room lined with all kinds of navigational objects, brass gadgets, and several rows of trophies wired against the recently varnished walls. The room smelled of jasmine polish.

"A beautiful room," Samuel said, feeling uneasy, like an interloper at a private party.

"Yes, it's my pride. Some of these doodads go back three, four hundred years. Like this spyglass and compass, Bluebeard and Francis Drake stuff. I'm especially proud of these trophies. When you see my fat ass I bet you don't think of me as a great bowler, but back home I was the 'Sparemaker' because there weren't no split I couldn't make. I'll show you my technique later."

A sudden swell hit the boat, slamming Samuel into the wall.

Lewis shook his head. "You've got to roll with them, kind of sense when they're coming."

Almost immediately, another wave hit the boat—this time Samuel shifted a few steps, but didn't lose his footing.

"That's better, Mr. Sammy. Go on, sit down," Lewis said, taking the bench anchored to the wall. He craned his neck toward an opening on the right-hand side. "Lincoln, where's the grub? I'm hungry. And bring in another set of crockery and silverware for our guest!" Turning to Samuel, he added, "It ain't silver, but what the hell. It holds the food," and chuckled.

A barefoot boy, no more than fourteen, came out of the kitchen with a casserole which he placed on a metal plate in the center of the table. The smell of cooked fish and onions wafted into the air. He then placed a silver bell on the table and disappeared.

"So what brings you to Central America, Sammy boy?" Lewis asked, snagging a piece of fish from the casserole. "Love or fortune?"

"Neither, really. I'm looking to get a decent job—"

"I hope you're not planning to stay in Puerto Barrios—don't think I wouldn't mind the company of someone like you—but if you'll pardon my French, the town's a shithole."

"No—I'm going to Guatemala City. My cousin Heinrich lives there. I'm hoping he can help me get settled."

"Is that so," Lewis said, somewhat disinterestedly, ladling stew onto each of the plates.

Samuel picked up his fork, worked it into the sauce, and stabbed a chunk of fish. As he was about to stick the fork in his mouth, he glanced at Lewis wiping white sauce on his chin with a slice of bread and nearly gagged.

"Your cousin one of these coffee barons? I hear the Krauts own all the plantations in Guatemala."

"No, Heinrich runs a clothing store."

"Ah, I see, this fancy stuff runs in the family! I hope you don't mind my saying this, Berkow, but you Yids sure like to wear fine threads . . ."

"Yes," he replied, face flushing.

"I'm glad you told me. I really don't care if you're a Jew. Anyway, I'm pretty good at sniffin' these things out." He put more stew on his plate though he hadn't finished his original serving. "To my mind, Jews are people, that's what I always say. Zemurray, the Company boss up in Boston, is a Jew from Ruuumania! *Sam the Banana Man.* Now I know some people say he's uppity, but I don't think he's got a lease on that . . . Damn this fish—it's deee-licious. Snapper. That Lincoln Douglas is finally learning something."

Samuel said nothing.

If outward appearance determined character, then it seemed that Alfred Lewis had none. The clothiers in Germany taught their salesmen that people judged you by what you wore. All the same, Samuel was stuck with this man, for better or worse, for hours to come.

"I'd eat something if I were you."

"Actually, I had a late lunch on the ship before we reached Colón . . ." Samuel felt a bit deflated—why should he speak? Couldn't he just say he was exhausted, excuse himself, and go to his berth?

"Suit yourself. This could be your last good meal."

"That's what they said on *Das Baurenbrot.*"

"Was that the ship that brought you to Panama? Bet you ate well there. Four square meals a day. Must be something to travel in style, have all those penguins waiting hand and foot on you . . . Yeah, but that stuff isn't for me. I'm no good playing the fancy man, never was."

It wasn't just Lewis's crudeness but also those black rings on his neck. Samuel suspected the man wore dirt as he himself might wear a silk tie or a woolen scarf. Maybe Lewis believed that dirt was emblematic of his openness—he certainly flaunted it like someone would a diamond necklace.

Suddenly he stretched his arms and burped aloud. "Ah, nothing like bountiful chow to keep a man happy." Lewis looked at Samuel as if waiting for him to rekindle the conversation.

"What exactly is your line of work, Mr. Lewis?"

"Alf, Alf."

"Yes, Alf."

Lewis licked his lips. "You've of course heard of the United Fruit Company?"

"No, not until now."

"Them's my bosses. Puerto Barrios is home base, but I spend my time scooting along the ports of Guatemala, Honduras, Nicaragua, and Panama. I tell the home office what we need in terms of machinery and stuff like that—which one day I might explain to you. But mainly I oversee the ship-ment of bananas."

"And where are they shipped?"

"Well, they mostly go to New Orleans where they're weighed, pack-aged, and shipped to points north. But I do more than write numbers in a book. You see, the Company's a pretty complicated network—we operate railroads, steamship lines, plantations, commissaries—really whole towns, thousands of people. I make sure things go smoothly at port. If there's any trouble, I'm authorized to step in. Got my own telegraph system hooked up to this boat. Now I'm going to tell you something, Sammy. Nothing's off the table for me—strike busting, bribery, paying someone off to quell an insurrection." Lewis smacked his lips. "A man's got to do what he's got to do to keep the business operating . . . And you know, those kinds of things happen often . . ."

"I can imagine."

"You *better* imagine. Let me tell you another little secret. Why just last year we—that is, the Company—paid the president of the Guatemalan Congress eighty thousand smackeroos to swing votes our way on a bill that gave us exclusive leasing rights on fifty miles of land along the Motagua River. Fifty miles! You can grow quite a few bananas there, let me tell you. Enough to feed the whole United States. It was some stunt. The home office is still buzzing about it. Eighty thousand smackers."

"And you had something to do with that?"

"Ah, I can't take all the credit, but I played my role. Old Sam the Banana Man sent me a special commendation for my help and a bonus to boot."

"But aren't you afraid someone might try to blackmail you later?"

Lewis slid his plate under Samuel's untouched one. He stretched back, his black necklace glistening. "Afraid, Sammy? Why would I be afraid?" He exploded in laughter.

"In Germany those things aren't done. And if they are, well, no one would talk about them—certainly not to someone you just met."

"Hold your horses, Sammy boy. I've told you—you're not in Germany anymore, not for one minute. Why, you aren't even in the U.S. of A. This is a *different* world. Here, you grease a few palms—and I don't mean trees! A few dollars here and there and all of sudden, things that couldn't be done are done. Weakness gives the locals an excuse to walk all over you, and they will." Lewis's pupils contracted. "Let me tell you something: here you've got to be a fox, quick and sly! The natives are snappy, always looking for a way to get something from you. You've got to stay a step ahead of them. And then you have these busybody unionists—Communists by any other name—sneaking around, stirring up the locals. We're always on our toes. If they plan a field meeting, we invite the pickers to a barbecue, stuff like that. Why, you're a German! I'm sure you've had the same kind of problems back home. That Hitler guy, he knows how to deal with it."

"Excuse me, Mr. Lewis, but I don't think you can compare Hitler—"

Lewis cut him off. "It's not an easy problem to solve. The natives have nothing, or next to nothing, and the Reds offer them the sky. But the wise ones know darn well they either work for us at our wages or they starve—

and you know what, Berkow? They're right! Sure, we can try to help out—a school here, a hospital there—but what good will it do them? Most people only think with their stomachs or their peckers, and a couple of blows to the head help them understand." He paused for a second. "I've shocked you, Sammy boy. Maybe you've got more liberal ideas?"

Before Samuel could answer, Lewis scanned the dining room and brought his face closer. "When I came down here, I was like you. Keep a man's belly full, his house stocked, give him an even break, and most likely he'll turn out good. That lasted about a day. Things are different down here—it's a completely different ball game. I've studied the situation. Got it down to a science. I've come to believe that a little ache in the belly helps a man work best—a little tug in the guts makes him beg for the next meal. Here, there are no free rides. You have to make sure that your enemy has no idea what you're planning next."

Lewis snagged a piece of cold fish from Samuel's plate. He held it in front of his nose and shook it like a lure. "Just this," he began with a whisper, "just this, and a man will actually kill for you." He held the dripping chunk for another second before gulping it down.

Samuel shifted in his seat. The world this man was describing seemed like a nightmare. He should've stayed in Panama, gotten used to the terrain and the customs, he thought. Better yet, maybe he should have stayed in Europe, rigged his way on a boat to London or Amsterdam. "Life's very different here," he said, not so sure of his own words. "I see that, Mr. Lewis—Alf. I appreciate your advice."

"That's nothing but the voice of experience. It takes time to adjust to the way things are done here. But I can tell you, Berkow, that the faster you do, the less trouble you'll have later on. You've got to roll with the punches. You know: when in Rome, do as the Romans. If you don't mind me saying, take off that coat for starters. Put on something a bit more casual. Dressed like that, you're begging to be clipped by some scum."

Lewis stretched back against the wall and yawned. "I'm damned tired. Some booze?"

"I'll take a cup of coffee, if you have it," Samuel replied, taking off his tie and putting it on his lap.

Lewis winked at him. "That's much better, Sammy." He rang the bell on the table and the servant who had brought them the stew reappeared.

"Lincoln Douglas, a coffee for the gentleman, you hear?" he said to the boy in Spanish.

"Sí, señor," the boy answered, turning to leave.

"Hey, not so fast!"

The boy bunched his shoulders.

"How many times do I have to tell you not to overcook the fish?"

"Pero, Señor Lewis—"

"Shut up!" Lewis growled. "How I hate your damn whining. How long did you cook it?"

"Like you say. Twenty minutes."

"Well, the fish was rubbery and the broth had no taste."

The boy sputtered a few apologies, but Lewis turned his head away. He pushed the plates to the edge of the table—the boy had to hurry to keep them from falling on the floor—and then waved a hand in the air as if shooing flies. "Take these away, now!"

The boy stacked the plates without raising his eyes. As soon as he was beyond earshot, Lewis smiled triumphantly. "I'm getting so good at this." He pulled out a fat stump of a cigar and matches from a drawer in the table. "Say, you want some bourbon? Got a case of Kentucky last week."

"No thanks."

"Suit yourself." Lewis fumbled trying to get a stick out of the matchbox. He lit his cigar and took three quick puffs. He then bent down and pulled a bottle of Jack Daniel's and a glass out of the cabinet behind him. He poured himself a large drink and smiled happily.

Samuel felt he was coming down with malaria or cholera or some other such disease. He felt alternately hot and cold. As he began standing up, he felt weak-kneed. "If you don't mind, I'm going to turn in—"

Lewis's beefy arm stopped Samuel. He started humming "Camptown

Races" and shook his hand with the cigar as he sang, *"Doodah, doodah."* After each puff, he would pour himself another glass. But after four shots of bourbon, his tongue—tired of galloping—paused.

"You know, Berkow, sometimes I miss home. Pittsburgh. Even those stinking, belching smokestacks. I think of going back, getting resettled. The comfy life—a nice wife to keep me warm, the coffee-and-slippers routine. There are days I wouldn't mind it at all . . . Did you ever marry, Sammy?"

"Yes, many years ago," Samuel answered. And just then he saw Lena in his mind's eye, putting on a chinchilla coat over her beaded dress with the low back. It was her favorite party dress.

"Didn't last long, eh?"

"No," Samuel confessed. The wound was still raw.

"Figured as much. I was also married," he slurred.

"Were you?"

"Bet you don't believe it."

"Why shouldn't I?"

"Yep. Lasted nearly ten years. No children, though we often talked about it, Esther and me. A train at a railroad crossing . . . hit her. Wham-o!"

"I'm sorry to hear that," Samuel said with real feeling. "It must have been a terrible blow to you."

Long seconds ticked by. Lewis had his eyes closed and nodded. Samuel's nose itched, but he refused to scratch it. Dishes clattered in the kitchen. He wished he were anyplace but here.

When Lewis reopened his eyes, they swam in their sockets, without life preservers. "You believe everything I say, don't you, Berkow?"

"I beg your pardon?"

"You can't believe everything you hear," Lewis sang out, raising his glass to the air. "Well, it's all a goddamn lie, this horseshit about the railroad crossing. I never get around to telling the truth. But you, Berkow, I feel I can trust."

"Thank you." Samuel sensed that Lewis was toying with him.

"Don't thank me, Sammy. It's just that now I know things about you—and this kind of has you in my pocket."

Samuel didn't know what to say. He wondered what Lewis meant. The part about being Jewish?

Lewis went on talking. "You see, buddy, back in Pittsburgh I worked in a foundry casting railroad ties. Hard and dangerous work, and hotter than hell, I can tell you that. Well, one of these chain slings was carrying a steel tie when all of a sudden the tie slipped and landed across my chest. I had a concussion, broke seven ribs and had second-degree burns across my titties. It's a miracle I wasn't crushed—six weeks in the hospital, but I survived. Esther and my best friend Red visited me most every night. I'd say that they brought me back to life. I was grateful to them. But by the end of my stay, I felt something strange was going on. There was too much staring between them, and then this knowing kind of look like they had just gotten discovered with their hands stuck in the cookie jar . . ."

"I don't understand."

"They had been screwing around behind my back!" Lewis roared, shaking his glass in Samuel's face. "Do you understand that, my little Kraut?" Before Samuel could say a word, Lewis had resumed his account. "Well, the day I was to leave the hospital, they were supposed to pick me up together and drive me home. I still needed a wheelchair and Red offered to carry me to the car. I was waiting in my room, clean, dressed, and shaven, but the bastards never came."

"They left you?"

"You can imagine how I felt. Sometimes a man's got to forget certain things, but I couldn't do it. I can't do it. I keep hearing their voices bolstering me up, encouraging me to walk around with the crutches—it just gnaws on me. So the hospital drove me to my empty house, and I had to put up with all these smiling neighbors helping me—they all knew what had happened. They dressed my wounds, did the shopping, cooked for me as if they were the Lord's apostles . . . Is this boring you, Berkow? If it is, I'll just shut my trap!"

"No, please go on." Perhaps a show of sympathy was all he wanted.

Lewis's face was beet red. He grabbed the bourbon by the neck and stuck the bottle into his throat. "I swore if I ever saw hide or hair of either of them, I'd kill 'em. *Pow, pow, pow,* right between their fucking lying eyes . . ."

"A couple of years passed and I never saw them again." Lewis raised his shoulders with a sign of indifference. "I heard nothing. Or rather I heard nothing that was louder than something . . . But then one day, they got cocky and sent a Christmas card to one of my neighbors. The postmark said they were living in Canton, Ohio, the stupid fucks. So I checked out the tax rolls and street directories and phone books, and I found the address of the place where they lived—with a baby girl. That January, I took a leisurely drive across state lines. I parked outside their perfect little home and waited. I waited a long time, till one morning when Red came out of the house, I just blew a ton of lead into him. Must've been three or four shots. *Kapow, kapow, kapow, kapow!*

"Esther knew who had done it, but she wasn't about to say anything to the cops. Red was a bootlegger and a numbers man on the side, and that's where the coppers' investigation stopped. I'm not ashamed of what I did, Berkow, I would do it again. No shame what-so-ever!"

"So they never suspected you?"

Lewis chuckled. "Did you think I'd just stay there and wait for them to come looking for me? Hell no, I got the hell out of there, made it all the way down to Honduras before I stopped for breath . . . I don't know why I'm telling you this, Berkow. Maybe because you're a Jewish Kraut and you don't know who the fuck you are and you're scared as all get out to be here. You wouldn't breathe a fucking word of this to anyone, would you?"

Samuel shook his head.

"There you go," Lewis said, folding his arms on the table and squeezing his eyes. "Sometimes I think of their little girl who had nothing to do with this betrayal, but then I see Esther. I can't say I still loved her back then, but the bitch really deserved it. Do you still love your wife, Berkow?"

Samuel grew rigid. "I often think of her—if that's what you mean."

"But do you still love her? I mean after all these years?"

"Maybe I do." There was so much he still couldn't admit to himself about Lena.

"Yep," Lewis nodded, "that's what makes it worse."

CHAPTER TWO

The sleeping quarters were two cubicles next to the dining room. Lewis's room was on one side and across the hall was the guest room—a small cabin with a table, two bunks, and an open porthole. Samuel's suitcase was wedged against one wall, and the bottom berth had been prepared for him. A stumpy candle burned away on the table.

Samuel took off his suit and laid it across the upper bunk, putting his long-sleeve shirt on top. Normally he would've slipped into his pajamas, but the torrid night made it impossible, even with the window open. After weeks at sea and the stifling heat he'd had to endure since reaching the Caribbean, he longed for the cold of a Hamburg winter, the icy breath, the down comforter, the thick feather pillows.

He went to the bathroom at the end of the hall and heard Lewis, through his closed door, snoring like a clanging furnace.

Back in his room, Samuel blew out the candle and settled into bed. He bore his head into the pillow, pounded it with his fist to make a cavity for his head. He felt exhausted, but somehow he could not sleep. Was the bed too narrow and lumpy? Was he just too tired? He should've accepted Lewis's offer of bourbon to relax him.

After twenty minutes of tossing, Samuel got up. He put on his shirt, slipped into his Ballys, and shuffled out of the room. He crossed the dining area and climbed the stairs back to the deck.

He was half naked, but who would care?

The tightness in Samuel's chest eased and he could finally breathe.

He made his way to the rail of the steamer, which was anchored some four hundred yards from the coast. The stars were spilling out of the darkened sky. Had there been a moon, Samuel would've been able to see something more than the occasional flash of light from the shacks on the shore and what seemed to be the dancing of shadows against a streetlight.

Feeling slightly chilled, Samuel pulled his shirt tighter around him.

Lewis's confession and all the talk of marriage had addled him. When he closed his eyes, Lena suddenly appeared, coltish, as she had been when he first met her at the Alster Pavilion that January evening. Lena was quite thin, and her trademark was the coral cigarette holder, which almost always seemed to be dangling from her lips or her hand, with or without a cigarette. Samuel himself didn't smoke, but anyone would've tolerated this vice, just to be beside Lena and smell her perfume.

Samuel gripped the railing tighter. A dozen years had gone by—twenty-four times the length of their marriage—and still his heart was raw, a violin string aching to be plucked. He saw her in a series of flashes: dining with her and her brother in Hamburg; flirting in a Viennese parlor on Berlin's Kurfürstendamm. Samuel opened his eyes—puffy clouds sat on the horizon and water quietly splashed the sides of the freighter.

They had met at a masquerade party. Samuel was living in Berlin at the time, but had gone to this Hamburg party—a request of his father's—to see if he could come up with fashion ideas for the new spring season at their stores. There were all sorts of women dressed in feathers and sequins, gaudily so. He had bumped into Lena at the towel table by the bathrooms downstairs—she was radiantly tanned.

"Oh, so sorry," she had said.

"It's quite all right," Samuel had answered, accidentally touching her arm.

"You aren't Charles Laughton, are you?"

He had laughed.

"But you look so much like him—you only need a cigarette!"

"That and much more. Unfortunately, I don't smoke."

She wore a velvet hat cropping her black hair and a thin lace veil over her face—she was pretty and fresh and all of nineteen. He had been through the Great War, was a veteran with oodles of experience: handsome and fit, to be sure, but at least ten years older than her.

"No, you do look like him—have you seen him in *Piccadilly*? Only British films make it to Capetown," she said tipsily, raising her veil. She had blue eyes.

"So you're from South Africa."

"Yes, touring the continent with my older brother," she said wistfully. "Max is my protector. We've had so much fun. So many parties, but I must confess I don't know how you stand this miserable cold and snow. Our next stop is Berlin—which everyone tells me is magical, but even colder still."

And so it had begun. If he had only controlled himself at the Alster Pavilion, they would have met, exchanged a few words, and gone off, each on their own. He should have just accepted her compliment—he resembled George Raft more than Charles Laughton, but never mind, he had been taught to accept a compliment—but he had stupidly countered by saying she looked like Marlene Dietrich, all but the color of her hair. Somehow his wayward arrow had hit the bull's eye—Lena squealed with joy, jumped up and down, squeezed his hand, hugged him tight, and gave him a kiss on the lips.

Beyond the gusts jangling the ships rigging, he could still smell her perfume: lilac. That fragrance had bewitched him. On her neck, behind the ears, on her wrists. That night he had offered to guide her and her brother through their remaining days in Hamburg and then off to Berlin, where he happened to live.

Their romance had been a kind of whirlwind, the one time in his life when Samuel had surrendered to the moment and acted impulsively. That evening at the Alster was followed by two weeks of wild merriment—fancy dinners, visits to jazz clubs, nights of singing and dancing, finished out with nightcaps of Courvoisier and Grand Marnier, a debauchery of sorts. Lena loved being with an older man, one who knew how to dance, who treated women with respect, a man who had fought in a war, had four bullet wounds, who knew how to make love deliberately to her body.

And the day before Lena and her brother were set to sail back to South Africa, she insisted that they get married at once. So they did. Max, entranced by the homosexual clubs in Berlin, had abandoned his chaperoning once Samuel appeared. He was off on his own escapades, thinking that at least Lena—crazy, impulsive Lena—had found a Jew to marry, a rarity in Capetown and maybe this, only this, would keep his parents from killing him when he returned to South Africa alone.

On the day her brother Max set sail, Samuel and Lena went off by train on their honeymoon to Prague, Vienna, and Budapest.

Still to this day, trains, gutters, castles, expensive hotel rooms, all smelled like lilac to Samuel. It was love, not infatuation, he had believed.

But two weeks later, they were back in Berlin. It was February—the sky was constantly gray and low and the days began and ended in a moderate drizzle. Samuel had to go back to work. The wind blew in icy licks, and Lena had no interest in visiting the Brandenburg Gate or going to museums, especially not alone.

The criticism of him had begun quite innocently: *You look silly selling ties across some dirty counter,* she would say when she visited him at the store. Then it became more personal: *I don't mind your father visiting, but must your friend Klingman stay with us every time he comes to Berlin? I hate his beady eyes, the fact that all he does is criticize and complain.* Lena never listened to Mozart or Brahms, she never picked up a book to read. *Samuel, couldn't we move into a larger flat near the Kurfürstendamm? I am frozen by the time I make it down to the shops there.* Lena had no girlfriends and made no new friends in Germany after her brother left, yet she would say: *And, well, I feel humiliated inviting my girlfriends to such a dark and dank apartment. Couldn't we find a larger one with more light?*

By March the complaints began piling one on top of the other: *I hate this Arctic climate. All the people here are stiff and cold. All you do is work and at night you're too tired to go out. I can't stay here all day. I miss my parents. I miss the beach. I was thinking of taking a cruise home . . . I'll be back by May, in six weeks . . .*

Samuel slammed his palm on the ship's railing. He should have put his foot down and said: *No! You must stay with me, Lena, you cannot go alone. You're my wife. If you need something to do, why don't you get a job or go to school?*

But he was too hurt to say any of that. He had fallen in love with a face, a perfume, stupid conversations, and a pair of blue eyes. The fact of the matter was that he, a man who had been alone all his life, suddenly felt afraid to be alone.

"Please, Lena, please don't leave me," he begged her as she brushed her dark hair on the stool by her powder table. She then took a cotton ball and began removing the makeup from her cheeks with an astringent.

"It's only for six weeks," she replied, not looking at him through the mirror.

"I don't want you to go."

She glanced up at him and saw that his eyes were watery. Rather than soften her, it made her angry, terribly angry. Without knowing where it came from, she blurted out: "Samuel, you're a good-looking man, but frankly, you're also such a bore."

Samuel was stunned. Instead of answering her, touching her, he simply turned around and went to look out of the grated window on the other side of the bedroom. He tightened his fist, as if he were squeezing his heart into a ball.

The next day Lena left.

When Klingman came to visit a few weeks later, it was clear that Lena had taken everything of measure in her two trunks and had no plans to return to Berlin. Klingman asked his friend why Lena had left, and Samuel had merely shrugged, mumbling that sometimes a healthy plant, when transplanted, comes down with an unsuspecting disease. "Better to have it back in its native soil than have it die."

Samuel felt the warm breeze blowing and looked up. There was a seagull sitting on the rim of the smokestack and though it was huddled in its wings, he felt the bird eyeing him, perhaps smiling. He was such a sight, in a long-sleeve shirt, underwear, and Bally shoes. Even a strange bird could see it.

He was tired of thinking of Lena, tired of Lewis, a man he had just met several hours ago. All the talk about what Samuel should and shouldn't do, what he should and shouldn't know. The crowning blow had been Lewis's sordid confession of how he had killed his wife's lover.

The sea stank of rot, not lilac, a kind of stagnant soup of oil, dead fish, and putrid dreams. Still, Samuel knew that he was living through danger-ous times—this was not the moment to simply sniffle and weep. He had left Hamburg just in the nick of time—Kristallnacht had happened just nine months earlier—the "party" in Europe, as Lewis referred to it, had already begun.

The last few weeks in Hamburg had convinced him that only war would stop Hitler. Samuel really had seen too much bloodshed. But it was Uncle Jacob who had forced his hand, gotten him to leave Germany, not the gun-ning down of those two Hasidic Jews.

So he was on a tramp steamer headed for Puerto Barrios. From there, he would take the train to Guatemala City, where his cousin Heinrich would help him get an apartment and a job. He would honor the moment: once and for all he would plant his feet firmly on the ground—no more excuses for leaving, for abandonment, for shifting about.

Samuel went back down to his room. The moment he crawled into bed, he dropped to sleep.

CHAPTER THREE

What's taking you so long in the shit room?" Lewis asked. "Got the runs?" Samuel was leaning over the sink, his elbows deep in soapy water. "I'm rinsing out a dirty shirt," he said, opening the door. He was surprised: No *good morning*. No *how did you sleep?*

"Why are you doing your own washing?"

"I always wash my own things—ever since I was in the army."

"Not on my ship, you don't."

"Why not?"

"Because I say so. It's not right for a white man to be washing his clothes. Don't you have any idea how it looks to others for you to be doing your own laundry?" Lewis spat out of the porthole above the sink. "I'm surprised at you, Berkow. I thought you were smarter than that."

"I don't see what this has to do with intelligence." He could feel his blood beginning to boil.

Lewis grabbed a dirty rag from a nail. "Okay, not intelligence, but what's right and wrong. Now, dry your hands, Berkow. My boy will finish up here."

Samuel took the towel, scratching his head. Lewis turned around, whistled a song out of tune, stuck his head in the kitchen, and shouted angrily in Spanish.

When Samuel finished dressing, he entered the dining room with the towel in his hand just as the servant appeared with two cups of coffee and a small basket of sweet rolls on a tray.

"Put the tray down on the table," Lewis told him. "I want you to wash the shirt in the sink before you polish my trophies."

"Sí, Señor Lewis."

"You know where to hang it to dry?"

"Sí, by the smokestack."

"Below it, below it, cabrón, or it'll stink of kerosene," Lewis said, slapping the boy on the head.

The servant touched his head, bowed, and left.

"Sit down, Berkow. Grab a bite. You hardly ate last night. And sorry to have snapped like that, but you should really know better. You're nearly my age, Berkow, not some dumb kid."

"You don't need to tell me, Mr. Lewis. I was raised with maids and butlers."

"Well, that's all good and well, Berkow. I'm happy to know you had a comfy life in Krautland. But here, let my boys do their jobs. Let's sit down before the coffee's cold."

Samuel noticed he still had the towel in his hand. He looked around, then started back toward the bathroom.

Lewis stopped him. "Dump it on the floor."

Fortunately for Samuel, Lewis had a backlog of work to do before coming to port in Guatemala and he stayed at his desk in his room. Samuel spent the morning inspecting Lewis's gadgets and trophies in the dining room, none of which made much sense to him. Samuel wasn't mechanically or nautically inclined, and he knew nothing about bowling or other sports.

Later, he went back to his own room, clipped and filed his nails, and repacked his one suit back in his valise. He took a cold shower in the bathroom, but after a lifetime of cold showers, the tepid water that dripped out of the shower head was hardly bracing. Samuel shaved, put on cologne, and then donned a pair of slacks and a long-sleeved white shirt—he realized he had only brought long-sleeved shirts.

Despite Lewis's friendly advances, Samuel didn't trust him. Twice already he had seen his cheerful surface shatter into fitful rages. He believed that the American cared for his company, but was there an ulterior motive? Was he being overly suspicious? Maybe it was a good idea to keep his true thoughts in check and not reveal anything else—Lewis knowing he was Jewish was more than enough and could have gotten him stoned or killed in Germany. In any case, Lewis was all too happy to prattle on, especially when the liquor loosened his tongue, and Samuel had sensed that there was an advantage to the man's acceptance of silence as wholehearted agreement. Maybe he could escape with frequent nods, playing the role of devoted or compliant apprentice. That's it—he would make sure that Lewis saw him as the novice, desperately in need of guidance. It would be all too foolish to dismiss Lewis's friendship—offered so openly—especially without knowing what snares awaited him in Puerto Barrios.

Samuel had had his fill of feasting, waltzing, singing, and crude comedians on *Das Bauernbrot*, which in truth he had witnessed more than partaken of. The ten-day journey from Hamburg had been a bizarre celebration, as if the three hundred passengers on the Hamburg-Amerika line had no idea that war was raging in Europe and Jews were being transported by the trainload to concentration camps. Thanks to his Uncle Jacob, his own mother had managed to escape Hamburg on the *St. Louis* one month earlier, and though the ship was turned back in Cuba and Miami, eventually she had made it to asylum in Rotterdam. Samuel wished that his mother had made it to Great Britain, a land he had learned to love after he had been interned in a prisoner-of-war camp during the war, but at least in the Netherlands her German would be understood.

His father was dead, but his mother was safe, and their son was heading to the New World.

The skipper steered close to shore on his northward path, sometimes snaking between islands. More than ever, Samuel wanted to be as peaceful as the serene water that stretched all around the *Chicacao*. Whenever an upsetting thought or image came to mind, he would take a deep breath of salty air and everything would be fine. Though he could only see a blur of fronds and leaves on the shoreline, and an occasional series of wooden shacks, some of them on stilts, he felt comforted to be so near to land and to be able to say, *There, there it is.* Whatever he would find there would be better than the burning of Jewish homes, businesses, and houses of worship in Germany—the seizure of property, the expulsion to forced labor camps, the beatings, the rapes, the theft of millions of deutsche marks. And when the *Chicacao* dropped anchor near a fishing village, Samuel was shaking with happiness, despite the sweltering heat—Puerto Barrios didn't look bad at all—but it was false elation. The *Chicacao* only waited for a tender to bring out some packages and Company mail. The stop was momentary, and then the steamer sped off past reefs that shimmered their elkhorn and fire corals like amber necklaces under the clear water.

The *Chicacao* made good progress in the calm August weather, and by sunset it entered Amatique Bay. The breeze died down once the engine was lowered and the steamer glided over the water. The last rays of sunlight were oblique, turning the bay waters milky green. As the ship edged toward land, the shores to the left and right settled like welcoming arms around it. Off in the distance Samuel could see larger ships, many tin-roofed buildings, and a half dozen coils of burning gas and oil spiraling smoke into the sky. As if his pleasure boat were coming to the end of its Danube River journey in Vienna or Budapest, Samuel felt compelled to go downstairs and put on his best suit. As his father had always said to him, since he was a child: *Always dress for the occasion—arrivals in new towns are such occasions.*

He grabbed his suitcase and dragged it upstairs—he was sure that Alfred Lewis would scold him for handling it himself—and waited by the railing of the prow. The twilight air was heavy; he could feel the sweat pouring out of his body. No matter, he smiled outwardly, pleased by the prospect of finally being on land. Still, he felt a persistent anxiety. What if the New World wasn't that different?

The Puerto Barrios harbor was protected on three sides by land and had a single wooden pier that extended four hundred yards from the shore into the deeper water. The steamer's engine was switched off—a backwash of waves swirled about the prow—and the boat coasted over the weedy water to the pier. Three ships were anchored in the bay. Samuel shivered as he recognized the red and black German flag hanging limply above one of them; were the Nazis everywhere?

The *Chicacao* drifted toward its mooring on the pier. Samuel scanned the steamer for Lewis, but he was still nowhere to be seen. Three of the crew members, Lincoln Douglas among them, stood across the deck laughing and waving to the hands on a small steamer that chugged out of the harbor. Samuel broke into a sweat. A cuchuchito bird cawed out, sounding like a small dog barking. The putrid smell of the harbor reached into his nostrils, almost making him gag. Fireflies flashed in the darkening night.

Samuel stuck a finger under his collar and scratched his neck. How had he imagined Puerto Barrios? Tropical gardens? A British club with tennis courts and an eight-hole putting green, giant villas, smiling people wearing khaki shorts? Or had he expected endless sandy beaches, girls with hibiscus flowers pinned to their hair paddling out in canoes to welcome him ashore? Ukuleles? Sweet pineapples? A welcome committee and a band?

Straining his eyes, he saw a range of rickety houses rising on wooden stilts and stone pilings extending along a marshy beach, plantain and banana groves cropping up to the shore, a few rusting buildings on the verge of being swallowed up by dense vegetation. Instead of soft breezes, gas fumes started to burn his throat and eyes. He looked up—turkey vultures, flashing their silver-tipped wings sharp as stilettos, wheeled in the darkening sky. All of a sudden huge horseflies buzzed in Samuel's ears, circled his exposed neck and hands, looking for a spot to crash land.

As the steamer reached its berth on the pier, Samuel saw a crew of stevedores loading bananas onto a dockside ship, their black bodies glistening, working tirelessly like oiled pistons. Yes, the shacks, the workmen, the grunting sounds were not part of a king's welcome. Even the few windwhipped coconuts he saw seemed to be shaking their heads at him. So this is Guatemala, Samuel shuddered, not a tropical paradise—Lewis had warned him to lower his expectations, and he was right. He'd have to begin adjusting to the landscape.

Still, Samuel felt he had no right to complain—that would be a travesty. He had made it out of Hamburg, by the skin of his teeth, thanks to his uncle's willingness to bribe a few German officials. Back in Europe, his fellow Jews were being picked up, beaten, shipped out to labor camps in the frigid fields of Eastern Europe, at the same time that Hitler was showing the world that few countries were willing to accept deported Jews, especially from Poland.

Samuel pounded the railing of the ship, as if finally waking up: he was, after all, a refugee, not a vacationing tourist returning from an afternoon cruise on the Elbe.

CHAPTER FOUR

As soon as the gangplank touched down, a swarm of barefoot kids raced and tugged their way up to the freighter's deck carrying glazed figs and guavas. Several of them crowded around Samuel and spoke to him in English.

"Shoe shine? Real cheap!"

"Don't listen to him, mister. He doesn't even use shoe polish."

"Taxi, señor? The only one in town! Good service!"

Meanwhile, the crew secured the *Chicacao* to the dock pilings. When they finished, they bunched together and began eating the fruit they had just bought. They snorted and laughed, quite amused to watch Samuel trying to fend off the children with his umbrella.

"Please, leave me alone." Samuel needed silence to navigate his arrival in Puerto Barrios—he wished he could muzzle the kids so that his arrival could be more gracious.

A boy with stumpy arms pulled on his coat. "Hey, mister. Money for my sick sister?"

"He has no sisters! He's a bastard."

"You like black women? I take you to Livingston."

"Scat! Shoo!" Samuel snapped, spinning away from them.

"Scat, shoo!" mimicked a thin boy, older than the others, with a hint of a mustache on his upper lip. "He must think we're flies!"

"At least you, Guayo," teased a shrunken boy with a protruding lower jaw.

"Shut up, garbage mouth, before I pull your lips off," Guayo said, pushing the smaller boy to the ground. "You're nothing but a flea."

"At least I'm a flea with a brain."

"Yes, flea brain!"

The two boys started chasing each other around Samuel who simply put down his valise and sat on it. The boy named Guayo grabbed the homburg off his head.

"Look what I got! Look what I got!" He threw the hat in the air and the other kids ran after it. Samuel made a vague effort to stand up. "I beg of you."

"Hey, get away! Leave that man alone or I'll beat the crap out of you!" thundered a voice from the shadows. Suddenly, all the movement on the deck stopped. Samuel's homburg was dropped on the wooden floor. Lewis came into view, and the kids scampered off the boat yelping and howling. He had an alligator skin bag slung over his shoulder and a double-barreled shotgun in his hand. He was shaking his head. "These kids," he fumed, "they have nothing to do but fool around. I'd like to crack their skulls!"

"Thank you . . ." Samuel began. He went over to his hat, picked it up, dusted it, and pressed it back on his head. He walked over to where Lewis stood and extended his hand.

Lewis waved him away. "Forget it, Berkow. They didn't hurt you, did they?"

"No, I'm fine. It's all so new to me." He was embarrassed to say that he had expected to be welcomed by his cousin Heinrich or some consular official, as he would've been in Europe. "To be honest, I don't know what I was expecting."

"Nobody ever knows what's around the next turn," Lewis said. "And here it's a bit worse. I told you that Barrios is a shithole—but it's where you are now. You've got to get with it, Sammy boy, get ahold of yourself. Say, where you staying?"

"Any decent hotel will do."

"Whoa, now you're asking for a blue moon!" Lewis touched his chin with the butt of his rifle. "There's only one hotel—the International—that's worth a plug nickel." He pointed into the darkness. "It's owned by a German from Cobán—that's what I've been told—but I'll be damned if he's ever stepped foot in the place. You can't miss it, Berkow. It's straight ahead at the end of the pier, in front of a crappy little park. It looks like one of these southern haciendas that's been ferried down from some plantation in Louisiana. Any of these scroungers on the dock can take you there. But don't expect linen tablecloths and porcelain. Like I said, it's the International, but there's nothing international about it."

"Thanks, Mr. Lewis." Samuel couldn't get himself to call him Alf—it felt disrespectful. "I'm grateful for everything. The free ride, the advice—"

"You'd do the same for me," Lewis interrupted, as he walked past Samuel. Halfway down the gangway, he turned around. "I've got to do some work at the commissariat—send off a few telegrams to the home office in Boston, sign some papers. It should take me a couple of hours. Why don't I join you for a drink at your hotel, say at eight?"

"It would be my pleasure."

"Till later, then. You won't have any problems if you keep to the path. I've got to hurry, Berkow, otherwise I'd bring you to the hotel myself. Toodle-oo." Waving his hand in the air, he continued down the gangway.

Without glancing down, Samuel lowered his left hand to pick up his valise. He found himself gripping a shoulder and jumped back.

"That's me you're holding," said a little man, barely three feet high.

"I'm sorry."

"Don't be. I have a way of sneaking up on people. I'm a licensed tour guide—I'll take you to your hotel," he quipped in a precise, deliberate English.

Samuel surveyed the little man. He barely reached Samuel's belt, and his eyes seemed to cross at the bridge of his nose. His head comprised over half of his body.

"Do you know the International?"

"Of course I do." He pulled a net bag with a leather head strap from his waist pocket and looped it about Samuel's suitcase. In one motion, he slipped his granite forehead through the strap and jockeyed the suitcase onto the lump of tight muscle and bone on his back. "Just follow me," he ordered, tugging on Samuel's coat. He trundled down the gangplank like a snail carrying an oversized shell.

Umbrella in hand, Samuel staggered after him, keeping his eyes on his feet so as not to trip on the wooden crossbars. Years ago, he had marched through the frozen terrain in the Hallerbos forest in Belgium with his military gear—compared to that, this should have been a cinch.

"First time here?" the dwarf asked from under his load.

"Yes, sir," replied Samuel, thinking it would be his last. Tomorrow he would be in Guatemala City bringing his shirts to be washed and ironed, his suit pressed.

"Staying long in Puerto Barrios?"

"Long enough to take the train to Guatemala City. Do you know when the next one is leaving?"

"No, wouldn't know," the man huffed.

At the bottom of the gangway, their steps leveled and they walked along the pier stacked with huge wooden cages and green tarpaulin. A crowd rushed toward them till the dwarf shouted something in a language Samuel did not understand.

Gusts of hot air blew, bringing wafts of grease and fried food to his nostrils—Samuel couldn't wait to get to his hotel room and change.

"I want to go first to the train station, please."

"Do you, now?" the tiny man said, not slackening his pace.

Floodlights washed over the pier. About thirty yards from the *Chicacao*, Samuel and the dwarf passed six or seven Carib men busily working near a huge white freighter docked on the far side of the pier. Wearing no more than rag strips around their waists, they were hoisting four-foot green banana stems onto giant slings. These, in turn, were raised by pulleys onto the loading deck where more stevedores placed the fruit on conveyor belts that dropped them down into the ship's ventilated hold.

The tiny man stopped to trade words with a set of workers who were unloading piled bananas from flat railroad cars further along the pier. A well-dressed man with straight black hair and a walnut-sized nose was pointing to piles of yellow bananas, urging a laborer to dump them into the harbor waters with his pitchfork. "These'll be rotten before the ship makes port," Samuel heard him say in English.

Samuel was uneasy. He knew he had entered a new world where his previous experiences meant nothing. In the trenches of war, it had been the same, but he'd always had lieutenants and captains who told the troops what to do. Here, no one would be directing him. He closed his eyes as if that gesture, like a magician's wand, would somehow erase the world before him. But the droning generator, the one that powered all the lights, mocked his effort like an inner voice. His years as a soldier, a salesman, an export agent, a bank teller, a night clerk at a hotel in Berlin were over. Nothing had prepared him for the floodlights, the abrupt animal screams, the natives working and grunting like galley slaves, the sweat, the filth, this little man who had somehow taken charge of his affairs—

A scream broke out, electrifying the night.

"Oh Lord, save me!" howled a man, grabbing his forearm. "The devil's got me, mon, the devil's goin' to take me away!"

He let go of his arm, slamming his body against a railroad car. A six-inch snake slithered away on the wooden planks, trying to get out of the light. Samuel and the dwarf backed off. In a single motion, the man who had been pitching ripe bananas into the harbor lifted his pitchfork high into the air and jammed it down, piercing the snake. Then the man directing the work crew flung his machete at the snake and lopped off its head. The headless body writhed away.

The snake-bitten man got up. His face poured sweat; a bubbly froth came out of his mouth. His eyes couldn't focus, simply rolled around in their sockets. One of his mates ripped off part of his loincloth and tied it just above the bite on the man's arm.

"My luck," the man moaned softly, rolling over on top of the snake's head. "I'm goin' to die. Forget it, mon, it's no use. The Lord's already holdin' my hand."

The mate who had produced the tourniquet sunk down, pinned the man with his knees, and made a wide and deep cut along his upper arm with the tip of a scaling knife. Then he put his mouth to the wound and began sucking and spitting.

A crowd of fellow workers—outshouting one another to explain what had happened—formed a tight circle around the two men, blocking Samuel's view. The tiny man tugged on his coat.

"Come on, let's go. I already know what's going to happen next," he said, chuckling. "Puerto Barrios has some of the strangest creatures you'll ever see. We've got scorpions that can bite through wood. And tarantulas too, bigger and hairier than coconuts!"

"Do you think the man's going to die?" Samuel gulped.

The dwarf looked across the pier. "*Will he die?* the man asks?" He looked to his sides, as if on stage and addressing an audience. "Should I tell him the truth? Okay. If I'd been bitten, I'd be dead now. You too, my friend, would be dead and we'd have to plan your funeral with none of your family! But these Caribs have tough hides and blood thicker than mud."

"Horrible, just horrible." Samuel shifted his umbrella to his left hand and pulled a handkerchief out of his back pocket to dry his face. Over the harbor noise he could hear the bitten man still moaning fitfully. Samuel licked his lips—they were salty from the sweat streaming down his cheeks. He swallowed hard to keep from vomiting.

The dwarf resumed his tottering walk and Samuel hurried to keep up. As they reached the shore, the pier widened considerably to accommodate wooden cargo sheds and what appeared to be steamship and telegraph offices. Further on, Samuel saw the only concrete building on the pier. A United Fruit Company sign was clearly illuminated; Alfred Lewis was most probably working inside.

At the end of the pier, a dirt road took over from the wooden planks. On one side stood a small guard house. As they neared the booth, the dwarf whispered: "Give me twenty dollars."

"What for?" Samuel asked.

"To bribe this fool, what else? Do you want to spend hours at the immigration office answering a hundred stupid questions and then still have to pay off another man? I'm trying to save you time and money! Put the bills inside your passport. Make sure they don't stick out. Do you hear me?"

"But that's bribery!"

"Nothing's bribery in this country, my friend." The little man snapped then turned around to smile at him. The strap holding his suitcase dug deeply into his forehead. Samuel felt a sharp kick to the leg. "Don't be stupid, mon. You could be here all night. Be quick about it!"

Samuel shook his head. He opened his wallet, took out a twenty-dollar bill, and folded it into his passport. When they reached the booth, the dwarf let Samuel go before him; the guard took the passport and smiled. He thumbed through the pages, found what he wanted, examined the visa, and stamped the passport.

"Bienvenido a Guatemala, Señor Berkow. Esperamos que le vaya bien."

"Gracias a usted, señor, por vuestra gentileza," Samuel said in his best Spanish. He smiled politely, slipping his passport back into his inside coat pocket. The visa, which had received no more than a passing glance, had cost his Uncle Jacob thousands of marks . . .

When the dwarf reached the gate, he gestured for Samuel to wait up ahead. "Noches, Tacho," he said to the guard.

"Noches, gusanito. ¿Por qué hay tanta bulla en el muelle?"

"Lo de siempre. Una barbara amarilla picó a uno de los estibadores."

"No me digas. ¿Y seguro que no fue un gusanito que lo pico?"

"No te creas. ¿Todo bien?"

"Así es. Gracias por el pisto. Te debo una. ¿Quieres tu parte ahorita?"

"Después, después. Paso a verte más noche."

"Que les vaya bien."

Samuel knew some Spanish from having spent two months with his sister in Mallorca. From what he could tell, the guard and the dwarf were in cahoots and planned to split the twenty dollars. He felt anger surging up inside of him at having been clipped by them. But he told himself to calm down, that he should stop worrying about little details—he was finally on land, soon he would be in Guatemala City. No point in making a fuss.

Relieved, Samuel began walking jauntily up the road, figuring that the tiny man would catch up to him. He passed several mule carts and an old black Packard on the side of the road. As he passed the car, he noticed a black swastika decal on the side rear window.

Samuel edged closer to have a better look.

"Taxi, mister?" a voice said in English, blowing smoke toward him.

Samuel looked inside and saw a casually dressed figure slumped in the front seat. He couldn't make out the man's face because of the cigarette smoke.

He felt sick to his stomach. First the ship with the German flag in the harbor and now this swastika on a car. Were there Nazis everywhere in the world?

"Long walk into town . . ."

"No thanks," Samuel said.

Just then the dwarf whistled. Samuel glanced back and saw him pointing to his left. "Come along, this is the shortcut to your hotel. That gravel road was built by the Fruit Company bastards—that's why it goes from the pier to the train station and sidesteps Puerto Barrios!"

Samuel rushed back to him. "But didn't I tell you I wanted to go to the train station?"

"I told you it closed at sundown."

"Are you sure there aren't any trains to Guatemala City tonight?"

"I'm quite certain."

"Awhile ago you said you didn't know. And now you are sure. I would like to take the very next train there, if that's at all possible."

The dwarf looked up at him. "You would, would you?" He shook his head. "Well, I would also like to see the Church of Notre Dame. And I wouldn't mind taking the ferry to London, but I can't. That's the way it is. Like I told you, there's no train to Guatemala City tonight. Maybe there will be one tomorrow afternoon."

"Surely, there must be a schedule."

"Surely, there must be, but I'm not paid to know it. Now hurry along. Do you think your suitcase weighs nothing?"

"Please. Why don't you let me carry my own bag?"

"I've got it, can't you see? Besides, how would it look for a man dressed like yourself to be seen carrying around his own luggage? Not very well, indeed. Come along now. We have to hurry if we want to get across the little wooden bridge to the hotel. When the tide rises, it gets quite slippery."

Samuel followed the man up three wooden steps joined with side planks to a series of loosely fitted boards set on stone pilings. The long bridge ran parallel to the bay and passed the elevated wooden shanties he had first observed from the *Chicacao*.

As they walked along the bridge, Samuel peered into the houses. Candles on little dishes threw phantom shadows against the walls. Laughter and talk blew out, accompanied by a child's occasional giggle.

These stilt houses comprised a town within a town and were connected to one another with swinging wooden transits. Samuel saw that the last stilt house was the neighborhood store. Penny candy jars sat on a rickety counter; behind them were skewed shelves dotted with canned goods and paper-wrapped staples. A cat pawed a couple of fish heads on the store floor, which was covered in trash. A dog came to the door of the shack and poked its head out. It had a mangy coat and what seemed to be a broken leg.

"How can people live in this filth?" Samuel asked in a low voice, his throat tightening again.

The dwarf kept walking. "How? Well, what did you expect? Pretty little houses with picket fences and flowers?"

Puerto Barrios was a port city; Samuel had of course been aware of this prior to his arrival. It didn't need bustling docks on the scale of Hamburg or Rotterdam, but this was nothing more than a miserable assortment of wobbly shacks stuck like matchsticks along the shore.

His hotel had better be different. "Is all Puerto Barrios like this?"

"Hmm, in a way. It has bars and restaurants and whorehouses. Anything a man needs. You'll get used to it. Believe me."

I don't plan to get used to anything here, Samuel thought to himself.

Once past the last shack, they walked on in silence. Under normal circumstances, Samuel would've wanted to ask the dwarf many things—his name, how he managed to get settled in Puerto Barrios, where he had learned English. He would have been interested, as well, in asking the little man his opinion of Mr. Lewis. And more personal questions too: What was life like for a dwarf? Did his parents love him the way parents love a normal child?

But for now, silence was better; it was enough of a chore for Samuel to keep his footing. He certainly would've preferred the longer route by the railroad station—that way, at least, he would have gotten the schedule, seen a bit of the town instead of skirting the mangroves. But he had committed himself to the dwarf, who was now his guide. More than his guide, his one and only pilot—for in truth, Samuel was completely in his hands.

A strong foul stench now greeted them. "Oh my God, what's that odor?"

"That's right," said the dwarf. "Brace yourself—we're approaching the toilet facilities. The lavatories. In street parlance, let's just call them the shitholes!"

To their left, four toilets with molded seats had been carved out of a huge tree trunk. Below them ran a creek which flushed the excrement right into the bay. A nifty idea, to be sure, but something had gone wrong—either the creek had been diverted upstream or had dried up, and the stench was overwhelming.

Samuel clasped the railing not to slip, but he stumbled against the tiny man who had stopped momentarily to shift the suitcase further up on his back. Samuel tripped and fell, facedown, onto the bridge's wooden planks. His umbrella flipped into the dry creek below.

"Hey!" yelled the dwarf, falling to his knees. "Do you want me to fall into this crap? You think I have no pride?"

Samuel stood up, unhurt, and looked at the man. He wiped his mouth slowly with his handkerchief and held his breath. He felt embarrassed by his clumsiness—surely the army latrines had stunk just as bad, and he had tolerated it. What about the time the army officers had urinated on him and his fellow soldiers as a prank while they slept rolled up in the frigid night?

"I'm very sorry," he began uneasily, breathing in and out through his mouth. "I was choking. Are you hurt?"

The moon was rising over the bay to the east. It was a huge moon, a giant milky pearl really, suffusing the darkness with white light. It was quite beautiful.

Samuel stared at the dwarf—the leather strap dug into his melon-shaped head. He was sweating profusely and his eyes poked out like fishhooks shimmering in blubber.

My God, Samuel thought, *this little man is monstrous—no one can love him. No mother, no father—no one on earth.*

"What are you looking at now?"

Samuel ran his hands through his hair. "Nothing at all. I—please, Mr. . . . I don't even know your name."

"Mr. Price to you."

"Please, Mr. Price. Let me carry my own valise. I don't know why I let you take it in the first place. No, I know what you said, about how it looks here. In Hamburg it would be the same. But really, I am accustomed to taking care of myself. I don't really need any help. I'm sorry for all the inconvenience."

"In-con-ven-ience. Now there's a big word for a German. My, you are quite educated, we can see that," the dwarf laughed, spreading out his arms as if about to do a two-step. "You do have a way with words."

"I'm so sorry—"

"Don't be. What's there to be sorry about all the time? Have you never seen a dwarf? Haven't you ever smelled shit before? What did you expect to find? Sewers out here? Cobblestone streets and gas lamps? Is that it, Mr. Berkow?"

Samuel threw up both hands. "I don't know what I expected."

"Of course you don't. And this is why you need to trust me. I can see very clearly that you're a confused man, somewhat out of his element."

Samuel shuddered. Why had the little man said that?

"I'm right, aren't I? You don't know who you are and you don't know where the hell you are or where you're going. You could be in the China desert or in the middle of Africa. You, my friend, are completely lost."

Samuel said nothing.

Mr. Price clapped his hands. "All right then. Now that we've established that, let's move along. I'm sure you'd be surprised to know you're almost at the one and only Hotel International!" He spun around on his heels and started walking again.

They went down some steps and took a dirt path that cut through a wooded area of thick ceibas and tamarinds. Samuel heard screaming animal sounds above him. He glanced up, scanned the trees, thick with leaves. A flurry of brushing noises followed, then there was more screaming and something smacked down beside them.

"The howler monkeys are having a party." Mr. Price bent down, felt along the ground. He picked up a pulpy object and gave it to Samuel.

"What is this?" he asked, holding it in his hands.

"Breadfruit. We grind it and then combine it with dried coconut to make johnnycakes."

Samuel examined the breadfruit. As soon as he pressed it, phosphorescent worms gushed out and he dropped it to the ground in disgust.

The little man shrugged. "Suit yourself," he said, resuming his walk.

The footpath brought them to a treeless park with a stone band shell in the middle. A couple of pariah dogs, more bones than flesh, snoozed open-mouthed on the steps.

Beyond the park there was a green three-story wooden building. Above the entranceway, there was a veranda supported by two stone columns. Swinging from the top of the columns was a sign that read, *Hotel International*.

The little man stopped in front of the steps. He looked around as if admiring the grand architecture of a newly discovered Mayan temple. "The Ritz of Puerto Barrios," he said.

Samuel nodded. He was beginning to understand Mr. Price's odd sense of humor and that made him happy. What made him happier still was that he had been as good as his word—he had brought him to the hotel quickly and safely and without any further deception.

The Hotel International could be crumbling for all Samuel cared at this point. No matter what it was, it was exactly what he needed.

CHAPTER FIVE

S amuel followed the dwarf up the three steps of the veranda and entered the hotel through flapping screen doors. The lobby had little furniture—most prominently, a half dozen dusty wooden chairs set facing each other on a jute rug. Each chair was flanked by waist-high metal ashtrays overflowing with cigarette butts. There were dramatic murals on both sides of the lobby depicting the same Mayan scene of bare-breasted women offering a quetzal-feathered chieftain libations and plates of food. A route map of the Hamburg-Amerika line hung on the back wall above the front desk.

There was no one working the desk. The dwarf tried to set down Samuel's suitcase behind him, but the weight flipped him onto his back. He flapped his arms to the side to regain his balance and, as if to cover for his bungle, slipped quickly out of the headstrap, jumped to his feet, and blared: "Hey, George! Where you hiding? Come on out, mon. Time to get off the john. I got you a customer."

A few seconds later, a very dark man stepped out from a scrim curtain behind the counter. He rubbed his face with his two big hands, shook his head, and yawned loudly.

"How's things, Mr. Price?"

"Oh, you know, not bad." The little man folded up his net bag and jammed it into the space between his pants and his waist. "Not as many clients come by ever since there's been all this talk of war. But oh well. To get to the point: this gentleman would like to spend the night here."

The clerk glanced at Samuel. "How do you do?"

"Just fine," replied Samuel.

George pulled out a hotel register from under the counter and started opening drawers searching for something.

Samuel opened his coat pocket. "I have a fountain pen, if that's what you're looking for. Do you need my passport?"

"That won't be necessary. I just need you to print your name here. And then I will need four quetzales—dollars will do—for your room. You'll find a towel in the bathroom and a piece of soap."

"All I need is a bed!" Samuel announced euphorically. He was so happy to be back in civilization, poor as it might be.

The clerk raised an eyebrow. "That you'll have."

Samuel wrote his name, put his pen down on the counter, and took out the bills from his wallet. His Uncle Jacob had not only bought him his ticket, but had given him fifty dollars in cash to get started. He was about to slip his wallet back into his trousers when he felt a tug.

He looked down and saw Mr. Price opening and shutting his hand like a clam. "Let's hand some of that over here."

"I beg your pardon?"

"I beg *your* pardon," the dwarf mocked. "That will be four dollars for my escort services."

"But that's impossible! You only carried one bag. Why, you were with me for no more than fifteen minutes."

"You forget that I got you through customs and saved you from being scalped by the boys and the taxi driver. My rates are standard."

"But that's what I am paying for this room."

"I couldn't care less about your other expenses. As I said: my rates are standard. You better pay me now or I'll have George call the police."

"Don't involve me in this, mon," the clerk said, shaking his hands in front of him. "I don't want to lose my job."

"Oh, don't worry, Georgie Porgie. I'll call the police myself. They are all my friends. It is amazing what a little money will do. And besides, there's no great love of foreigners here in Guatemala, and certainly not for some

German who is unwilling to pay a dwarf for standard services, I can tell you that."

"All right! You win!" Samuel took out four more dollars, thinking that it was safer to settle accounts with a thief than to create a scene.

Mr. Price snapped the bills out of his hands. "It's a pleasure doing business with you." He stuffed the money into his front pocket. "And what about my tip, George?"

"Just a minute, Mr. Price."

The clerk glanced nervously at Samuel. "I need your signature next to where you printed your name. Here, along this line."

Samuel uncapped his pen. He noticed that the register had few recent entries. As he began to sign his name, he heard two loud whistles.

"What's that?" he asked distractedly.

"That's the train for the capital, sir. It leaves every night at seven," said George.

Samuel banged his fist down. "But I wanted to be on that train!" He glared down at the dwarf.

"Well, I guess you missed it," Mr. Price chuckled. "You still might catch it—if you want to take a taxi to Bananera . . . Then again, you could also fly."

"You lied to me, Mr. Price."

The dwarf scrunched his face dismissively. "I'm not paid to recite the train schedule, you know."

"I've done nothing to you to deserve this treatment."

"You think because you have a bit of money that this entitles you to full services."

Samuel's upper lip began twitching; he felt his head throbbing and a slight pressure in his chest. Before he could do anything, the clerk put his paw on Samuel's hand and said softly: "It's not so bad here for one night. Sometimes there's a train leaving in the morning with Fruit Company personnel. I'm sure they would let you on it. Now, would you like a room facing the bay or the jungle in back?"

"What's the difference!"

"I'll give you a bay room at no extra cost," said the clerk, closing the register.

"I'm waiting, George," Mr. Price chimed in, thumping his foot.

George looked at him with blank eyes. He opened the drawer where he had placed Samuel's money and flipped two large coins to the dwarf.

Mr. Price leaped for the coins and snagged them in midair, one in each hand. His chest hit the wooden floor and he slid across. Then he stood up and dusted himself off.

Samuel was furious, but chose to ignore him. He was asking the clerk if the hotel had hot water, when Mr. Price tiptoed over and poked him in the ribs. Samuel jolted up, bashing his fingers against the edge of the counter.

The dwarf had a defiant smirk on his face. "Hey, how about a little company tonight? A girl or maybe a young boy if you prefer, to while away the hours? What do you say to a bit of fun after such a long voyage?" He swiveled his squat hips, thrusting his pelvis back and forth.

"Get away from me, you disgusting little bastard!" shouted Samuel, trying to clutch the dwarf in his hands. The little man scooted out of his way, but stumbled against the suitcase.

"Please don't hit me. I was just kidding."

Samuel's kick landed on the dwarf's back, sending him and the suitcase across the wooden floor. They both ended up next to one of the ashtrays.

Mr. Price pushed himself up slowly. There was a small gash just below his cheekbone and dust on his greasy face. Still, the little man smiled through his pain.

"You'll pay for this, you European monster." He stretched his neck and lobbed a ball of spit toward Samuel. It missed him, but landed on the counter. "I should've left you on the pier alone with all those kids—then you would've understood how grateful you really should be. You fool! You stupid fool!" He ran his mouth across his shirtsleeve, jerked up his pants, and sauntered out of the hotel.

"Sir, if you'll—"

"What do you want from me? More money?"

The clerk dropped his eyes. He lifted a panel from the counter, allowing him out into the lobby, then walked over to pick up Samuel's suitcase.

Samuel beat him to it. "I don't need your help!"

"No, please, sir," implored the clerk softly, trying to hide the foolish grin that formed around his mouth whenever he was nervous. "Let me help you with your bag. I had nothing to do with Tom Thumb. You can see that he's a bit sick." He tapped a finger against his forehead. "Most of the boat passengers miss the train as well—it's been like that for years. You have to plan to stay at least one night in Barrios. We never know when the next train is leaving—"

"But I told Mr. Price I wanted to go to the station first."

"Yes, but it's too late for that now. You might as well take it easy—no use getting more upset. That will only make things worse for you."

Samuel eyed George incredulously. He didn't know who he could trust. Alfred Lewis? George?

He felt lost.

The clerk blinked several times. "Let me give you a hand."

Samuel finally relented, letting George take his bag. "You're right. I must be calm. You said there might be a train tomorrow morning, yes?"

The clerk shook his head. "You can't ever be sure of the trains," he warned, as they walked together to the stairs. "Things go easy here, the Barrios way. You can't make things happen. The Company would like to change that, but you can't change people who would rather throw out a fish line than work. You're not with the Company, are you?"

"The Fruit Company? Not at all, Mr. . . ."

"St. Lawrence. Geoffrey Quincy St. Lawrence. My family's originally from the Bahamas, but I was born in Punta Gorda in British Honduras. My mother is Garifuna from Honduras. My friends all call me George, my father's name."

"Pleasure to meet you, George." Samuel felt that perhaps he had finally met a gentleman.

"Likewise." The two men shook hands warmly on the landing between floors and then continued climbing. "How is it that you speak English, Mr. Berkow?"

"I also speak Spanish, but not as well. I was in England for nearly two years during the Great War. Then a few years back, my sister moved to Mallorca, an island off the coast of Spain. Well, I would visit her for weeks at a time. You might say I have a way with languages. Naturally, I speak German, my mother tongue."

"Interesting," nodded the clerk, "very interesting."

At the top of the stairs, they swung left and walked down a long and wide corridor protected by a wire screen. At the end of it, George set down the suitcase. He pulled out a ring of keys and said, "This is it," then thumbed through it and slipped one into the door lock; the tumblers screeched and clicked. George held the door open to let Samuel into the room.

Samuel groped momentarily against the wooden wall, searching for a light switch.

"It's not there. Go to the center of the room and pull on the chain."

Samuel found the chain and pulled. The bulb went on, barely infusing the room with light.

George hoisted the suitcase onto a rickety writing table. "Should I say that you don't want to be disturbed?"

"What a thought!" Samuel laughed. "No one will be looking for me," he said, stretching. Then he remembered: "Actually a Mr. Lewis may stop by around eight o'clock."

George frowned.

"Is something wrong?"

A weak smiled formed on the clerk's lips. "Nothing at all. I will let Mr. Alfred Lewis come up to your room. By the way, your towel is on the bed and there's a pitcher of water by the bowl."

"And the shower?"

"Well, that's down the hall, back near the stairs we took. The toilets are there too. And the bar and dining room are downstairs, to the left. Rest up, sir."

"Here, this is for your help," Samuel said, pulling a few coins from his pants pocket.

"That's not necessary, sir. I'm the night clerk, not a porter."

"Please, I insist."

"Well, I appreciate it." The clerk pocketed the coins and left.

Samuel walked after him. "Won't I need a key?"

"No, I left the door unlocked."

"But what about thieves?"

"You don't have to worry about that here."

"And the other guests?"

George blinked back at him, sighing. "There are no other guests except for an old priest who won't bother you."

"You never have guests?"

"Oh sure, lots of them, especially when a pleasure ship comes in. Just not today. None this week. But we will keep the kitchen open—for you. Will you be eating here tonight? I imagine you'll be with Mr. Lewis."

Samuel nodded.

And with that the clerk left.

In the privacy of his own room, Samuel finally felt at ease. He took off his suit jacket, so sopped with sweat that it was like a second skin, and folded it over his chair. He felt a lightness in his being and did a little waltz around the room.

He went over to his bed, mere canvas strung between two sidebars and a straw mattress covered with a white linen sheet. He pushed down on it with his fingertips and it sank to just inches off the floor. His pillow was also stuffed with straw and a bit flat. He tried puffing it up, but it simply collapsed in his hands.

Glancing up, he saw two horseflies chasing each other around the thirty-watt bulb. And next to the light chain was another chain that activated the ceiling fan. He pulled down on it and the creaking blades began to go around so slowly that he imagined he could touch them and not be hurt.

Samuel gazed into the mirror hanging just above the wash basin. He winced—is this what he really looked liked? No wonder Lewis had laughed and the dwarf had jeered! He looked like a hollow man on the verge of collapse.

If he had been in Germany, Samuel would've showered and shaved, but here in Puerto Barrios, at the edge of the jungle in the middle of nowhere, he felt a mere touch-up job would do. He washed his face in the tepid pitcher water. He took out his tortoise-shell comb from his toilet case and proceeded to comb his hair back, leaving a wide part down the middle. He spread his lips and examined his gums: good, they weren't bleeding, always a sign of bad nerves. He filled his only glass with water from the jug—it might have been potable, but it still had a moldy smell to it.

All of a sudden Samuel felt his legs weaken. He went over to the light chain, pulled it down, and sunk into bed.

A short nap would do.

Chapter Six

Samuel lay on the bed with his arms crossed behind his head. He was exhausted, but could not get himself to sleep. He felt charged up—images raced through his mind as if they were cards flashed before his eyes. Worse still, he couldn't get himself to focus on a single detail since he had arrived in Puerto Barrios. Just as soon as a face zoomed into focus—Lewis or Mr. Price or the clerk named George—some other vague face or gesture would blast it from his mind.

Samuel saw himself walking determinedly through a snowy landscape of thick trees and tangling vines. There was smoke and a terrible stench like the rear of a butcher shop and he tried to figure out where he might be. He was wearing a light brown uniform and a pair of Ballys and yet, somehow, he was able to trudge through deep drifts of snow. His stomach hurt so he decided to stop and unbutton his shirt—there was caked blood all over his undershirt and stomach. Obviously he had been shot.

He needed to find a hospital. He kept walking until the snow gave way to piles of flak jackets and boots in smoldering fires. He suddenly heard the voice of Field Marshall Dieter Rausch, his pug-nosed, no-neck commander, shouting orders at him above a deafening noise of mortars and shells that hacked the ground. Samuel stopped, and he felt his shoulder take another bullet. Despite this, he continued walking until he lost consciousness and fell to the ground like a perforated balloon. He curled up in a bush, hoping that the brambles would fight off the wind that attacked his wounds. Where was he? He recognized the Hallerbos forest of Belgium—and soon he knew that his troops would carry him back to the field hospital behind the battle lines. And now it began snowing heavily.

He was not quite asleep. Though the noise was deafening, he heard one of his German comrades speaking stonily above him as if through dense glass. *Das ist aber schade. Berkow ist tot, ganz tot. Gehen wir jetzt! Hier kommen die Englische soldaten.* Samuel tried to protest—*I'm not dead, can't you see? Please take me back with you*—but his words refused to issue out of him. He let his helmeted head drop comfortably into the snow as if it were the softest of pillows. Was this death? To witness things, to be able to hear and see what was going on, but not be able to cry out. No longer noticed. People prancing about you, even talking about you, but being incapable of being heard. What a horror!

Then there was a lull, the late light of the day weakened, and he felt himself now losing consciousness as if forever. Before passing out, however, he saw his mother sitting on a park bench—was it in the Botanischer Garten or at the entrance of the Hagenbeck Zoo?—looking at six-year-old Samuel trying to read a plaque that had lots of words and dates and showed two snakes swallowing each other by the tail. Scared, he ran back to his mother, but then she, like his German comrades, disappeared. And again, as he was about to pass out, he heard yet another voice, a bit more shrill, telling him that snakes were charming creatures, silky and slithery, nothing compared to tarantulas. *And if you want to know pain, invite a scorpion to sleep in your bed! Tee hee.* The voice was coming from a dwarfish man with black rings around his neck.

Samuel did not like this man, but there was nothing he could do.

Then he felt something crawling on his cheek. Was it the deadly scorpion? Black, slender, with the finest of features. Nothing could be more beautiful. Ah yes, the only one of God's creatures capable of simultaneously killing his enemy and himself with his very own stinger. And Samuel, it had to be noted, had been born in late October . . .

He opened his eyes and batted away a horsefly that had landed on his ear. His room was dark. He turned to his right side on the slinglike bed. He heard furniture being moved on the floor of the room above his and then a voice chanting some kind of prayer. Hadn't the clerk told him that the hotel was empty, absolutely empty? Ah yes. Just his luck to be in an empty hotel and have a crazy priest above him.

Then it was quiet again, except for the clinking of his ceiling fan.

Samuel remembered part of his dream—after all, he had replayed his war experiences hundreds of times. It had been a miracle that the following morning after having been shot three times, a British regiment found him alive, one of the few survivors of the previous afternoon's carnage. They could have left him there, a brown caterpillar dropped in the snow, but several British soldiers challenged fate and carried him back behind their lines. A slow death, he had thought, as he felt his nearly lifeless body being jostled about. What could they do for him and his perforated lung?

Later he would learn that several medics had operated on him in an army tent. Despite the anesthetics (they could only give him a bit), he had rolled his eyes for hours and his body had writhed in pain. The British doctors had patched up his lung, pulled out three bullets from his porous body, and mended him shut. He couldn't be moved for a week but somehow managed to survive the whole surgery; when he finally came back to full consciousness, he was being transported back to England on a military vessel along with other German prisoners. He imagined that soon he would be walking the seashore in Dover, gathering pebbles.

But he never walked the seashore because he was a prisoner of war. In Harwich, northeast of London on the coast, he recovered from the bullet wounds he had sustained during what had been a suicidal German attack.

Two weeks in Harwich and the good doctors sent him to a detainment camp outside of Warford in the Chiltern Hills—the mountain air would do him good, would help his lungs recover. There were few prisoners there, and because Samuel learned English rapidly, everyone suspected that he was not a hardened soldier. In fact, he loved the British and said as much and soon he was made an orderly. He worked in the hospital serving meals to the other injured prisoners, and though he had to sleep under lock and key, he was basically free. When the Treaty of Versailles was signed a year later, he wanted to stay in England, but the armistice had strict rules for repatriation. The best he could do was to get a letter from the hospital stating that he needed to go to a mountain region, perhaps in the Alps, for another six months of treatment. The doctors and nurses were sad to see him go.

Samuel was sent back to Hamburg by boat along with five hundred other prisoners. Rather than be seen as heroes, the veterans were treated— as they had been as soldiers—like expendables by the German authorities. He received thirty devalued marks from the Veterans Administration, wooden-soled shoes, and, yes, a paper suit, for almost having lost his life serving his country. The German commanders insisted that Samuel go to a sanatorium in the Alps—but at his own expense.

Samuel closed his eyes. Even now, twenty-odd years later, he didn't know why he had enlisted. He came from comfort and he hadn't been a particularly defiant adolescent, though he didn't cherish his mother's complaints about her husband's philandering ways. His father hadn't tried to stop him, he merely questioned the logic of it all—the usual clichés about duty and patriotism—not that Samuel shouldn't be patriotic, but what did attack and counterattack have to do with him? Had his school friends been regaling him with exaggerated stories about the glories of war? His father had said, *Yes, I know, we are patriotic Germans first and then Jews, but what do you think your death will prove? If I were you, Samuel, I'd stay in school, and if you're drafted, drum up some false medical excuse . . . Better a live coward than a dead hero. I know my German people—life is expendable, and Jewish life, well, it has very little value for the Kaiser and his advisors.*

It was his mother who had been most upset by his decision. Were his parents and sister so horrible that he preferred war to them? It wasn't proper for the son of a successful businessman—the importer of fine leatherwear, haberdashery goods, and French lingerie—to be chucking away his future for a cotton uniform and combat boots. She had grabbed his fingers, laid them across her soft, lotioned hands, and scolded him for wanting to ruin them with calluses and sores. *And for what? So you can spend your days clean-*

ing your rifle or polishing your boots for the fourth time in a week? You're a young man with a future, Samuel, use your head! And through all these discussions, his mother seemed more concerned about what her lady friends—the Jewish tea-and-torte crowd—might think of her son than she was about his health.

Samuel had wanted to get away from home, and enlisting seemed like the best way to do it. He knew that he wouldn't be "on his own" in the army, but at least the voices barking orders were unknown. He was tired of the apartment in Hamburg, the daily fighting of his parents and sister—another poseur, siding with his mother. His father Phillip Berkow was coarse, vulgar, and unserious—*I make money, so what?*—and he had no culture to speak of (unless going shopping was culture).

Even his good friend Achim Klingman had thought Samuel was bluffing—that is, until Samuel had shown up at the Goldener Stern Café brandishing his enlistment papers. Up to then, it had been just loose talk, the bravado of their classmates who felt that to serve one's country was not only a duty, but almost a religious calling. *Samuel, how could you have done something so foolish? The army is full of drunken louts; it's no place for Jews. If your mother was driving you crazy, you could have moved in with me.* Maybe Klingman was right—well, in a way—but all he could do was shrug. If he had been pushed to supply reasons, he would have said that he was bored by school, felt his life was going nowhere, didn't have an interest in going to university, and was too young to start working at his father's store.

Perhaps, all he sought was adventure. *Man isn't a turnip*, he philosophized, *so why should he stay rooted to one place?* His destiny was to be like a piece of driftwood, floating on the ocean, resting on reefs and islands, until finally he hit solid land . . .

Rather than be tugged apart by his parents' contrary expectations and the usual evenings of bickering, he preferred to weigh anchor and go off on his own. Samuel respected his father for being the kind of person he could never be. His father, forever the extrovert, was a jovial man who gathered friends around him as a bird gathers twigs. It was true that he handled Hamburg's finest imported apparel—this should have pleased his mother—but that wouldn't change his clowning ways. Phillip had learned the difference between sheer and taffeta for his trade, between suede and horse leather, not because he attached any social value to it (in fact, he couldn't care less), but because it offered him the opportunity to be his own boss and, naturally, to flirt with the wives of the men who came to his shops to purchase fine accessories.

His father refused to enter his rightful place in Hamburg high society, preferring to remain on a first-name basis with carriage operators, laborers, icemen, coal sellers, even street sweepers. Didn't he offend the *haute volé* by always sitting next to the driver whenever he rented a one-horse carriage? Wouldn't he greet great dignitaries and boozers alike in the same manner? Hadn't he refused to come back from the corner tavern to greet the mayor of Hamburg when he wandered into his store?

Samuel's mother would never forgive him for that—for not being more proper, more dignified. His inability to discern the difference between truly remarkable people and the lower class drove her nearly insane. Samuel could forgive his mother her snobbishness, the air of *ancienne noblesse* that she loved to flaunt, which had nothing to do with birth since her family hailed from a village near Kraków. He could forgive her frequent asides when she belittled people—merchants and clerks—who she felt were below her dignity, but he could never forgive her for the way she treated his father, as if he too were unworthy of her respect. With her constant jabs, which his father either deflected or eventually faced, she had reduced their married life to bad theater that Samuel was forced to witness.

At a certain point, his father was eating at home no more than once a week and Samuel sometimes noticed him flirting with the cashiers and servers at bakeries and perfumeries. Samuel had no illusions about the state of their married life; he readily admitted, for example, that love had been squeezed out of their relationship if—and this was crucial—it had ever existed. He had viewed their marriage as something brought about by convenience, habit, or even family meddling, but it irked him to witness the day-in, day-out bickering. As a teenager, he still hoped that, at least for his sake, they would come to understand and accept their differing notions of civility and etiquette so that a workable truce could be achieved.

Was it too much to want there to be peace at home?

Yes, yes, yes. It was true—the squabbling at home made his leaving so much easier, and of course there was a war to be fought. So he stupidly enlisted, and like all German foot soldiers, he suffered the indignity and sadism of the officers who ruled over them—degrading them, forcing them to march around in circles in the bitter cold, just to test their mettle. Release hens from the hen house and pigs from their sties just to see the soldiers sinking their boots in mud and filth to try to recapture them.

So after his six months in the Alps, with his lung scars healed, Samuel found it impossible to go back home to live in his parents' apartment on Lutterotstrasse. He rented a flat in the Reeperbahn area. It was a huge apartment, though unbearably noisy because it was in the red-light district, full of drunks, sailors, pimps, and whores. He figured that his father would leave him alone and that his mother, scared off by the neighborhood, would refuse to come and visit.

But she insisted that he dine with them at home every Monday and Friday—he was a veteran, a former prisoner of war, and still just twenty-two years old. When his father mentioned that he would be opening a store in Berlin and wanted someone trustworthy to run it, Samuel made the move.

And that's when he met Lena. Then, after the fiasco with her, his movements read like a peripatetic's travel brochure: Bern, Geneva, back to Hamburg, Amsterdam, Paris briefly, once more back in Hamburg. When his mother went to Mallorca to visit with his sister and brother-in-law after his father's death in 1936, Samuel stayed in Berlin till Kristallnacht—the Night of Broken Glass—in 1938. With the Berlin store burned and ransacked, he returned to Hamburg.

Samuel scratched his scalp and sighed. He was exhausted from churning up all the dead leaves of the past. That stupid dream of going off to war and seeing the world had started it all: this idea that a new environment would somehow reveal how he should conduct his life. And as miserable as Europe had been, it was now far out of his reach. Yes, the past had been full of obstacles and cul-de-sacs, but there at least, the difference between friend and foe, helper and destroyer, had been crystal clear.

Here, in Puerto Barrios, he was lost in a swirl of confusion. Samuel closed his eyes and tried to forget.

CHAPTER SEVEN

A **little after eight, there was a rapid series of knocks on his door.**
"Berkow? Are you in there? What the hell's wrong with you?"

Samuel struggled up. He swung his legs over the edge of his bed and sat there, rubbing his eyes; his lips were dry and sticky. "Who is it?" he managed.

"Alfred Lewis, dammit! I've been banging on your door for the past five minutes!"

"I'm sorry, I must have dozed off."

"Well, why don't you meet me downstairs at the bar once you're ready."

"Fine," Samuel answered. He heard Lewis's *clippitty-clop-clippitty-clop* footsteps fading down the corridor.

His chest and shoulders ached, his legs felt weak, unsteady, as if about to buckle under him. He pulled on the light chain, and even the dim bulb seemed to hurt his eyes. He couldn't get his mind cranked up, as if it were clogged by some sleeping drug.

At the wash basin, he splashed warm water on his face. How unrefreshing. He flattened his clothes as best he could with his hands and headed out of his room. He had no choice but to leave the door unlocked.

Moths circled slowly around the hall bulbs, as if tired of batting giant wings. It was a muggy night and Samuel couldn't escape the dreary feeling that had parked itself in his heart. Was it sadness or gloom, or just plain hunger? He had eaten no more than a few biscuits in the last twenty-four hours. Perhaps a nice glass of wine and some roast potatoes would stir his appetite, though he was certain not to find it downstairs. Yet, he had to eat to nourish himself, no matter how bad the food tasted.

A schnaps would do him good.

At the landing by the stairs, Samuel bumped into a tall, drawn man wearing a black robe that reached down to the floor. Pockets of white hair issued like weeds from the furrows of his face. He was going upstairs, but seemed in no rush.

"Another hot night," the man said in Spanish. "Like sleeping on coals."

"Yes, I can hardly breathe," Samuel answered, noticing that the man's eyes were very red. He had an unpolished silver chain around his neck, which held a three-inch iron cross. So this was the priest who lived above him.

"You would think it would be cooler sleeping thirty feet off the ground. What's the point of having a room facing the bay if it's as hot as the ones facing the jungle? What about your room?"

Samuel shrugged. "The fan does little to help the circulation . . . Father."

"He calls me *Father*." The man smiled and clasped his cross. "The faith of the uninitiated, to be sure. I was a Man of God, and still am in a way, but I am no longer a priest. It's a rather long story. Father Cabezón at your service, on his way to Delphos. Would you like to join me for a drink in my chambers?"

"Some other time, perhaps, Father Cabezón. I have a previous engagement."

"What a formal man! And how strange—I have never heard of anyone having a previous engagement in Puerto Barrios." He smiled again, revealing long yellow teeth against red, inflamed gums. He examined Samuel. "Obviously, sie sprechen Deutsch. Ich spreche nur ein bisschen. We must get together some night and talk."

Samuel rubbed the back of his neck. "I'm leaving tomorrow on the first train."

"What a shame! I would've liked to discuss the Old World with you, perhaps give you some insights into Puerto Barrios. It has its charms, but mostly of the satanic kind. I should warn you—it isn't so easy to leave here. There's always something pulling you back. That's been the case with me."

"Oh, I am leaving tomorrow. That's certain. As sure as the sun rises."

The priest nodded slightly. "It most certainly does rise, though you can't always see it. And there's a point of discussion: can you be certain something happens when you can't even see it? Religious leaders have long pondered that question." Noticing Samuel's impatience, he added: "Now run along to your engagement. By the way, what's your room number?"

Samuel stepped past him. "It's at the very end of this hall."

"Below my room! What a coincidence. I hope my chanting won't disturb you. There are times when I am consumed by the desire to pray. I shall have to be a little bit more considerate." Before Samuel could answer, the man had begun bounding up the stairs two steps at a time, holding his skirt up with his hands.

At the bottom of the stairs, Samuel turned right and made his way to the bar, which consisted of a long cedar wood counter facing half a dozen stools and a couple of tables further out on the floor. A fan as drowsy as the one Samuel had in his room sputtered overhead. There were three people there—Lewis closest to the lobby and two dark-skinned men sitting down the other end of the bar, quite apart from him. The bartender was at the far end, attending to something Samuel could not see.

Samuel cleared his throat as he entered.

Lewis lurched his head. "Berky!" he yelled, tapping the stool next to him. "Come over here and rest your dogs."

Samuel sidled up to him, giving no more than half a glance to the other two men hunched over their drinks—he now recognized that the clerk George was one of them. George glanced blankly at Samuel and then looked back down at his drink.

"So whaddya think of our tropical showcase, eh?"

Samuel sat down on a stool. Lewis was drinking bourbon straight from the bottle and drawing heavily on his signature cigar. His body gave off an odor of sour oats.

"I don't know what you mean by tropical showcase."

"Well, Berky, I don't think we want to get bogged down in technicalities. In semantics. Call it a showcase, a warehouse, a whorehouse, a cesspool, a honey bucket, the biggest shit dump you've ever seen, a pigsty, a dung heap. Call it what you want, my friend, but don't ever think of this shithole as your home!"

Samuel gazed down the counter. George met his look, shook his head, and looked back down. It was obvious that Lewis had been drinking for quite a while.

"Is something wrong, Mr. Lewis?" Samuel whispered.

"Wrong, Berky? What could be wrong? Or maybe you see things differently. Oh yes. Those lovely flowers on the tables, the fine linen tablecloth, friendly broads bringing you drinks? Nice flowers, eh? Ah, and the wonderful party music!" Lewis reeked of booze.

"Perhaps you're tired," Samuel said.

"Course I'm tired! Been coming in and out of this shithole for more years than I care to remember. Mind you, each time I come back it has more low-down cantinas, more stragglers and bums, the ugliest whores you've ever seen. There isn't a decent blade of grass in this ornery town. I've got to stop coming back here, Berkow, and move to a civilized place. Mozo, bring this man a glass—on the double!"

The bartender took a glass from under the counter and strolled over to where Samuel and Lewis were sitting. He cradled in his right arm something wrapped in a white towel. He put the glass down and poured Samuel a drink out of Lewis's bottle.

"Make it a double! A triple! Whoa! Them Germans can drink." He wrangled the bottle away from the bartender and held it from him. "Here's mud in your eye!"

Samuel took a sip and winced at the taste, but ended up swallowing his drink in two gulps.

"Whoa! Whoa! Now there's a man!" whooped Lewis, glancing right and left down the bar. "Set him up again!" And he poured more bourbon, spilling half of it on the counter.

Samuel smiled uneasily. The drink had dizzied him a bit. Suddenly the towel that the bartender was carrying moved, and a creature stuck out its horny head. Samuel jumped back.

"What's that?"

Lewis kept drinking and glanced at the towel. "Don't be scared, Berky. It's what the natives here consider their poodles. Go ahead and touch it. "

"I would rather not."

Lewis reached over to touch the animal, and the stool almost came out from under him. "It's just an iguana, for Christ's sake. A big lizard these hill-billies tame for pets, maybe even fuck with, for all I know. Come to Papa," he said, trying to yank the iguana out of the towel.

The animal desperately stretched its legs, bristling its dorsal fin, trying to escape Lewis's grip. It had brown leathery skin and a tail that had been severed. Its eyes were green.

"Let it go, mon!" shouted the bartender, yanking back. The iguana opened its jaws and gave a strange yipping cry.

"I'm not going to hurt it, you ape!"

The bartender cuddled the iguana like a baby in his arms, tickling its throat with his wide fingers. The iguana arched its back in pleasure, nodding its undersized head. It almost seemed to purr.

"Get your fucking iguana away from me!" Lewis said. His arm inadvertently struck his bottle, which skidded down the counter a few feet, gushing bourbon on George and his friend, then exploded on the bar floor. "I'm sick of it anyway. I'm sick of this hotel, this poor excuse for a bar. I'm sick of all of you!"

"No one is forcing you to stay here," the bartender replied.

"Well fuck you, then."

George walked over to Lewis. "I think it's about time you go to bed."

"Are you throwing me out, Georgie Porgie?" Lewis snarled. "I haven't even had my dinner yet."

"Please, Mr. Lewis—"

"Shut up, Berkow. This doesn't concern you. I'm having a private conversation with this half-breed over here." And turning to George, he added: "Who do you think owns this hotel or this miserable town? Or, for that matter, you?"

"Nobody owns me. Like Willie says, you shouldn't touch what's not yours."

"PPssshhaw!"

"We're not just rugs you can step on."

"Is that so?"

George shook his head. "You are drunk, Mr. Lewis. Go home."

Lewis got off his stool and brought his face to within an inch of George's. "I could have you arrested for saying that. I could have you dragged away from here and have you cutting bananas for the rest of your life until you rot like the scum you are!"

George slapped his face with an open hand. Lewis fell against his stool and teetered. George's friend ran over, wrapped his arms around Lewis, and held him tight to keep him from falling on the floor.

"Let go of me, you dumb black bastard!" Lewis screamed, trying to grab the man holding him.

George wrapped his arms around Lewis's head and began dragging him out of the bar while his friend still held him.

"You'll pay for this, you oversized zombie!" Lewis tried hooking his legs around George's like a blinded crab. "I will have you both executed." His head was flush against George's chest, his chin in the crook of his arm. He glanced at Samuel, who seemed paralyzed by what was going on. "You too, Berkow. You don't know who runs this town, you dumb Jewboy."

Samuel stared at Lewis. The word *Jewboy* swirled in his throat like a loose piece of metal.

"Rrrrrahhhrrr." Lewis made a desperate stab with his free hand to reach his hip pocket. George felt the motion, grabbed his hand, and smashed it hard against his raised left knee. Lewis's hand went limp and a small gun dropped to the floor; a shot fired. The bullet bounced off the fan and perforated the tin ceiling.

"You miserable apes!"

George tightened his grip around Lewis. "I should just break your neck. No one on this earth would miss you."

"You wouldn't dare. I'd have your head in no time," the American barely whispered.

George looked angry; he clenched his fist and was about to slam it into Lewis's face. But he hesitated, his hand floating in midair, as if he had just realized the truth of his threat. He let go of Lewis, letting him tumble to the floor, then picked up the gun and shook the two remaining bullets out of the tiny cartridge. He put the bullets in his shirt pocket and threw the gun behind the bar.

"You can pick it up tomorrow, Mr. Lewis, once you sober up."

Lewis crawled on his hands and knees till he found a chair. He gripped the seat, pulled himself halfway up, sat down, and pointed a finger around the bar. "You'll be sorry for this." He stood up and brushed the dust off his khaki pants. "I'm somebody in this town, you know. You're going to be sorry you ever touched me."

Without saying another word, Lewis wove his way out of the hotel.

George walked slowly back to the bar, dug the bullets out of his shirt pocket, laughed, and then flung them across the room.

Samuel was shocked and disgusted. On the freighter, Lewis had certainly expressed his biases, but he expected him to be a bit more tightlipped or measured in the company of those he so caustically berated. Here, at this bar, he had simply lost it. He also couldn't understand why Lewis, who up until that point seemed to be so caring and deferential, had all of a sudden lumped him in with the others. Samuel knew that he couldn't trust Lewis because he was unstable, but he had almost thought of him as a guardian of sorts.

Samuel picked up Lewis's stool and carried it over to where George was now sitting. He was watching the bartender dropping purple berries into the mouth of the iguana, who swallowed them whole. No one seemed to be in a talking mood, but he felt the need to disassociate himself from Lewis.

"Mr. Lewis shouldn't drink so much."

George looked up. "It's his routine. For days he's calm, and then he starts becoming crazier and crazier like the clouds of a storm. This happens every few weeks or so. Tonight, well, it began after you checked in. He came here and started drinking, and making all these strange faces and talking really loud."

"He was acting crazy, mon," added the bartender.

"But why? I don't understand."

"Look, Mr. Berkow. As I said, it's happened before. This time it was just a bit worse. You know, I was here in Barrios when he first came. In fact, I carried his bags off the ship. Back then, you could talk to the man and he would listen."

"He was all ears," the bartender said. "Always asking questions."

George nodded. "One after the other. He was friendly, eager—maybe because the big wheels like Dexter and Hoolihan paid him no attention. They thought he was a pest, always wanting to be a part of them. When the Company announced that it would move its headquarters inland to Bananera, I remember Lewis began packing up all his files. But they told him he wasn't going. He was left in charge here."

"They cut him off, George. That's how I would put it."

"You could say that's what happened. In Bananera they have these huge mansions and swimming pools and, well, here there are the storerooms and the ships. Little by little, Lewis started to become mean and nasty. The drinking didn't seem to help. At first he kept to himself, but then he began to threaten and complain, sometimes for no reason. He began spitting and barking at everyone, as if nobody listened to him and he owned the whole damn town. Then there was the strike by the dockworkers and he was told to put it down. He had to pay off some soldiers. People were killed. It was ugly. And, well, he was never the same after that." George pointed to his glass. "Pour me another shot, Willie."

The bartender complied.

"But that's no excuse," Samuel offered. "He said some very vulgar things."

George swallowed his drink and winced. "Don't you worry about it. He'll be all dried out in the morning. And if he remembers what happened, he'll be here falling over his heels and apologizing. And if he doesn't, then it's as if nothing happened."

"Amnesia," said Willie, tapping his temple.

George looked intently at Samuel. "Listen to me. You take my advice. I'm talking to you as a friend, if you can believe that. Get the hell out of Puerto Barrios as soon as you can. Believe me, it's not a good place for you. I've seen too many people come into town wagging their tails and then within a month they're falling on their faces. It happened to Lewis. It happened to Father Cabezón."

"Poor man," Willie added, again tapping his temple.

"I met him on the stairs."

"He's a strange one," said George.

"Well, I couldn't understand what he was saying. I tried."

"The hotel priest got here long before I came. He used to have a small congregation. Willie, you were here. You tell him about it."

The bartender bent down and placed the iguana in a wire cage on the floor, then poured himself a glass of rum. "Father Cabezón came from Quetzaltenango, a big city in the Guatemalan highlands, to become the headmaster at the Santa Elena School. That's when it looked as if Puerto Barrios might become a decent town. But then when the Company moved its headquarters inland, things went downhill. Cabezón was a responsible priest when he arrived, a good director, but he began drinking and neglecting the school. The heat bothered him, and then some parents said he was visiting brothels. He didn't show up at the school for days at a time. It was a very small school with three or four classrooms and the nuns were happy to run it themselves. Still there were complaints, but the Church did nothing— what did they care about what went on in Puerto Barrios, hundreds of miles from civilization? But then the priest got arrested. He was accused of selling cases of illegally brewed rum to army officers in Zacapa and Cobán—he had probably insulted someone at one of the brothels who wanted to exact revenge. There was a big fuss and the bishop of Guatemala City had to intervene. I know that Father Cabezón was forced to give up the school . . ."

"Was he defrocked?" Samuel asked.

"I don't know. All I know is that they took away his school and took away his church. But they surely didn't take away his money. For the past five years he's been living in this hotel. Sometimes I hear him saying Hail Marys and Our Fathers in the middle of the night. Other times it sounds as if he is thumping about his room on one foot. Dancing, maybe. Strange smells float out of there. He can shake his maracas for hours!"

"And then there are the candles." George grinned. "Once a week, on Thursdays, we have a big open-air market by the band shell. Indians come in from all around the country to sell stuff for Puerto Barrios, Livingston, and Saint Tómas de la Castilla. Old Cabezón sets up his little booth of trick candles that light back up when you blow them out. Some Indians, a group of Lacandones who live deep in the jungle, say that Cabezón is the son of Kinich Ahau, the Mayan sun god. They make pilgrimages just to buy his candles and receive his blessings. Maybe that's how he can afford to live in this hotel and spend his money on the prostitutes at the Delfos Bar in town."

"Ah, that proves he's no longer a priest!" Samuel said. He felt oddly lifted by the conversation, as if it provided a bit of a respite from his recurrent dark thoughts.

"The man's crazy. Was he wearing a robe when you saw him?"

"Yes, he was. A black robe."

"Well, priest or no priest, the Church leaves him alone because they don't want any trouble from the Indians who believe he's a God. In a way, it probably benefits the Church. In the end, it's all harmless."

Thunder suddenly cracked, and the bar lights flashed off and on.

"I think we better call it a night. Go to bed now, Mr. Berkow. Get yourself some good sleep."

Samuel, sensing that his company was no longer wanted, got off his stool, leaving the whiskey that Willie had poured him untouched on the counter, even though his throat itched.

"You're right. I have a long day tomorrow. I'm taking the train to Guatemala City."

"Good for you," said George.

"Good night, George, Willie, and, ah—"

"Kingston's his name, but don't expect him to answer. He was among the dock workers that went on strike, but one of the soldiers ended up smashing his voice box."

The man looked up, flashing a lame smile. Samuel noticed that he had two doughy scars creasing his neck.

Samuel nodded and left. Again he felt bile rising up his throat.

As he walked through the doorway, he heard a shrill, inhuman cry behind him as if the throat of an animal had been slit. He lingered for a second at the foot of the stairs, heard a second wild cry, covered his mouth, and went up to his room taking the steps two at a time.

Chapter Eight

Samuel closed the door, wiggled out of his shoes, and collapsed in bed. It couldn't have been much past nine, but he felt engulfed by fatigue, by the desire to sleep and forget. Lewis, the dwarf, the priest, the iguana—it was all too much for him. He had expected something different when the *Chicacao* entered Amatique Bay.

Puerto Barrios reminded him of what he had felt after enlisting in the army—a dose of a bizarre reality, but a reality nonetheless.

An explosion snapped him out of his stupor. Samuel went over to the door and opened it. Beyond the screened corridor, lightning blazed in the sky like swords crossing in battle. Suddenly the wind picked up, shuffling leaves and fronds, making the corridor screen billow. A furious rain began swirling and falling from many directions.

Samuel walked over to the screen and held his breath. The rushing wind abruptly died down, was gone, at best soft gusts barely rippled the screen. What sounded like a wild pig grunted from behind the hotel. Frogs, high up in the trees, made quick clicking sounds.

There had been no storm, except perhaps in his mind. What was wrong with him? Next he would be sitting at the dinner table with his dead parents or accompanying Lena to the Alps for a skiing weekend. Again he cocked his ears. Nothing. He shook his head, trudged back into his room, and sat on the rattan chair by the desk, confused.

This new world was playing tricks on him, to be sure. Heinrich had made it sound so different when he wrote to his father. Samuel remembered certain images and observations from the letter:

You can't believe how fertile the land is. You sprinkle seeds on the orange-brown soil and within days shoots are pushing up. You only have to stretch your arms to pluck ripe plums from the treelined boulevards. It is another Garden of Eden. For twenty-five cents you can buy a hundred oranges. There's a green fruit called aguacate that is creamy and smooth—three for just a nickel—and tastes delicious, with lemon juice, salt, and a kind of parsley called cilantro. There are: Purple mountains. Talking birds. Flowers growing wild everywhere. Mangoes. A fruit called papaya that grows to a meter in length, weighs up to three kilos, and tastes delicious with a hint of lime.

And the climate, Father, especially in the countryside. The air sweeps through your body as if it were a colander—I'm becoming a poet! No clouds in the sky for six months at a time. Every day you awaken to dazzling light. No snow, no blizzards. The tour conductors say this is the country of eternal spring—and so it is. Your bad moods are forever on vacation.

Guatemala City is ideal. Well-maintained colonial structures and new modern buildings going up every day. Cobblestone streets have replaced the dirt roads. Movie houses and restaurants on Sixth Avenue and fancy cabarets that could rival Hamburg's are opening up every month.

President Ubico is an admirer of Mussolini and even dresses like him, with his uniform and high boots. He is no Hitler, but it is indisputable that he believes in order: no beggars, no prostitution. The city is so clean you can eat off the streets.

A businessman's dream. Electrical appliances, imported fabrics, canned goods from America. You can import and export anything and retire comfortably within twenty years. Five quetzales a month, and you get a live-in maid to clean and cook for you seven days a week. Three daily newspapers. Imported German magazines. Life is progress. A Frankfurt Jew has begun importing pickled herring and sprats, wonderful gemütlichkeit—I am so happy that I decided to come here. My only fear is that Guatemala will one day be overrun with Polish Jews, as our beautiful Berlin was, thus feeding anti-Semitism. All those black frocks, beards, and side curls aroused such resentment from the working-class Germans. But so far, these are only my fears . . .

Had these been his cousin's very words?

Why hadn't Heinrich said anything about Puerto Barrios when he wrote to his father to tell him that Samuel was welcome to join him in Guatemala? Surely his cousin had passed through the port on his way to the capital—the heat, the filth, the hustlers trying to swindle him, the scruffy kids? Just beyond the hotel, there were probably packs of beggars and chiselers and gun-toting thieves.

Samuel opened his valise. At the top were his silk pajamas. He put them on and lay on top of his bed, which was already a tangle of sheets.

Why hadn't Heinrich at least warned him? Yes, yes, he had said, *Do not expect too much help from me.* This comment had embarrassed his Uncle Jacob, but Samuel knew what to expect from his cousin. The only male children in the Berkow family, as boys they had been inseparable, living so close together, the two sides of the same coin darting off on common escapades. They were the two rails of a train track—bending, dipping, and turning together, but always with the same amount of space between them.

There was jealousy between Uncle Jacob and his brother Phillip because Samuel's father had been so much wealthier. Heinrich also felt that his freedom was hemmed in by his mother Gertie and his three sisters. Samuel was aware of his cousin's feelings, tried to be the best friend that he could, especially after his mother died of cancer. He would lend him money, pay his way when they went rowing near the Alster Pavilion or would go to the movies and stop off for dessert at a café in St. Pauli. But what else could he do? Trade places with him?

When Samuel enlisted in the army, Heinrich stayed in Hochschule to finish his studies in business math and accounting. If before the war their friendship had begun to fail, certainly after it there was little friendship left. When Samuel visited his Uncle Jacob's house, his girl cousins would sit at his feet, pepper him with questions about the battlefield, and beg to see his wounds until he embarrassedly consented. By this time, Heinrich would have hurried upstairs without excusing himself to do something like finish studying for a licensing exam. His sisters frankly didn't care. They found their own brother to be unbearable and self-centered . . .

After the Great War, when the German economy was in a shambles, Heinrich worked with his father at his lamp store. As soon as he could, he began his own import/export business, though he could have easily joined his Uncle Phillip's firm. Jacob's relationship with his son became strained. He couldn't understand why Heinrich wanted to compete with his uncle for the same customers. And strangely, Samuel's father didn't worry about competition—the more, the merrier. Samuel defended his cousin to his uncle, saying that Heinrich needed to make his own mark in the world.

"Just as when I joined the army—Heinrich wants to set out on his own."

Samuel did not tell his uncle that his own son loathed him for his lack of enterprise, but kept up cordial ties simply to keep peace in the family. By 1930, thirty-two-year-old Heinrich was becoming a rich man in Germany, but then something ugly happened—he was accused by Hamburg's municipal assessor of having failed to pay duty on several shipments of belts and umbrellas from London. Heinrich denied the charges, but refused to contest them—anti-Semitism was beginning and it wasn't clear if he had committed a crime or whether some worthless soul was trying to blackmail him or take over his market. He simply sold what was left of the business and set sail for Guatemala in 1931.

When Samuel's father died of a heart attack in 1936, his uncle sold the lamp store and took over his brother's business, which was already in trouble. Anti-Semitic slogans soon were painted across the Hamburg store walls, display windows shattered, and Uncle Jacob told Samuel that it was time to leave. A group of Nazis had shown up at the store, threatened him on the trumped-up charge that he was selling deerskin gloves advertised as genuine calfskin leather. He was an old man now, his daughters having married and moved with their husbands to London and Amsterdam to escape the Nazis, and did not want to leave. But Samuel was young—why should he stay and suffer? His Uncle Jacob had written to Heinrich to put old grudges and the past aside. Yes, the cousins had their differences, who didn't? In times of need, wasn't blood thicker than water?

Jacob bought his nephew a ticket on the Hamburg-Amerika line for the boat to Panama. He gave him the equivalent of a thousand dollars in deutsche marks and fifty American dollars. How was he to know that the gestapo customs agents would confiscate the marks and threaten to throw Samuel in jail for leaving the country with illegal funds? Samuel had protested, but the agents just patted their guns. He surrendered his money, except for the dollars he'd hid in an old sock, and boarded *Das Bauernbrot*, lucky to be getting out alive . . .

Would his cousin see him through? Blood was thicker than water and thicker, too, than money. So what if Heinrich had never replied to his letter telling him that he was coming? One can never trust the mail . . .

Still, Samuel had been foolish to think that Heinrich would come all the way to Puerto Barrios to meet him. But now that they were on the same soil, they'd meet face to face, embrace, reminisce about their youth, iron out their petty little differences. Who knows, they might even work together and become best of friends again!

Was this naïve?

Samuel relished the thought.

CHAPTER NINE

Unencumbered by dreams, Samuel slept like a log. In the morning, as he washed his face in the basin of his room, he heard a brisk knocking. He dried his face and opened the door. Sunlight streamed in.

It was Lewis, wearing a freshly pressed light blue shirt and a small fedora on his head. His eyelids were thick and pasty. Before Samuel could say a word, the American began speaking. "I wanted to say goodbye before leaving," he said slowly, as if weighing each word. "The *Banana Reefer* is loaded up to the brink and will be setting out for New Orleans in another couple of hours. I've got to go back down to Puerto Cortés in Honduras for the day, to finish up some old business, then get back here tonight."

"Won't you come in?" Samuel asked, squinting.

"Nah, I can see you're busy."

"Not at all. I insist."

Lewis shrugged, walked into the room, and sat down on the rattan chair. He took off his hat, laid it across his lap, and began to twirl his thumbs nervously.

"I feel terrible for what happened last night. I talked to George this morning. He said I flew off the handle—not his words—and let my mouth run loose all over the place. Berkow, I hope I didn't come down too hard on you."

"You don't have to explain yourself," answered Samuel, leaving the door open.

"I'm not apologizing, Berkow, don't get me wrong." His little eyes narrowed and he paused. "I am not in the habit of apologizing for anything."

Samuel felt he had to say something. "Liquor loosens the tongue and isn't too particular about how things are said."

"Right-o," Lewis replied quickly. "I thought you'd understand. Look, I'm beyond making amends with George and Willie. That pickaninny Kingston? Well, he's another story. He was a good worker till he let some of those unionists twist out the little sense he had in his head." A smile slid across his face and he stretched his neck a couple of times. Samuel saw that he was cleanly shaven now and neatly dressed. "Berkow, you and me, well, we're cut from a different cloth. It may have to do with color."

"That may be, Mr. Lewis."

"I just came to give you some advice, straight-from-the-shoulder advice, the only kind I know how to give." Lewis kept fidgeting. "Sit down, Berkow. You're making me nervous."

Samuel sat on the bar of his bed, rubbing the towel, which he had placed on his lap. He knew he was being set up for a long sermon.

"Look, when I came to Puerto Barrios twenty years ago, there was nothing here. Well, there was this pier built out of rotting planks and natives living in their stilt houses under the palm trees. You'd have thought they were still living in the Stone Age, running around half naked. As you can imagine, things have changed. You have this hotel, though you might not think too much of it. We've put up some decent housing for the stevedores—wooden army barracks, that sort of construction—away from the water so that if a hurricane blows in, they won't all be wiped out. And in time, restaurants and cantinas and a few churches opened up. Ten years ago, it looked like we might turn this cesspool into a paradise." Lewis moved his chair closer to Samuel.

"One or two concrete buildings were built, for the mayor and the police. Why, we had a big old fancy whorehouse with girls coming from as far off as New Orleans and Gulfport, just for us Americans. The prettiest ones stayed for only a few months—malaria and whatnot—but never mind, we had a rollicking good time.

"We tried our darnedest to make a go of things here. We drained the swamps to get rid of the breeding grounds for the mosquitoes. We gave the workers plots of land so they could grow their rice, plantains, and beans. We truly tried building schools and churches and whatnot. I don't know if it was the diseases or the inherent laziness of the workers, but all we did was tread water. Then the Company decided to move headquarters inland to Bananera, so that the big chiefs would be closer to the banana plantations. Personally, I wouldn't have minded the change myself, but my bosses felt I should stay here and take control of port operations. Berkow, do you know what I'm driving at?"

Samuel touched his neck. He was hungry. Two days with no food. Yet all he could do was listen. "I'm afraid not."

Lewis tapped his legs. "Of course you don't. I can see it in your eyes. This is a new world for you. I remember the feeling. Hopping with hope, dreams of bliss, eh?"

"To be honest—"

Lewis quieted Samuel with a wave of his hand. "You don't have to fake it with me, I'm an old dog myself. But listen to me. It'll save you a lot of grief, especially when you are dealing with some of these unsavory critters who aren't even grateful to the mothers who gave them life. I'll give you an example. We put up a hospital in Quiriguá, which the natives can go to anytime they feel sick. We pay the pickers a wage, which they never had in their whole lives. We've built schools right out in the fields and tried to get schoolteachers to teach the children how to read. We've created hundreds, maybe thousands of jobs, pumped money into the economy, turned jungle into fields—did I tell you that there's a nine-hole golf course in Bananera?"

Samuel shook his head.

"Amazing, really, to see this short little grass growing and have sand dunes in the jungle. Well, all the Company has ever asked for is to have the right to do business as we see fit without interference from the government. There are some busybodies who go around stirring up the workers by claiming that we own too much land; that we meddle in politics to get laws passed that only benefit us; and that we deal brutally with the workers. Well, they don't have a clue what it's like to try and keep this banana business going. If it's not Panama Disease or sigatoka attacking the crops, it's malaria or scurvy attacking our employees. If it isn't disease, it's a worker riling up the other workers instead of putting in a day's honest labor. Berkow, you have no idea how many headaches we have. Have you heard of Ubico?"

"I think my cousin mentioned him in a letter."

"Well, he's the big boss in Guatemala, the president. I gotta laugh when he puts on his military uniform with all these medals making his blue shirt sag and goes clopping on his horse down the middle of the streets as if he were Napoleon. Berkow, it's a sight.

"Anyway, the highland Indians call him *Tata*—something like *Pops*—because he's a half-breed like most of them and he knows them inside and out. Why, this year we had a vagrancy law passed that says the Indians must actually get jobs and make money or else they'll be forced to build roads for the country. No more idling around, growing crops in your yard, practicing your Indian mumbo-jumbo, cutting off the heads of chickens. And to show his good faith, Tata cancelled the debts of all the Indians—something I wouldn't mind him doing for me!

"This is the kind of legislation that will produce results. Free labor won't work in Guatemala like it does in the States. If meddlers had their way, they'd take back the lands that we acquired legitimately and parcel it out. But them Indians plant just enough corn to keep their families alive—they have no idea how capitalism works. I ask you, is this any way to run a country, having people living in their little huts and praying to stones?"

"Mr. Lewis, this is all so new to me. What do I know? I'm from Hamburg. What you're saying makes sense—"

"I knew you'd agree!" Lewis beamed. "You're an intelligent man. Someone I can talk to."

Samuel felt hot inside. He felt like rushing out of his room and jumping into water. Or better yet: going to the train station!

"You see, Berkow, I need you to understand me. Despite what I may sometimes say—I'm not careful with my words like a university professor—I care very much about the natives. I believe that everyone should be lifted out of poverty. I do. I even have a personal letter from President Ubico thanking me for my help in drafting and instituting the vagrancy law—to be honest, all I did was make a trip to Guatemala City with several dozen envelopes that Sam the Banana Man asked me to bring him. Old Ubico liked that and I got a bit of a kickback, to be honest . . . So to show all my gratitude, I've decided to will my money in my mother's name to a small Protestant mission on the Guatemalan side of the border with Honduras, to be used to educate the Indians so that they drop their heathen ways. It's an uphill battle, but it'll be my small way of giving thanks. I certainly don't want Esther to get ahold of my money!"

"That's generous of you."

"Yep," Lewis said, breathing in as he spoke, "I've no wife and no children, so what the hell." He placed his hat back on his head. His shirt was already patched with sweat. "I just wanted someone else to know how I feel deep inside. No one but Esther ever did, and you remember what she did to me. You do understand, Berkow, don't you? People get the wrong impression of me."

Lewis stood up, and Samuel followed. Lewis was so overcome with emotion that he raised his arms to hug Samuel, but then clumsily dropped them to his side.

"Bye, Berkow. You'll be heading inland today?"

"Yes, on the train."

"The trains," Lewis said, bobbing his head. "They're terrible. We own them, but can't find anyone responsible to manage them. Conductors are always hitting the bottle. Must be boring work, I guess. Well, if I don't see you again, best of luck. Write to me when you get to the capital. Who knows? I may have to go there soon to deliver a few more envelopes, if you get my drift. And if you come through Puerto Barrios, look me up. I'd be glad to see you again."

Samuel held open the door. Lewis stepped out into the corridor, turned around, and gave him a fake jab to the face.

"So long, buddy. Keep your chin down and your guard up. And don't forget my advice. It comes from experience." And off he went.

Samuel shook his head: Lewis had begun by asking him for permission to give him advice and ended up delivering a full speech. No matter what the situation, Lewis was always searching for an audience.

Samuel was pressed for time, but felt too deflated to begin traipsing around Puerto Barrios. He slumped into his chair and stared into his palms, unable to rally his strength.

He remembered the time he had gone with his Hochschule friends to visit a palm reader. All the preliminary hocus-pocus had bored him, but his interest had perked up when the gypsy indicated the significance of each crease in his hand. She prophesized financial ups-and-downs, but improving prospects if he ever decided to stop traveling so much. As to love, the lines were inconclusive—they pointed out much heartbreak, betrayal, though if he could learn to trust, he would find a loving mate. If he wanted to have a long life—which was possible—he needed to avoid conflicts, develop some sort of quiet hobby like chess or stamp collecting, and live far from the sea . . . He could learn to avert conflict and misunderstanding by developing calmness, poise, and balance.

With his left forefinger, Samuel now traced the lines of his right palm. He couldn't remember which line stood for what—at the time, the gypsy had been so explicit. Now they all seemed to run in circles, merge, veer off, shatter into so many fragments and wrinkles. He sneered, as if this would dismiss the palm reader's prophecy from his mind. Besides, what could a puckered woman with too much cosmetics and weighed down by trinkets know about his future?

Patience is the best remedy for trouble, she had said.

White light was pouring into his room. Samuel walked into the corridor and gazed out. A pair of frigate birds soared high in the milky sky above Amatique Bay. Beyond the shabby little park and the dense vegetation along the shore, he could see the *Chicacao* still flush against the long pier. Across from it, standing huge and monumental, was the *Banana Reefer* surrounded by tiny stick figures—stevedores loading the last fruit into the hold of the ship. Funny, the pier was so close by—no more than three hundred yards from the gatehouse, where he had bribed the immigration agent, to the steps of the hotel. The walk had seemed so endless last night, desolate. For a brief moment, he forgot how he had made it to the International Hotel—had Lewis accompanied him or had he come by carriage or taxi? Now he remembered Mr. Price—a nasty little man with no pride. His body tightened with rage.

Samuel went back into his room. There was an oval mirror with a carved frame just above his chest of drawers. He glanced at himself. He was still handsome, some might say. His dark brown hair, though receding, didn't have a fleck of gray. He touched the skin around his cheekbones—it was a bit loose and there were small bags under his eyes. Such beautiful eyes, Lena had said, green like fine China jade.

Despite the weight in his heart, the world still offered him infinite possibilities. That was it—Samuel had to seize the reins and not be afraid to take the big step. He shouldn't live like a mole in the recesses of darkness.

Samuel stepped back from the mirror, still admiring himself. Though he had a boyish, slender build, he had the bad habit of bunching his shoulders and leaning forward as if unreasonably burdened by responsibility. His nose in this downward posture seemed too fleshy and dipped, but if he straightened, tilted his chin upwards, he seemed altogether dignified. Lena had been right—with a little bit of grooming, he could have joined her brother and kept company with the Prince of Wales. It was in part a question of his wardrobe, for sure, but most of all his posture: *Stand up straight, chin up, let your lips hide your crooked teeth!*

For a final few seconds, Samuel stared deeply into the mirror, as the gypsy had into his palm. How horrible! He saw a shrunken old man with choppy white hair staring back at him. A dark mole crowned his forehead. His face was textured like burlap, and the corners of his mouth pulled down in a sour, glum expression.

He closed his eyes and groped for the towel he had left on the bed. When he found it, he brought it back to the mirror and draped the towel over it. He certainly didn't need to see himself in this figuration.

He remembered that after his grandmother had died, all the mirrors in the apartment were covered for the sitting of shivah—yes, some Ashkenazi ritual that went back to the Middle Ages. Some more hocus-pocus. Mirrors, dwarves, stupid gypsies, a man named Kingston with a smashed voice box, a pet iguana—where was he, he questioned himself bitterly, part of a traveling circus?

Samuel went over to the sink and poured himself a glass of water from the pitcher. He then poured a bit more water into the wash bowl, dipped the towel into it, and scrubbed the back of his ears. Now he was clean.

And for one of the only times since his war days, he didn't shave. He simply didn't have the spunk for it. Besides, who would even care?

He was ready to go out and face the world. He placed his passport in his shirt pocket—it would be dangerous to be picked up without proper papers—and stuffed all the dollars he had into his pants. He latched the door shut from the outside, knowing that if a thief got in, he had no real protection. He did this simply to keep the door from flapping in the wind.

As he walked down the corridor toward the staircase, he started humming "Himmel und Erde"—Sky and Earth—which was literally a recipe of apples, onions, and potatoes, but also a lovely German song which somehow made Samuel feel bold and confident.

From somewhere in the bay, a horn sounded.

The *Chicacao* had steamed out.

Day had begun.

Chapter Ten

It was already late in the day. Samuel should have gone directly to the train station, with suitcase in hand, but instead he sauntered into the hotel dining room. He was hungry, but it wasn't that. He felt that he wanted to sit down and eat as if to prove to himself that he was entitled to be properly served. He settled himself at a table along one wall and waited as if he had all the time in the world.

The light blue room was spacious and airy, with a high wooden ceiling, like those dance halls so popular in Berlin in the 1920s. While he waited for the waiter to bring him a menu and take his breakfast order, Samuel recalled that his first official date with Lena had ended in a club called the Top Hat in the Reeperbahn. They had arrived around midnight, after dinner and a variety show at La Boheme, and danced tangos—the new rage—till five in the morning. Lena danced dramatically, hooking a leg around Samuel's, bringing him closer to her face and her downcast eyes. And whenever Samuel tried to kiss her red lips, Lena would open her eyes, her sparkling green eyes, and spin Samuel gracefully away from her. This sort of tease continued, on the dance floor and at their little candlelit table, till all the other couples left and they were alone.

The musicians were putting down their instruments when Samuel called the violinist over and offered him a fat tip to play a private serenade for them. He played a Grieg solo and as they listened to the plaintive violin, they held hands and sipped apricot brandy. Samuel was particularly happy, having played the role of the attentive gentleman: gratifying Lena's whims even before she pronounced them, combining elegance and flair on the dance floor, and tipping generously.

When the solo had ended, Samuel escorted Lena arm-in-arm out of the club. It was morning. The city, under clouds and fog, was already charged with life: street sweepers were sweeping paper and leaves into piles, milkmen rattled empty cans in their wagons as they made their deliveries. Samuel whistled, waking up the driver who had dozed off atop his cabriolet in front of the club. They climbed into the cabin and he asked the driver to take the long way along the river to Lena's brother's apartment. Snow had begun falling, swirling in the air like feathers, leaving no more than a light dusting on the streets and sidewalks. At seven, he tried kissing Lena on the mouth, but she turned, so that his lips landed on her cheek. As he moved away from her, she grabbed him by the shoulders and put her lips and tongue on his mouth. They stood quietly deepening their kiss by the open oak door as if no one else on earth existed.

When they parted, Samuel asked: "Do you love me?"

Lena looked at him and answered: "Very much." She then laughed aloud, childishly so, and scurried into the house.

Samuel had stayed glued to the spot, snowflakes falling on the rim of his homburg, glaring at the bronze knocker on the closed door.

Happiness finally seemed within reach.

He could still feel the imprint of her thin red lips on his now scraggly face. He had rushed home—showered, shaved, and changed—ready for the workday. He had arrived at the store in a daze: the manager couldn't understand his gaiety, the salesgirls teased him about his new devil-may-care attitude. He was floating on air, like a snowflake lifted by a gust, twirling and spinning, without a worry in the world.

Now he touched his lips and shook his head. He had needed a woman to confide in, a warm bosom where he could rest his head. Lena had listened attentively to him recount his war experiences and also his complaints about his bickering parents, but she had smiled and made light of them, as if his complaints weren't so serious. Lena loved to caress his arms as he spoke, petting them, but she didn't listen all that carefully. He blamed it on the fact that she was years younger, that she came from a sunny climate, that her parents had protected her from all ills. How could she possibly understand? She was lighthearted, bubbly, and, yes, superficial.

It had been a mismatch from the start.

Samuel bit softly into his finger. After Lena went back to South Africa, he had closed the spigot of his feelings. He vowed never to let them gush again. When his body needed attention, he would go to one of the whorehouses in the Reeperbahn, the finer ones of course, not too close to the docks. Once a month would do, no more, because he always felt dirty later, as if somehow satisfying his sexual urges in exchange for money was beneath him. For days afterward, he would be gloomy and demoralized, until the sexual urge arose again and the cycle would be repeated . . . Yes, Germany was a long way off, much further than the thousands of sea miles that separated it from Puerto Barrios. What proof did he have that it even still existed?

And here he was in Puerto Barrios. He listened for dishes to clank in the kitchen, but it was eerily quiet and no one came to take his order. He glanced around the dining room. Each table was decorously set with linen tablecloths and napkins, porcelain, and silverware.

Much as he regretted doing this for reasons of simple etiquette, Samuel picked up his knife and began to tap lightly on his goblet. No one came. He took up his knife again and started drumming on his plate with it.

The noise brought George in from the lobby this time.

"Can I help you, Mr. Berkow?"

"Good morning, George. Yes, I'd like to order breakfast. Nothing greasy—I haven't eaten for days—just some toast, marmalade, and coffee, no milk. Perhaps a boiled egg."

George tightened his lips against his teeth. "I'm sorry, Mr. Berkow, but the kitchen's closed. As you know, you and Father Cabezón are our only guests and, well, our kitchen is on a schedule." He let his head swivel around the room till his eyes settled on a wooden column a few feet away. Samuel read the sign on the column:

Se sirven las siguientes comidas a las siguientes horas
Desayuno de	*7:00 a 8:30*	*Precio:*	*$0.75*
Almuerzo de	*12:00 a 14:00*		*$1.00*
Cena de	*18:00 a 19:30*		*$1.10*

Sólo podemos atenderlos durante estas horas.
Gracias
Gerencia Hotel International

"But it isn't quite eight-thirty, is it?"

George scratched his head. "I'm sorry, but it's after ten, sir. I'd get you something to eat, but the cook's gone until noon and I have to watch the front desk."

"Oh, I see," Samuel replied. "Well, never mind. I wasn't so hungry, anyway."

"It's the heat that does it, sir."

Samuel tapped his plate with his fingers. "I suppose you're right," he said gloomily. "Well then, can you direct me to the train station?"

"It's not far. Do you remember your way back to the pier?"

Samuel frowned. "I'm afraid not."

George pointed to the front door of the hotel. "Come with me. I can at least set you in the right direction."

Samuel got up and the two men walked across the dining room to the lobby. Kingston was sweeping the floor by the entrance. "I didn't know he works at the hotel," Samuel whispered.

"He doesn't—officially. Since the strike by the stevedores, I let him do some work for me here. I give him his meals and he feels he's doing something useful." George held the screen door open for Samuel to pass onto the veranda.

"What happened during the strike, if I may ask?"

"It's no big secret," George began, "but no one really wants to discuss it anymore. The workers asked for more money, and the Company said no. They organized a meeting during a lunch break and some soldiers came to break it up. Lewis was there and he ordered them back to work. The workers refused. There was some shoving and pushing, and Kingston got squeezed toward the front. Bullets flew and three workers were killed. Kingston was badly hurt. The workers claimed that Lewis had instigated the shooting, but there were no outside witnesses. The judge was paid off and the case against the soldiers was dismissed. That was it!"

"And Kingston received no compensation?"

George stared at Samuel. "You must be joking."

Samuel felt slightly embarrassed. "Everyone should respect the law," he answered. "And there are people who must enforce the law. If you break the law, then you're punished. Innocent people must be protected."

"Is that the way it is in Germany?" George asked, without sarcasm.

"Well, not exactly. The law is there, but now we have some troublemakers who have overstepped it, taken it into their own hands."

"Exactly. There you have it."

Samuel shook his head and looked out. The sun had risen far above the bay palms and the huge leafless jacaranda that arched over the band shell in the park in front of them. The sunlight fell flush against his face, making his body feel hot all over. "Poor man, poor, poor man," was all he could say.

George merely shrugged. He shook a cigarette out of his pack, put it into his mouth, drew out a small box of wooden matches, and lit up. "At least he wasn't killed. And after the court case, Lewis gave Kingston one hundred dollars to let the matter drop. One hundred dollars can buy plenty of silence—not that he can ever speak again."

"I'm sure it does. So why did Kingston get involved last night at the bar?"

"Oh, that was different. Besides, all Kingston did was hold Lewis back and he would be too drunk to remember. What happened at the union meeting tamed Kingston for life. It should have tamed all of us, but there are still some workers who meet secretly with union officials. It's going to end badly, I'm afraid. To be honest, I should get out of here before I do something really stupid. What if Lewis remembered that I hit him last night? You would turn against me—"

"No."

"Please, Mr. Berkow, I know what I am talking about. If he remembered, I would be arrested and you would have been forced to testify against me. Certainly I wouldn't be here with you, talking and smoking, as if I had nothing better to do . . . Oh well . . . Something tells me that I am beginning to talk too much."

"Not at all."

George took a long puff of his cigarette and blew the smoke out immediately, without inhaling. He pointed across the park with the hand holding the cigarette.

"There are two ways to get to the train station. The long way is to follow this path along the front of the hotel until you hit the main road and turn right. Otherwise you can shoot across the park and pick up another path through the brush, which will get you there twice as fast."

"No more shortcuts for me—not after last night."

The clerk offered a foolish smile. "Good luck. Will you be back for lunch?"

"I don't know," Samuel responded. "First, I need to find out the train schedule. And then I'll decide what to do. I'll definitely be back to pick up my suitcase." He gave George a funny kind of military salute and left.

It was a cloudless day. Without thinking, he took the shortcut—the path across the treeless park. Samuel had left his hat in the room and now he felt the tropical sun searing his face and scalp. Last night everything had seemed murky, out of focus, but now everything was sharp and clear as if cut by a knife.

When he reached a spit of land that extended into the bay, he stopped and gazed out toward the water. He thought he could pass the morning sitting on a flat rock under an almond tree. It would be pleasant to sit quietly and watch the wavelets moving in geometric precision on shore.

Samuel was dawdling, and he knew it. Did he want to stay in Puerto Barrios for the rest of his life? Surely he hadn't needed eleven hours of sleep. Why hadn't he risen at daybreak and gone immediately, with his suitcase in hand, to telegraph his cousin that he had arrived, or gone to the train station to check the schedule? By now, he might have even received a reply from Heinrich. Was he secretly afraid his cousin might not be so helpful?

What was taking him so long to get the day started?

Samuel pressed his palms against the side of his head. His stomach gurgled noisily. He had to get a grip on himself. Yes, what had happened in the last day would be enough to demoralize anyone, but Samuel knew he had to snap out of this stupor which dulled his mind and made him dumb and drowsy.

He walked briskly down the path, ducking branches and thorns, until it merged with the gravel road. Here he turned left, past a wall of empty oil drums and broken crates stacked on the side of the road. Coming toward him were several Caribs lugging sacks of flour or cement on their shoulders; they broke formation for him to pass between them. He walked alone on this road tamped down by spilled oil. Squinting, he saw in the distance a conglomerate of wooden buildings—the center of Puerto Barrios—but now here, immediately on his right, was the train station.

He went up a couple of steps and entered a huge wooden structure with an arched ceiling. It had a few metal benches; otherwise it was clear of furniture. Across the room he saw a barred ticket window with a light on in front. He could make out a clerking sitting in there.

Samuel headed to the window and spoke excitedly: "I hope you can help me."

The man looked up from a magazine he was reading, but said nothing.

"Can you tell me when the next train leaves for Guatemala City?"

"Usually it leaves around seven p.m."

"Are you sure? I wouldn't want to miss it."

The clerk smiled. "You can never be sure."

"Don't you have to keep to a schedule?" Samuel asked, trying not to lose his temper. He had so many reasons to be angry, not least of which was because no one in this town seemed to know anything with any degree of certainty. It was all guesswork and supposition.

The clerk rubbed both sides of his unshaven face with his palms. "Sir, the schedule's posted in front of you." He pointed to the wall on his right. "But that doesn't mean we hold to it. It's been like that for years and I don't see why things should change now. It's mostly a freight train, with a couple of passenger cars."

"I don't understand."

"Look, sometimes the train arrives from Bananera at four, sometimes at six, and sometimes not at all. The cargo has to be unloaded, and then freight bound back to Bananera and Guatemala City has to be loaded. If you go through that door, you will see that the platform is already full of heavy crates."

"But that's impossible. A train must leave on time. What's a schedule for, then?" If he could only speak in German—his thoughts were coming out confused in Spanish—he knew he could make himself understood.

The clerk shrugged. "The train owners make money on freight, not on carrying a couple of dozen passengers to Bananera, Zacapa, and Guatemala City. Now, if you don't have any more questions, I'd like to get back to my work." He shifted in his seat and returned to flipping through his magazine.

Samuel tapped on the counter.

"What now?" the man asked without looking up.

"Let me speak to the station master!"

"The what?"

"Your supervisor! I demand to speak to him!"

The clerk looked up and grinned. "Sir, he's been in Guatemala City for the past week."

"Isn't there anyone else I can speak to?"

"No, not unless you want to drive to Bananera and talk to the supervisor there. I don't suppose you have a car. It's about sixty kilometers from here."

"This is no way to speak to a customer!" Samuel replied, digging his nails into his palms. "I shall file a report when I get to Guatemala City." As soon as he said this, he knew he never would. It was all so pointless.

The clerk grinned again, and shrugged.

Samuel felt his head pounding. In Europe, a station manager would have reprimanded, suspended, or even fired the clerk for being so curt and insolent. Such conduct would never have been tolerated in Germany, not even during the worst of times. In Germany, in Germany, in Germany, many things might have happened, but here he was thousands of miles away at the mercy of a brutish clerk who was clearly unsupervised and thus did what he pleased.

"I'll be back in a few hours. Perhaps you will have more information by then."

"This office is closed between twelve and two for lunch."

"Yes, I know, siesta time," Samuel said, his lower lip trembling. He turned around and walked heavy-footed across the station.

Outside, the sun hung straight above him. Samuel saw that the road he had just walked down was beginning to undulate from the heat. To his left was the pier and the government buildings, and to his right, the town itself. Samuel made a half-turn toward Puerto Barrios, then stopped, as if a hand had clasped him by the back of his shirt. It was Lewis's voice warning him not to mix with the townspeople because they were a rowdy bunch that carried guns.

"Besides, Berkow, anything you might want can be found within the confines of the Company buildings here on the pier," Lewis had said.

Samuel shaded his eyes. In the lumberyard across from the station, half a dozen men were lifting lengths of timber onto a flatbed car. Near them, several dogs—sacks of bones, for the most part—lounged around a brown puddle as if it were an oasis. One dog stood up, slurped some of the water, sniffed the air with its snout, and lay back down.

"I must get out of here," Samuel said aloud, his stomach clamping up. "I must wire Heinrich." He pulled his handkerchief out of his back pocket and mopped his brow

What was Puerto Barrios like? Unpainted wooden buildings, no sidewalks, no promenades, no streetlamps, no green parks, no smoky cafés, no dignity whatsoever! Raw sewage, filthy cat houses, beggars sleeping on top of each other in the shadows.

This was die neue Welt . . . aber die Leute, mein Gott, sie sind eine echte Schande . . .

Everything here seemed sordid and diseased, disfigured by creatures that merely howled and spat. Other than George, wasn't Lewis the most sensible man he had met here? And yet he was on the verge of madness: lucid one second, his mouth rambling about anything the next—

Samuel kicked a rock into a pile of cornhusks near the side of the road. A three-legged mongrel that had been lying there stood up, yelped, and simply hobbled away. Samuel bent down and picked up a rock, which he flung straight at the dog; it bounced on the road and hit the animal in the ribs. Again it yelped.

A Carib woman came out of a shack and shook her fist at Samuel. She wore a loose brown dress; a red and black bandana cropped her head. "What are you doing to my dog?" she demanded.

"I beg your pardon."

"That's *my* dog. You have no right to hurt it!"

Samuel bent down, grabbed another rock. "Get back inside your house."

"And now you threatening me, you crazy old man?"

Samuel snapped his arm. The woman shrieked, and rushed back inside her house. He made a vague motion to go after her—to do what, he didn't quite know—and then the fear of his own madness stopped him in midmovement.

Chapter Eleven

Samuel walked quickly back to the hotel. His eyes burned with sweat and his stomach knocked as if a bomb were ticking away inside of it. He passed a ceiba, dead branches raised to the sky, with a sign nailed to the trunk warning pedestrians and cars to look both ways before crossing the train tracks.

Once across, a paved road angled left. Out of curiosity, Samuel followed it for a few hundred feet till it dead-ended at a three-story building surrounded by fence palings and unkempt shrubbery. A sign was still legible across the boarded up entrance: *Club Pigalle: Herzlich Willkommen.* Was this the fancy whorehouse—girls from Finland, Germany, and Sweden—that Lewis had yammered about? He had claimed that ten girls comprised the stable, each solicited for her talents in a particular sexual pleasure.

Samuel laughed—Puerto Barrio's only paved road led to an abandoned whorehouse!

He turned around. When he reached the intersection, he bore left toward the pier. The gate was wide open, but the customs guardhouse of the night before was empty and dark. He walked on the wooden slats until he saw the commissariat and the Fruit Company offices. The telegraph office was right there in front of them.

As soon as Samuel stepped in, a dark-skinned man who sat at a table in the center of the room looked up. He had blue eyes, a swollen nose, and a goatee that hung three or four inches from his chin.

"Good morning," Samuel said. "I want to send a telegram to Guatemala City."

The clerk tugged on his goatee. "You're in luck! The telegraph's just begun working again. It was down for a week," he said in English. He put a sheet of paper in the typewriter. "Your name, please?"

"Berkow. B-E-R-K-O-W. Samuel. Do you want to see my passport?" he asked, touching his shirt pocket. "Or should I write it down for you?"

"No, I got it," the clerk answered, typing away. "And to whom are you sending this wire?"

"To Heinrich—H-E-I-N-R-I-C-H—Berkow. Same last name. Tienda La Preciosa. Sexta Avenida y Octava Calle. Zona Uno. Ciudad de Guatemala."

The clerk typed on. "Your father or brother?"

"What business is it of yours?"

The clerk glanced up. "I meant nothing by asking . . ."

Samuel realized he was still smarting from the railway clerk's rudeness. "I didn't mean to snap at you. The heat's too much for me . . . Heinrich is my cousin."

The clerk went back to his typing. Samuel could barely read the letters. "And your message?"

Samuel hesitated. "I'm not sure what I want to say," he said, embarrassed.

"Take your time," the clerk smiled. "If there's anything, there's plenty of time around here."

A dark scrim curtain fell across Samuel's mind. He paced back and forth in front of the clerk. A loose slat creaked. How should he put it? A wrong word, here or there, could spoil everything. Samuel's temples throbbed. What could he say to his cousin that would sound warm, humble, grateful, and still get to the point? Heinrich knew why he had come to Guatemala. It was no great mystery.

Arrived last night in Puerto Barrios. Will take train tonight to Guatemala City. Am in desperate need of work. Will take whatever is available.

He should say something about Uncle Jacob, even if it wasn't true.

Your father sends regards. Hope you are well. Samuel.

When the clerk finished typing, Samuel asked him, "When will you send the telegram?"

"In a few minutes—before I close down for lunch."

"And when should I have a reply?"

The clerk laughed. "I can't tell you that. What I do know is that your cousin will have the telegram delivered to him one hour after I send it. If you tell me where you are staying, I'll bring you the reply myself."

"That won't be necessary. I'll stop by later, if you don't mind."

The clerk laughed again. "Mind? Why should I mind? I appreciate visits. It's boring work to be here alone. Now that the Fruit Company has its own telegraph, this office will be shut down. If that happens, I will return to my house in Livingston."

"Livingston?"

"You've never heard of it?"

It sounded strangely African to Samuel and he said so.

"It does, doesn't it? It's a small fishing village across the harbor. I'm surprised you've never been there." The clerk snapped his fingers, pointing to the note he had just typed out. "That's right, you just got here last night." He offered Samuel a chair. "Why don't you sit while I send the telegram from my cabin in back? It'll only take me a few minutes."

The clerk disappeared behind the scrim curtain. Samuel sat down and immediately heard a stream of punctuated taps. He felt at ease with this man—despite his shabby dress, he seemed polite, good-natured, willing to please. Perhaps he had been educated abroad.

The clerk soon returned. "Livingston's at the mouth of the Rio Dulce up the coast. It was a Belgian settlement, I believe, before the British and the Germans came to Guatemala fifty years ago. They all left for the highlands after a few years—it was too hot for them, I guess."

"Did your family come to Livingston from elsewhere? Your blue eyes—"

"You noticed," the clerk interrupted, removing a stack of yellow papers from another chair and sitting down next to Samuel. "My mother's from India originally. A Hindu, but everyone calls us *coolies*. Her family came over fifty years ago to cut lumber and they stayed. My father's a Creole. He says I have cousins in South Africa with light skin and blond hair, but you wouldn't know that by looking at me. Just by my eyes."

Samuel laughed aloud.

"Did I say something funny?"

"No, it's just that in Germany, people have to verify the purity of their blood—as if that were a great accomplishment. I was just thinking that if everyone had been born looking alike, there might not be so much hatred."

"A wonderful idea, Mr. Berkow, but people are always finding something to hate. Even in a small place like Puerto Barrios. While the Fruit Company was growing, everyone smiled and was willing to be your friend—yes, as long as you took off your hat to the white people, there was no trouble. But when the Company moved its headquarters to Bananera, even your old friends began fooling you. Everything seemed out of control. No more trust, every man for himself. Maybe we should start over again here."

Samuel nodded. He enjoyed talking about the past, a glorious past, one in which his place in the scheme of the world was assured. It allowed him to access the dreamy wistful mood that he most liked, before his countrymen became brutes. He thought back to his own youth in Hamburg and re-membered how wonderful it had been at home, to be raised in luxury, even though his parents often quarreled. He would sometimes try to identify the exact moment when things began to deteriorate for him. Was it the declara-tion of war? So many things had gone off badly, it was too hard to remember.

"When I first came to Puerto Barrios from Livingston, every week a big white ship would arrive, filled with furniture, rugs and curtains, and dozens of passengers from New Orleans and Boston. There was so much excite-ment." The clerk waved an arm around. "Silk curtains from China once draped this room, and you might not believe it, but a crystal chandelier hung from the ceiling. Only fifteen years ago, Mr. Berkow, everything was still here. Now it's all gone, everything but this oak door, which is too heavy to move. Progress stopped, even reversed, so quickly. I should go back to Livingston, even if I have to survive on wild cashews. Here, there's always a smell in the air like bad fish, but you can never find out where it's coming from. Have you smelled it or am I just crazy?"

The clerk's openness was disarming; Samuel felt that here was a man to whom he could finally talk. "No, I can't say that I have smelled it, but I must tell you that these last two days have been very difficult for me. Less than a month ago, I was in Hamburg, Germany—taking streetcars to restaurants where I could eat well and drink wine. There was a philharmonic, an opera, elegant estates, promenades where the very rich paraded around in new clothes. There are so many new things here, I sometimes think I'm living through a bad dream. Especially in Puerto Barrios, if I may be so blunt."

The telegraph clerk put a hand on Samuel's forearm. "This is no place for you, Mr. Berkow. Things just happen here and you can't figure them out. For example, last week I saw a buzzard and wild dog happily chewing on a dead monkey as if they were the best of friends. Sometimes around sunset I've seen snakes flying through the air. It can all be a bit terrifying. You don't have to play with fire to get burned in Puerto Barrios. When you least expect it, a fire will come looking for you."

"I don't really understand what you mean."

"It would be useless for me to tell you to look around you, but we have birds that bark like dogs, flowers that bleed when you pick them. Strange things. Do you know which animal is the most dangerous here?"

Samuel shrugged. "Tarantulas . . . poison snakes . . . scorpions . . . I don't know."

The clerk smiled. "I like tarantulas myself. As a child, I would let them walk across my chest. As for scorpions, well, all you need is a broom to sweep them out . . . Ah, but the tiny, little green frog isn't so harmless in Puerto Barrios."

"A green frog? The kind that jumps around the water?"

"Well, a kind of green frog, only very malicious. You see, its urine will make your skin fall off. Its saliva can blind you if it spits in your eye; eating its meat will kill you instantly."

Samuel nodded.

"But there's still a more dangerous creature here, Mr. Berkow. I think you know."

"Oh, but I don't."

"Oh, but you do. I would take a snake in my bed, step into a lion's den, or be chased by a pack of wolves, but I would never want to be in a cage with a starving man. Never!"

The silence that followed seemed inordinately long. Samuel felt slightly uneasy, as if the clerk was expecting him to come back with some kind of profound retort. "I must be going," he finally said, standing up.

"The dangers in Puerto Barrios are often unseen. I didn't mean to frighten you. I hope you know that."

"Of course. But I am late for lunch."

The clerk rose and accompanied Samuel to the door, pushing it open for him to step out. "I'll stop by later, Mr. . . . ."

"Meena," the clerk replied. "But just call me Joshua."

Chapter Twelve

Samuel wanted to go back to the hotel, but the thought of eating alone and biding his time in the lobby with George and Kingston hovering about depressed him. Hunger was wearing him down: he wanted to eat something at the stands lining the pier that sold hot food to the stevedores, but he was afraid to get sick. In the end, he settled for a large fresh orange juice at a nearby stand, which only quenched his thirst.

He scanned the pier. Brightly dressed Carib and Garifuna women were making a beeline toward a red steamer, balancing huge covered baskets on their heads. It was the boat to Livingston. Dozens of Caribs were already packed into the boat, crouching under a piece of haphazardly strung canvas or lolling in the sun protected only by the rims of their straw hats.

Samuel thought that it might be interesting to visit the village across the bay. As he approached the steamer, heads turned to watch him. More heads turned when he struggled up the small rung ladder from the wooden pier to the boat. At the top, a deckhand offered Samuel his forearm; Samuel gripped it tightly and climbed over the side railing to the deck. Here he rolled his shirtsleeves up above his elbows and looked around. There was lots of jabber—adults talking to each other, children laughing and screaming amongst themselves. A scaly skinned toothless woman offered her shaded seat above the engine room to Samuel and moved out into the glaring sun. He felt embarrassed, but as no one said anything and the seat remained unoccupied, he went ahead and took it.

The novelty of his presence among all the black faces wore off as soon as six or seven Carib men tried to hoist a gas stove onto the steamer just above the captain's lookout post. It was comical to see them struggle to balance the stove and then ease it down on the captain's lookout, buttressed by some crated boxes so it wouldn't tip.

Sitting among the crush of bodies, waiting for the boat to push off, Samuel had a kind of epiphany: people in Puerto Barrios seemed to be either malicious or overly deferential. This had to be the result of the abusive power that the Fruit Company wielded, making friends, spies, and enemies by the simplest of actions. This woman, for example: why had she given up her seat? Had she been taught to cede her treasured place at the very appearance of a white man? And why had George and Joshua warned him not to stay in Barrios, when he hadn't even solicited their advice? They were looking out for him, that was all. And the tiny man, Mr. Price, who he wished he could forget—why had he heaped abuse upon Samuel? Was there something in his face that made people either pity or hate him?

Samuel was aware of the chatter around him, yet he felt enclosed in glass with hardly a sound or smell reaching him. He closed his eyes and drifted back to Hamburg. He was eight years old, hiding behind the sofa while his mother played Beethoven's *Appassionata* leisurely on the grand piano. His father and uncle stood by the bay window only a few feet away from him, watching the snow drift down and talking. He heard his father say that Samuel was too serious, much like his wife, so concerned with right and wrong that he couldn't allow himself to enjoy the surprises in life or even let out a sprawling laugh. His Uncle Jacob complained even more about Heinrich. *At least Samuel cares about people. Heinrich talks to them as if they are bolts of cloth, dogs rifling through garbage, ignoramuses not worth common courtesy. I don't know what has made him like that—the taunting of his sisters?* The two men stared out the window without talking. Suddenly, Uncle Jacob clapped his hands and said he must go. His father followed him to the door, handed him his old familiar coat and hat, and came back to the window. Meanwhile, Samuel left his hiding place and ran up to his father and hugged him as if he had been alone in his room and had just discovered his arrival. He wanted to apologize, to tell him that he laughs when he's with his friends and that he can be spontaneous, but before he could say a word, his father patted him on the head and pulled some pocket change out of his trousers. He placed a few coins in Samuel's hand, closed his fist tightly around them, and told him to put on his galoshes before he headed out to the corner store to buy candy. Samuel felt wounded, yet determined to obey his father: he put on his overshoes and took the elevator to the ground floor. Outside, he went down the building steps, slipping and sliding on the sidewalk. It was twilight and the gas lamps had been lit. At the store, Samuel pointed to a jar with chewy coffee balls, his father's favorite sweet and now his. A young attractive woman, wearing an apron and chic dark glasses, smiled at him as she scooped out a few dozen coffee balls and dropped them into a paper bag. At the cashier, he opened his hand to pay and the woman started laughing. Samuel glanced down, saw several buttons in his palm. The woman said never mind, your father will pay me later—*One way or another*, she said with a wink. He was so embarrassed that he ran home crying. Before he entered his building, he glanced up and saw his father smiling and laughing from the window above. He was the butt of his father's jokes too.

Samuel opened his eyes. Unknowingly, he had stood up and raised a hand in the air. Three girls were sitting across from him, pointing and laughing at him, hiding their mouths behind their hands. Samuel dropped his arm. The girls looked at one another, giggled, and buried their faces in their laps. The tallest girl, with piercing black eyes and very straight hair, stuck her fingers in her mouth and started making faces at him. Samuel bristled.

The two other girls joined the tall one in making faces. Samuel realized they were plotting to get the other boat passengers to turn against him. But why? He hadn't done anything to them, nor would he. What right did they have to mock him, a total stranger? Someone needed to teach them some manners, to respect their elders! Was this his calling? Well, why not? If their parents refused to control them, then he would have to discipline them.

"Stop it! I won't have you laughing at me! I don't have to take such abuse!" Samuel howled, lapsing into German. He raised a hand menacingly into the air. There was a lot of buzzing, maybe the engine had been started though the boat was still tied to the pier. The two younger girls immediately stopped their antics, grasping his tone, if not the meaning of his words. But the older girl, defiant and angered at his scolding, gritted her teeth and flicked out her tongue at him.

Choked with rage, Samuel lunged at her. The girl screamed, and hid behind her friends on the bench. All the movement on the boat had stopped, even the stove tottering above the captain's cabin. As Samuel tried to grab the girl and smack her with the back of his hand, a worker stacking sacks of flour next to the engine room held him by the back of his shirt.

"What are you doing, mon?" the man asked in English.

"She's laughing at me!" Samuel said, saliva flying out of his mouth.

The man tightened his grip on Samuel's shirt, forcing his arms to flail uselessly at his side. The passengers began to move away. Some, in fact, were so disturbed by what was going on that they started to take the ladder back down to the pier. A flurry of movement followed as Samuel twisted himself out of the man's hold. Voices buzzed in his ears, but he couldn't figure out what language they were speaking. He didn't understand Garifuna, but it seemed as if someone had said that the white man was going mad—addled brain, hearing strange voices. Others were laughing at his feeble elbowing.

"Let go of me, I tell you!" Samuel didn't know where he was or what he was doing, only that he had to escape. He may as well have been back in Germany, being forced into a boxcar that would eventually reach the gates of Sobibor or Bergen-Belsen. He tried to claw at the man's face, knowing that any minute someone might lunge at him and stick a knife into his chest. He remembered that it began with a stupid prank his father had played on him which had caused him much embarrassment, but then there was this thing with the girls laughing at him. Samuel was fed up with being ridiculed—by his father, Lewis, the dwarf, the train station master. He'd had enough.

But then he was struck by a novel thought—maybe there was a way to escape. Perhaps he could just die, stop being afraid, get it over with and put an end to this life of suffering.

The black man spun Samuel around, held him down against the side of the engine room. Sacks of flour broke his fall and white dust mushroomed into the air. Several people coughed, then it grew quiet. Samuel could hear, with his cheek pressing one of the bags, the bay water lapping the side of the steamer and his own heavy wheezing. He remained on the sacks, unhurt, not wanting to move, pretending to doze until something or someone more momentous than he decided to rouse him.

The man who'd been holding him before came over and stretched an arm down to him. "I don't know what's wrong with you, but I will help you up. Why are you acting this way? You better get off the boat before someone hurts you."

"But I did nothing—"

"Listen to what I'm saying," the man insisted. "I don't want to harm you."

Samuel shook off the man's offer to help and stood up on his own. His face and clothes were white, layered with flour. He could taste blood on his bottom lip. He wiped his mouth with his forearm and stared at the marbled stain, spit and blood. He then glanced at the other passengers shaking their heads in unison like a mute but concurring jury. Samuel bowed his head in shame. *Never, no never, have I acted like this before. What have I done?* He was disgusted with himself, thinking that not even Reeperbahn drunks and louts would behave like this, and all because a young girl had supposedly— he no longer knew for sure—made faces at him.

"I'm sorry," he said out loud to no one in particular.

"Throw the drunk off before he hurts somebody!" a man's voice rung out, sounding a bit like his father's when he spoke English. The crowd cheered.

Samuel saw only a blur of faces. "Yes, I'm going," he said, dusting himself off.

"Well, get a move on, now. The boat can't wait forever for you to decide what you want to do, you know."

Samuel nodded to what sounded like a familiar voice. The passengers opened a path for him. He took a few steps and slipped, but managed to keep from falling by grabbing the steamer's railing. No one stooped to help him.

"He's nothin' but a stumbling drunk," Samuel heard. He wondered if it was the voice of the woman who had originally given him a seat. That would be divine justice, for sure, but the voice was too manly.

Samuel stood straight again and climbed down the ladder slowly, measuring the distance between each rung before stepping. Two hands gently braced his back on the bottom rung and helped him onto the pier. Samuel thanked the man who had helped him, not taking his eyes off his shoes.

"Something has come over me," he said by way of explanation.

From the boat he heard the same voice saying, "He's a drunk, nothing but a drunk. Last night I carried his bags all the way to the International Hotel from the big pier and he tried to get away without paying me. Not only a drunk, but a crook!"

The familiar, squeaky intonation burned in his ears. It was useless to answer back and try to clear his reputation. He preferred a sullied name to arguing with the little man with no manners.

"If I were you, people, I wouldn't let that bum get away. You all saw what he tried to do—beat up on that poor little girl!"

As he shuffled along the pier toward shore, Samuel heard a roar as if everyone on the red steamer was now cursing at him. Any moment, he thought, they would pounce and kill him. What an odd way to go, having survived the enemy on the battlefield, Nazi hooligans in Hamburg, and end up alone like this, all because he imagined some girls ridiculing him.

Then a light went off in his brain—it was wrong to do what he'd done. She was only a child fooling around and he'd lost control, acted like a child beater. He deserved punishment. After all, the girl had such a sweet face. She could have been his daughter . . .

CHAPTER THIRTEEN

Samuel made his way to a stone bench under a leafy tamarind tree and sat down. The flour had congealed with the sweat on his face. He pulled out his handkerchief and tried rubbing off the paste which had hardened into a thin mask. He dropped his head into his hands. Who cared what he looked like now? He felt so helpless and hapless, at the mercy of his own erratic emotions. Each gesture seemed to be wrong and he had to admit that he, not some foe or goon, was responsible for his troubles.

His control over things was disintegrating and he was powerless to stop it. He was alone in Guatemala, lost in a maze of conflicting thoughts and feelings. He wished he had the peace of mind to dissect his life, examine each wrong turn, analyze the important incidents, but he couldn't concentrate long enough to sift out the wheat from the chaff. The dwarf, Mr. Price, had called him a drunk on the red steamer—he was wrong about that, but certainly he had lost the ability to react rationally to situations.

No, he wasn't developing the puffy eyes, the red nose, the lumbering gestures of an alcoholic. He was, however, well on his way to becoming a befuddled mumbler like Father Cabezón, incapable of relying on his own instincts. He had better be careful.

The clouds lay thickly over the water like a quilt. Samuel looked out over Amatique Bay and saw the boat to Livingston plowing along, riding over incoming waves. It wouldn't have been a good day for sightseeing anyhow—he would've gotten sick on the boat. Further in the distance, he saw curtains of rain sweeping toward Puerto Barrios across the water.

He knew he should get back to the hotel, but he couldn't bring himself to move.

Samuel felt desolate—like when he had returned from Berlin and discovered his mother had left his father and moved to Palma with his sister. As soon as he'd seen his father, he'd realized how the abandonment had aged him—gone was the gleam in his eyes, the humorous flashes in his conversation. His father had asked him to wait in the foyer as he retreated to get something from his bedroom. There was absolutely no spring to his step. In a minute he was back, holding the tip of a letter in his fingers as if it were a deadly snake.

The letter said that his mother was on her way to Mallorca. She acknowledged to her husband that they had grown apart and were so different that it was pointless to continue. She said she would send for her things and would appreciate Phillip boxing them up for her. She also insisted that her mind was made up and she didn't want him to come after her. She didn't want to see him ever again and she knew that he would be all right.

By the wear on the letter, Samuel realized that his father had read, crushed, opened, and reread it multiple times. His father had staggered into his arms, and Samuel tried to get him to sit down, but he'd slipped through his arms and fallen on the floor, crying fitfully. When Samuel tried to pick him up, his father resisted with the heaviness of grief and despair. Samuel didn't know what to do; he had never seen his father so defeated.

So after thirty-five years of marriage, his mother had finally initiated an act of rebellion. His father couldn't find comfort in anything, even struggled to get himself dressed. Going to work was out of the question. He was a broken man. Samuel came daily to take care of his father until he died in bed a few weeks later.

Berta refused to come to the burial.

When Samuel visited her in Palma, a week after he had buried his father, he found a woman hardened like a walnut shell, completely indifferent to her husband's passing. It was as if she couldn't even fathom what had happened.

How two months could change things. And to his surprise, his mother hardly acknowledged him, her own flesh and blood. She wanted to be left alone, to thumb through fashion magazines and drink chamomile tea at beach-side cafés. The only passion she showed was when she scolded Samuel for putting ice in an already cold drink—

A soft drizzle gave way to a downpour. Scores of Caribs and Garifunas raced along the pier, lugging carts and sacks to whatever shelter they could find. The stevedores crowded together inside the boxcars that had transported the fruit from Bananera. Samuel couldn't stay under the tamarind since it was peppering him with seeds and pelleting raindrops.

He stepped out from under the tree. To his right he saw the turrets of the hotel just under the cloud line in the distance and began walking in that direction. It took all his strength not to trip on the muddy ground and still keep an eye on where he was going. He reached the railroad tracks, and walked on the ties till he neared the hotel. He circled around several boxcars, crossed two empty tracks, and came upon a barbed-wire fence. He scanned it frantically until he found a tear in the fence marked by two steel drums.

His shirt clung like taffy to his body, his face was streaked with mud and flour, but he had found the trap door that would lead him to El Dorado! The crossing, unfortunately, would not be without peril since the opening was at a point where the bay washed up against rocks. But Samuel was ready for heroic action.

He placed his left elbow against one of the drums and lifted the top wire carefully with his right hand. Pushing down on the bottom wire with his left foot, he opened a space wide enough for his body to pass through. He arched his right foot over the wire and planted it firmly on a flat stone on the other side. Then he switched hands so that his left hand now held the wire and allowed him to slide his back under the barbs. When he had made it past, he sprung his left leg through the gap and plopped it down next to his other foot.

Samuel released the wire and the stone shifted. For a split second, he saw his body toppling on the wire. He twisted away, but his shift was too sudden. The stone slid out from under him and he fell on all fours into shallow water.

Samuel winced. He hobbled up, using a piece of driftwood as a brace. By stretching, he reached solid ground. He looked down at his badly scuffed hands—*Battle injuries*, he thought, laughing aloud. He bent down to examine his legs. His pants were ripped and muddied, his knees bleeding.

He felt ridiculous.

The rain was beginning to let up. He took a deep breath and walked over to an open shed littered with cracked railroad wheels and spokes. Punctured steel drums abounded and the ground was covered with nails and rusting tools. Discarded train and steamer parts were piled about everywhere, in careless heaps.

The hotel lights glowed in the distance; he was not that far away.

Samuel wiped his hands on his pants and then on impulse touched his shirt pocket.

"Oh my God! Where is it?"

Agitated, he searched through his pants pockets several times, turning them inside out, though he was sure he hadn't placed his passport in his pants. He tore off his shirt, squeezing it into a ball.

It's not here, it's not here, he despaired, throwing the shirt on a pile of rusting steel. Then he went back, picked it up, and began shredding the shirt by hand.

He snapped his fingers, turned, and walked over to the bay. He dropped bare-chested on the rocks and stretched his arms as far as he could into the shallow water.

"It must be here," he said aloud, "by these rocks! Yes, I had it on the boat. It must have fallen into the water . . . It's here, I know it is."

Samuel spent ten minutes raking the shore with his hands, but all he snagged were a tin can, a string of brittle wire, a bottle, and a fistful of oozing mud.

He was beside himself, fearing that without proper papers he would be jailed or immediately sent back to Germany—no one could stay in Guatemala without identification.

"I'm finished!" he cried, pounding the water over and over.

When he finally came to terms with the fact that his passport was lost to him forever, he stood up slowly. He was wheezing and panting. He lifted his arms into the air and then slammed his closed fists against his stomach. He teetered on his feet for a moment before he fell facedown onto the shore.

Chapter Fourteen

When it had begun to rain, George closed the register on his desk and came out onto the veranda of the International Hotel. He was proud of himself because he had predicted to Willie, the bartender, that there would be a storm today, confirming his theory that downpours always follow a full blue moon.

He pushed against the screen door, holding it open with his body. He welcomed the rain for it would disperse, at least momentarily, the foul odors that saturated the air in Puerto Barrios. His only concern was that the bad weather would force Alfred Lewis to return to port—he wanted the man with the egg-shaped head and the filthy mouth out of his life for a few days. The steamer sinking was too much to hope for.

George was fed up with Puerto Barrios. He felt it had become a magnet for malingerers and losers and he was sick of the lies he told himself to justify his remaining here. He should have left long ago. The town had become a cow with dried-up udders. When the Company had offered him the opportunity to oversee a guest house in Bananera, he thought that leaving was a betrayal of the dream that had brought him here in the first place. He hadn't been able to imagine himself living inland, surrounded by endless fields of bananas, in a Company town.

What a fool.

If he had any guts, he'd bundle up his things and go back to Punta Gorda and work the small plot of land still in the family name. It would be hard work battling the jungle, but at least he wouldn't have to prostrate himself in front of sneering, embittered men like Lewis.

But then, to return to his village empty-handed, well, that would be admitting to having struggled for twenty years for nothing. Not that his brother Buster, a lawyer in Monkey River, would complain—he had been begging him for years to come back home. Buster thought that the two of them could start a lumber business, since there was so much mahogany idly growing on their land.

No, George was trapped and he had nothing to show for it, other than a small house on the dirt road to Bananera he never stayed in, since he worked day and night at the hotel. This is why he advised newcomers to get out of Puerto Barrios before it was too late—vines grew too swiftly in the region, strangled everything.

He started moving down the steps of the hotel. The beauty of a hard rain was that it pelted everything equally and indiscriminately. In less than twenty minutes, deep puddles had formed in the park and mud was splashed on the sides of the band shell. He groaned at the thought of having to sweep the mud off the walkways afterward, but this too was part of his job. Since the swamps behind the hotel had been drained and the trees on the nearby hills had been cut, currents of mud swirled down unimpeded all the way to the bay whenever it rained hard.

George maintained the band shell on his own, though it had been ten years since any musicians played in it. The municipality had abandoned it, but George replaced the wooden slats on the floor and cemented the sides whenever they cracked from the elements.

That was the trouble with Puerto Barrios—one step forward and two steps back, a crazy dance in which no progress was ever made. It was as simple as that.

George lit a cigarette. Though the air was sultry, the sun was wedging its way through the clouds. In a matter of minutes, it would be out and everything would dry. The world was indeed mysterious.

Suddenly, a scream jolted him out of his stupor. The cigarette fell from his lips and before he could catch it, it bounced down the steps into the muck. "Damn," he mumbled.

When he looked up toward the band shell, he saw a creature the size of a small donkey trudging on all fours in the mud. George's chest started thumping. As it came closer, he realized it wasn't a donkey; it was too low to the ground. It was crawling on its elbows, holding a stick like a rifle in one hand and dragging a coconut shell by the hair in the other.

The rain had let up, but when the lightning flashed off in the distance, he saw the creature stop dead in its tracks, raise the rifle, and howl.

George went back into the hotel. The front of his shirt was wet. He shook his head. Maybe it was the hairy duende his mother had told him speaks a dozen languages and grants wishes to those who believe in him, or maybe it was Sismito who kills whomever he visits. Either way, he was not ready to confront a wild spirit.

When the creature climbed the hotel steps, George saw that it was simply a man and no errant spirit. He went to the screen door and opened. Upon being seen, the man stopped and snarled. He lunged with his stick and threatened to heave the coconut at George.

When Samuel recognized George, he simply put the stick and the coconut down on the steps and crawled on into the hotel. There was foam at the edges of his mouth and his eyes danced wildly inside their sockets. When he reached the foot of the staircase, he stood up and climbed the steps to the second floor.

George walked back out to the veranda, half in a daze. The storm, which had lasted all of fifteen minutes, had lifted and a ribbon of yellow light began streaking across the black, metallic water of the bay.

He would smoke a cigarette and then shovel the mud off the walkways. Later he'd sweep the lobby floor and mop it dry.

He pulled out several cigarettes from the pack in his shirt pocket, squeezed them till he found one that was dry. Cigarette in mouth, he rubbed his eyes—he could not fully believe what he had just seen, but in the end, what did it matter if it was real or not? His lips trembled. Puerto Barrios was cursed.

George put his hand to his cigarette and took quick, cheerless puffs.

CHAPTER FIFTEEN

Samuel had no idea what had happened other than that he'd lost his passport and walked back to the hotel when the rain stopped.

Once back in his room, he kicked off his wet shoes and peeled off his
ripped shirt and trousers. He wrapped a flimsy towel around his waist and
went down the corridor to the bathroom. There he saw a sign tacked to the
wall stating there would be no water until six p.m.

He went back to his room and used the remaining water in his pitcher to
wash the mud and hardened flour from his face. He then sat down on his bed
and rubbed his bruised legs. He knew he shouldn't be dawdling and should rush
back to the train station and telegraph office. Taking out clean slacks, a brown
short-sleeve shirt, and a spare pair of oxfords from his valise, he got dressed
again. Then he sat back down on the bed and resumed rubbing his legs.

He was worried to be without a passport since it would take weeks,
maybe months, to get a new one from the German consulate in Guatemala City—assuming they wouldn't put him off suspecting he was Jewish.
That's what Hitler was trying to prove to the world—that *no* country in
the world wanted Jews. And if the consulate refused to issue him a new
passport—that was a possibility—how would he prove to anyone who he
was? Without proper identification papers, he would have to toe the line,
remain completely inconspicuous, if he wanted to stay in Guatemala. He
knew nothing of the local laws, but the times required everything to be in
order—one false step and he'd be deported. Crooks or finaglers would have
him under their thumb if they learned he had no official papers.

But there was also a positive side to the loss. For one thing, the ties to his past had been cut. He was free to be whomever he wished. And he still had his cousin Heinrich. After a decade in Guatemala City, he must be well connected with the higher-ups in the government. He could ask a functionary to help his cousin get new papers. Connections and money opened up all kinds of possibilities. Samuel could change his name to something more Spanish-sounding like Pablo de la Vega or Roberto Gómez.

A lost passport was not to be sneezed at, but in the end, it could be a serendipitous opportunity for Samuel to remake himself.

There was nobody at the train station. Samuel felt relieved, however, to see palletfuls of boxed goods thronging the platforms. A card taped onto the clerk's window bars said, *Be Back at Two*, but a wind-up clock just above the booth marked ten minutes to three. Samuel was not rattled by the clerk's absence. The train would undoubtedly leave soon for the capital. Maybe he should go to the telegraph office first and see if Heinrich had answered his telegram.

So he headed toward the pier. He passed a man loping his way toward the center of town with a light straw hat pulled down over his face, carrying a sack on one shoulder and singing as he went along. On Samuel's right, he saw children playing with a litter of newly born kittens. A woman's voice rang out from a nearby shack—was it the lady who had taunted him earlier over the dog? And then a mutt came out of a shack, scratched its behind, and walked into a different hut.

Life in a normal town.

As he stepped through the open gate on the pier, Samuel flushed with nervousness. His hours of waiting, his days of uncertainty, would soon be over. He pulled back the oak door of the telegraph office and shouted, "Joshua, I'm back!"

Joshua was typing at his table in the center of the room. "Good afternoon, Mr. Berkow. How did your morning end up? Did you have a chance to visit Livingston?"

Samuel shook his head. "The boat was very crowded and I couldn't find a seat. And then it began to rain. I decided to go back to the hotel and wait. I got soaked as it was." He pointed to his new clothes as if Joshua would even notice.

"You were wise. It was one of those storms that sneaks in over the bay and threatens to destroy all these old wooden buildings. But look at it now," Joshua said, as he stretched his arms around himself, "not a trace of the storm. Not a one."

Samuel peered out the telegraph office's only window. A lone palm tree bristled in the wind. "Just lovely, just lovely."

"Yes, it is."

Samuel spun on his heels. "By the way, have I received a reply yet from my cousin in Guatemala City?"

"Why, yes," Joshua answered, drawing a hand down over his nose. "I've just typed the envelope."

Samuel took the envelope from the clerk, toyed with it for a second, first holding it toward the light and then shaking it as if it held jewelry inside. "You didn't have to seal it," he said.

"All the same," the clerk bowed, "I have to do things the right way."

Samuel stuck a finger under the glue leaf and slid it open. His whole body tingled as he seized the yellow paper and read his cousin's words:

Welcome. This is a bad time. No openings now, repeat no openings in Guatemala City. Spoke to Leon Fishman. Can use you as a ticket taker at Palace Cinema in Escuintla. Best I can do. Don't rush to get here. Enrique.

Samuel's back stiffened. "Where's Escuintla?"

Joshua pointed a finger in the air. "It's on the other side of Guatemala City, toward the Pacific."

"Is it a good town?"

"I wish I could find something nice to say about that place . . ."

"I see." Samuel crushed the message and envelope in his hand.

"I'm sorry for the bad news, Mr. Berkow, if that's what it is."

"Bad news? I don't know. It is news, but I am not so sure what it all means. I've never had a job as a ticket taker at a cinema before. My father used to say, 'No news is good news.'" Samuel let the balled-up paper fall to the floor and buried his face in his hands.

The clerk touched his arm. "Can I do something for you?"

Samuel pulled back as if from a flame. "Don't you touch me. Don't anyone touch me!" He pointed to the door. "I would be grateful if you would open it for me, please."

Joshua stroked his goatee, then held open the door and let Samuel stumble out.

"Mr. Berkow—"

"Please, Joshua. I want to be alone."

The clerk sighed and went back into the telegraph office. Samuel looked askance at the sky where the sun blazed like an orange yolk. His head throbbed as if a gong had just struck it.

So this was it—turned away by his own flesh and blood, without even a cursory meeting. Heinrich was in no hurry to see him. Now or forever.

No longer Heinrich, but Enrique, if you please.

Samuel gazed blindly at the thick, carpeted mountains rising above Puerto Barrios' two-story buildings. He suddenly conjured an image of his cousin sitting on a stool having his shoes shined in a parlor near his office in Guatemala City. He was impeccably dressed in cashmere and was reading a telegram that had just been brought to him by his secretary. Heinrich's brow was knit tightly—he was deeply annoyed. Why was Samuel so persistent? Heinrich had already ignored several letters, trying to wash his hands of the past, but now this telegram was staring him in his face. He was not going to fall prey to calls of conscience! He quickly dictated a note to his secretary and commanded her to send it off at once.

Samuel's stomach cramped and he curled up. He knew that neither words of solace nor childish optimism would ameliorate the pain. His Uncle

Jacob had been totally devoted to him—it had been no small risk to pay off the Nazi officials in Hamburg to make sure his nephew had a legitimate visa for Guatemala.

There was no other explanation for Heinrich's telegram—Samuel was explicitly being told not to come to Guatemala City expecting to be welcomed with open arms. *Taking tickets in a movie house. Probably on weekdays. Burning up in Escuintla.*

Samuel knew one thing—he would never, ever break his uncle's heart by letting him know that his only son, his heir, was a selfish and heartless louse. What would be the point? His uncle would never outlast the Nazi regime. Let him think that in the end his son had acted honorably as he had been taught.

What had he expected? Hadn't his friend Rolf Neumann written to him from Buenos Aires several years ago saying that immigrants—Jews, Germans, or Italians, it didn't matter—were so competitive that they spread vicious lies about one another's businesses to sabotage them? And it got worse. Threats, bombs, fires—even among brothers in competing firms—were common not only in big cities like Buenos Aires and Cordoba, but also in the provinces. Peddlers were ambushing peddlers.

Why would Heinrich—yes, yes, *Enrique*—be immune to such tactics and maneuvers? What a silly belief of blood being thicker than water.

Could fear of competition spark such cold, antiseptic words? Enrique must have ice water circulating in his veins! What interest did Samuel have in selling radios, batteries, and appliances to the middle class in Guatemala City?

No, this was payback time for something he had down to Heinrich thirty years earlier—it had to be that.

Samuel's tongue felt dry against the roof of his mouth. Every joint and cell in his body thirsted for moisture. Sanity was seeping out of his body like an invisible gas from the tiniest of punctures. How could he plug the hole before he went insane? Send Enrique another telegram soaked in blood and tears? What about sending him a photograph of himself, taken now, so he could see what his cousin looked like when he was thrown a noose instead of a life preserver?

Would that get Heinrich's stone heart to melt?

Joshua peeked out the door. "Can I get you a glass of water?"

Samuel smiled. "Water, did you say? The sea is full of water."

"Mr. Berkow, you're not making sense."

"I have no sense at all. No dollars and no sense. Ha ha. I feel better already. Please have a seat," Samuel motioned, tapping his crate.

Joshua took a bucket that had been catching water under the porch of his office, emptied it, turned it over, and sat down.

"I know I probably have no right to ask such a personal question."

"What is it?"

Samuel looked at him. "Joshua, have you ever killed anyone?"

"Killed anyone? How do you mean?" the black man asked.

"Oh, I don't mean in war. I've done that—at least I think I did it when we were fighting in Belgium. The snow was falling hard, the flakes were big and thick, almost the size of walnuts. We were told to keep shooting no matter what—I can tell you that the screaming of the bullets and howitzers was worse than that of the soldiers being hit . . . No, I want to know if you ever murdered a man. You have my word not to tell anyone."

Joshua stared at Samuel with level eyes. "There have been several occasions when the desire clutched my heart, reached down to the tips of my fingers, but there it stopped and a deep feeling of shame came over me. I don't think I could have lived with the guilt of killing someone even if I had gotten away with it. Or maybe I am too much of a coward. Too timid, I suppose."

"Timid?" Samuel shrugged. "I don't really think that matters. It isn't really a question of character. Maybe your religion or the fear of punishment kept you from doing it." He pointed to a guard standing in front of the guardhouse talking to two policemen.

"No, Mr. Berkow. I don't believe it was fear—certainly not of the army or police, all of whom can be bought off. Living in Puerto Barrios has taught me you can't have the luxury of being a private person getting along in your business. There's always someone who wants to squabble with you—for money or love or something stupid like a funny look. For certain trouble-makers, holding your tongue and walking away is worse than laughing in their faces. The Fruit Company made it that way for all the people here. And for us Caribs who are poor and black and only want to be left alone to eat and fish, it's worse. We are at the bottom of a heap with no way to strike back, not even by choosing silence. Like I told you, fire comes looking for you in Puerto Barrios and though the Lord is watching, He doesn't like to step in—"

"You're lucky to be a religious man."

"No, Mr. Berkow, I'm not religious. An English nun in Monkey River educated me, but Sister Roberta's sermons never worked for me. With God, I only choose to be on His right side and not break His rules and com-mandments. I don't think He kept me from killing a man. Something held me back when I was shoved around. And when I saw people I love being thrown to the ground, I closed my eyes. Maybe I just wasn't that angry. Or crazy. Or perhaps I knew that fighting back led to nothing. Or maybe I wasn't desperate enough."

"You think it all comes down to a question of desperation?"

"Yes, I think so. If you have no other choice or don't care what happens, whatever the circumstances—"

"The last straw."

Joshua nodded. "The last straw."

"There has to be a provocation—a reason to set it off?"

"Yes, I couldn't kill on impulse."

Samuel slapped his legs and stood up. "Neither could I."

The sun shone harshly on his face, accenting his wrinkles. "Well, Joshua, I have some things to do before leaving here. I don't think that I will be see-ing you again. I want to thank you for coming back out to see me. You have illuminated the truth. You see, I was beginning to think I was going crazy. Now I know what I must do. I have to get to Guatemala City and begin on my own. And now I know there's nothing that I wouldn't do to survive. It's been a pleasure."

"No, mine," the clerk countered. He quickly added: "But why are you asking me these questions?"

"I'm just curious. You seem such a thoughtful man."

"I hope you're not considering doing something foolish, Mr. Berkow. That would be a mistake. Guatemala has its own rules—it doesn't have a British court of law like in my home country . . ."

Samuel patted the clerk's arm. "Don't worry. I only wanted to know what you thought."

"Take care of yourself. And remember what I told you."

Samuel bowed his head. "About the fire? Yes, I will keep my eyes open— and a bucket of water by my side, just in case!" He waved goodbye to the telegraph clerk and headed down the steps.

Chapter Sixteen

Samuel walked a hundred yards down the road, crossed the railroad tracks, and followed a pink wooden wall for another fifty feet till he came to an opening leading to a field. As soon as he passed through the opening, a soccer ball rolled to his feet. He gave it a hard kick and the ball sailed into the arms of a boy playing soccer. On one side of the improvised field, four old men sat talking on a wooden bench. When Samuel walked by, one of them held a bottle to him and offered him a drink. Samuel shook his head and sat down by himself on a spit of grass and leaned his back against a leafless cypress tree.

He took even breaths as he watched the boys running up and down the field, screaming and shouting at each other. It was music to his ears; he closed his eyes. Samuel knew that for some people, killing was as natural as, say, sweeping crumbs off a table or emptying an ashtray. It was a casual, but necessary act. If Heinrich were to appear before him right now, he would happily break his neck.

Only once before had Samuel felt the impulse to kill outside of the battlefield. He had been sent to Amsterdam in 1934 by his father to negotiate a better price for the leather gloves he was importing wholesale and reselling to other German retailers. Spielberg, the glove manufacturer, was from Berlin originally, and their discussions on pricing were rife with questions and comparisons about how the Jews of Berlin, Frankfurt, and Hamburg were faring under Hitler's chancellorship. They were far apart in price; after much dickering, no agreement had been reached. Spielberg invited Samuel to dinner and, hoping to cement the deal, Samuel accepted.

Spielberg lived alone with his cook and housekeeper in a comfortable four-room flat in a wealthy Amsterdam gracht. Over drinks, he expressed his belief that the current anti-Semitism was a passing cloud that would blow over. It was merely a political tactic by Hitler to gain support of the unemployed populace and force President Hindenburg—"the old man with hemorrhoids"—to finally retire. Once Hitler had consolidated his power, the baiting of Jews would stop—he would have a free hand to freeze worker salaries and lower business taxes, which would finally pull Germany out of its ten-year economic depression.

Samuel had countered by saying that he didn't share this confidence in Hitler, and besides, the situation had gotten so out of hand that a retreat from anti-Semitism would not end it. Spielberg wagged his finger in Samuel's face, saying that he had reliable information to the contrary.

Samuel raised his eyebrows and held his tongue, and it paid off. After dinner, over tea, the contract was settled at the price his father had originally proposed. He was overjoyed—even Uncle Jacob wouldn't have done so well—and finally he was able to relax with his host. He found himself volunteering guarded tidbits: which Jews were leaving Hamburg; which were simply transferring the titles of their businesses to trusted gentile friends; and which were bribing officials so that the harassment would stop.

Spielberg brought out a pad and started taking notes. When Samuel questioned him about this, Spielberg said that he was one day going to write a book—"Of course changing names"—of how the Jews of Germany were able to survive the depression.

Samuel found this all a bit strange, but didn't think more of it.

When he was about to leave, Spielberg's housekeeper announced the arrival of one of his friends. Spielberg insisted that Samuel stay and join them for cognacs—the best Remy Martin! Samuel gave in and followed his host to the foyer where a tall, thin man was slipping out of his overcoat, shaking the wet snow off his hat.

Samuel's throat tightened when he saw that the friend was dressed in full Nazi uniform, down to the boots. Watching Spielberg hug the man like a long-lost brother sickened him. When Spielberg cheerfully introduced him to the Nazi, Samuel didn't know what to do. Maybe he should get a knife from the kitchen, but then again, he was in Holland, a foreign country. Instead, he impulsively thrust out his hand and slapped his host across the face, toppling him to the floor. He then yanked his coat from the closet and stormed out of the flat without saying another word.

Outside the snow was swirling, falling softly into the gray waters of the surrounding canal—Samuel felt proud of himself. If he'd had a gun, he would have killed both men right there. He didn't care if the contract for the leather gloves went through. He knew his father would be proud of what he had done.

Samuel opened his eyes. The sun was setting quickly and the soccer boys were hurrying home.

CHAPTER SEVENTEEN

The door to Samuel's hotel room was ajar. No one was there, but he suspected that someone had gone through his valise because his robe was draped over his bed and there was a pile of white handkerchiefs on the bureau. The chambermaid had tidied up his bed, placed fresh towels on his chair, emptied his washbasin, and refilled the pitcher. She had even washed and ironed his mud-streaked clothes!

He sat on the edge of his bed and scratched his hands, which were all of a sudden itching. The fan sputtered stupidly overhead, wheezing as it turned. In a matter of hours, many things had changed. He couldn't go back to Europe now. It was gone forever. There would be no chance to relive episodes of his life, imagine a different outcome.

Lena had called him a bore. Perhaps he was. He certainly didn't want to spend every night of the week dining with illustrious people, drinking and partying too much, laughing at stupid vaudeville acts where men dressed up as women. But no matter what he thought or said, the truth was that he had loved Lena, and when she left him, she, of course, had broken his heart.

Samuel spread out the objects in his pocket on the bed—a handful of German coins, worth nothing in Guatemala, only souvenirs. Eighteen dollars in his wallet, which would cover his train ticket, a first night in a fleabag hotel—he could bear it—and a few cautious meals. Meals? He had survived for days on air, droplets of water. Maybe he could learn to survive without eating! And if he were about to starve, better to be in Guatemala City, so that the stench of his rotting body would reach his cousin Heinrich's nose.

He had to get out of Puerto Barrios right away, where the heat and humidity seemed to unglue any heartfelt gesture. He needed a good dry climate and the capital was rumored to have it: no more dampness clinging like a leech to his lungs. What business did he have in the tropics where, according to Joshua, there were howling birds, poisonous frogs, flying snakes, giant lizards with spiked tails?

He was a cultured man. As a teenager he had sung in the Hamburg Boy's Choir. If forced to do it, he could still play Chopin on the piano, missing just a few notes of the polonaise.

He stretched out in his bed and fell asleep. His eyes fluttered open a few times, and he became aware of his hot pillow and the flies in his room. He dreamed of falling into a lion's den, strangling the animal with his bare hands, but then being unable to climb out.

When he awoke, he glanced around the room. Feathers from his pillow speckled his bed. Samuel switched on the light, trundled over to the bureau, and removed the towel covering the mirror. Quite an appearance! He had cotton stuck to his face, as if he had slept in a chicken coop. Fine lion it must have been to leave him looking like this.

No wonder people jeered at him.

He undressed and rushed to the bathroom, with a towel wrapped around his waist. Inside, he went over to the shower, unlatched the door, and entered. Three or four wispy spiders scurried away into the chinks of the wood. He hung his towel on a dowel outside the shower door and closed it.

It was stuffy inside the stall. He pulled down on the chain, and a boxful of warm, sulfuric water fell over him. It must have been months since someone had showered there. He washed himself with a piece of green soap, working up a rich lather on his skin, while the water box refilled, making a throaty gurgle. Samuel repeated this several times until he was completely cleaned. His last pull on the chain brought out barely enough water to cover his face. He waited another few minutes for the box to refill, but nothing happened, so he dried off the remaining soap with his towel.

Back in his room he packed quickly, throwing all his clothes helter-skelter into his valise. Then he shaved for the first time in days using the new water from his pitcher. He put on a pair of blue trousers with double pleats in the front, an old alligator skin belt, and a white silk shirt with little wedges and brocaded buttoned cuffs. He stuffed a clean handkerchief in the left breast pocket of his camel hair coat and set it down on the bed.

He admired himself in the mirror. He was proud that he hadn't even nicked himself shaving; there was a fine softness and a sheen to his cheeks. When he dabbed Kolnisch Wasser on his face, his skin turned rosy. With threads of saliva, he flattened down the few unruly eyebrow hairs.

He cocked his homburg slightly to the right of his part—riding just over his right ear—so that he looked almost like a movie star. After pulling down on his shirt cuffs, he slipped into his camel hair coat and placed his valise next to the bed—it would take no more than a few minutes to check out.

Now he was ready for the Puerto Barrios train station.

CHAPTER EIGHTEEN

Night settled quickly over the town, calming the throngs of blackbirds and swallows that whistled and jabbered as they circled above the palm and flamboyant trees.

Set to conduct himself like a gentleman, Samuel approached the ticket window at the train station. The clerk was snoozing open-mouthed in a chair, with his dirty feet propped up on his desk. He did not hear Samuel tapping on the ledge.

"Ahem," he said, pressing his face against the bars.

The clerk stirred. His tongue came out to wet his lips.

"Can you help me now?"

The man opened one eye. "What is it? I'm not a mind reader."

"When's the train leaving for Guatemala City?" asked Samuel, wondering if the man even had a mind.

The clerk lowered his feet and stared blankly at a brown card on his desk. "The train's getting in late tonight—let's see—and leaving at six in the morning."

Holding in his disappointment, Samuel said: "Very good. And must I purchase my ticket beforehand?"

"You can buy it on the train—that way you know what you are paying for." The clerk cleared his throat and spat on the floor behind him.

"So when should I be here?"

"Look, I've already told you when the train's leaving. What more do you want?"

Samuel bit down on his bottom lip; he was happy that the patient German in him was winning out. He would only quarrel with his equal.

"How long is the ride to the capital?"

The clerk scratched his neck and yawned. A bottle of aguardiente, half empty and corked with a dirty rag, stood in full view on a shelf behind him. Thirst seemed to tug at the man's throat—he looked as if he wanted nothing more than to swill down some more liquor and doze until the train trundled in.

"The tracks are in bad shape near Zacapa from the earthquake we had two years ago. Normally it takes twelve hours, but it could take a day."

"I see," Samuel replied, again hiding his disappointment. He carefully went down the platform steps and stopped at the bottom. Glancing up, he saw stars in the airless black sky.

In less than twelve hours he would escape this nightmare. But what if a worse nightmare awaited him in Guatemala City? Nothing had been as he expected, and he would need all his wits to survive.

But he would get by, even if it meant stooping to wash dishes, sweep floors, or take tickets at a movie theater in a sweltering town named Escuintla. The worst was behind him.

The moon shone brightly. Here and there a lone firefly sparkled like a flitting gem before vanishing into the saw grass. Toward his right, he could see shadows snapping at the doorways of the slat-board houses in town.

He knew Puerto Barrios was pestilent, but as an act of defiance, he wanted the townspeople to see him dressed elegantly, to show them he had not capitulated, much less been defeated. He wouldn't be like a dog limping off with his tail tucked between his legs. In fact, he even relished the idea of running into the tiny Mr. Price.

So he headed toward the center of town. After walking less than a few hundred feet, the road sloped up and then leveled where the shacks began. At the first one, he tipped his hat to a group of Caribs sitting on a wooden porch and they waved back to him. As he moved along, the huts bunched together. Samuel could see that they were miserable wooden hovels, neither screened nor sealed, with corrugated tin sheets for roofs. The smell of wood burning and pungent stews widened his nostrils, tightening his stomach like a wrench.

The feeling of hunger was familiar, like the one he'd felt during those delirious hours in the Belgian forest when he had no other choice but to wait for death to overtake him. He had stayed conscious by cataloging merchandise that he might have ordered for one of his father's stores: ten dozen Martin belts from London; forty embroidered silk handkerchiefs from Finland; thirty boxes of bon-bons from Di Capio's in Rome; three dozen umbrellas from Apinal. He had become so confused, he remembered, that eventually the Martin belts were from Finland and the umbrellas from Rome—he had mixed up the quantities as well—but the only thing that mattered was staying awake. When he couldn't repeat the orders anymore because his brain had almost ceased to function, he chewed on a pinecone he had found in the snow to remain conscious. He bit down on the wooden bits as if he could somehow squeeze nutrition out of them. And around him, his blood had begun to ooze from his uniform and jacket and turn the snow into a red marbled tomb . . .

At the intersection, Samuel veered right. On the corner stood the wooden Palace Hotel: six floors of rooms and a façade of painted half-nude women. The hotel and all its windows had been boarded up, but there was an open cantina on the ground floor.

Samuel peered in, craning his neck beyond the folding accordion screen that had been put up to block the view of curious interlopers. He saw several round tables with fat candles on them and pine needles carpeting the floor. He heard lots of laughter and the scratchy sounds of an old record on a turntable.

A fleshy woman in a yellow shift and open sandals came to the doorway and looked out. She ran her eyes over Samuel, deepening her stare. Casually she fiddled with the straps of her dress until one shoulder was bare. She then leaned against the accordion partition, still playing with her strap.

Samuel watched her hungrily. The woman coiled her tongue out of her

mouth and threaded it along her red lips before straightening up and placing a hand squarely on one of her shapely hips—she was challenging him to
give in to his desires.

As the music tempo inside slowed, her free hand snaked down her
throat to the neck of her dress, her rounded belly, settling on her crotch
like a brown starfish.

Samuel's groin stirred. His palms grew wet and he began sweating as
the woman let her fingers rub softly against her dress. He wanted to leave,
but found himself drawing closer to the woman, like an iron filing to a magnet. When she slipped her right foot out of her sandal and stroked her other
leg with the sole of her foot, he thought he was going to explode.

Samuel was nearly upon her when the music wound down and stopped,
though the record continued spinning. The scratching needle pulled him
from his dreamlike state, slowly chilling his desire.

The woman seemed suddenly unnerved. Had she also heard the record creaking? She was reaching out to touch Samuel's arm when a crash
sounded from inside, followed by lots of loud talk and laughter. Someone
changed the record, and several sassy trumpets blared loudly as a new song
started playing.

Si nos dejan,
Nos vamos a querer toda la vida.
Si nos dejan,
Nos vamos a vivir a un mundo nuevo.
Yo creo que podemos ver
El nuevo amanecer
De uno nuevo día,
Yo pienso que tú y yo podemos ser felices todavía . . .

It was a lovely ranchera, sung by a man and a woman, about loving one
another for the rest of their lives, if only people would leave them alone. A
new dawn was coming, a new day, and happiness would be theirs . . .

Swept up by the music, Samuel closed his eyes and began taking steps backward. When he opened them again, the woman was next to him with her dress gathered in her hand around her navel. She wasn't wearing underwear so he stared at her black pubis and her flabby thighs. She grabbed him, pulled his face close to hers, and kissed him on the mouth. He allowed himself to be kissed, his thoughts drifting to Lena.

When he opened his eyes, he saw the aging prostitute in front of him. Without a glance or a word, Samuel turned around to leave. The woman dropped her dress, stepped out of her shoes, and walked quickly after him. She caught his left arm and twisted him around. He tried to push her away, but she was strong and pressed her open mouth against his for a second time, placing his hands on her breasts.

"Let go of me!" Samuel yelled, grabbing his hat as it fell away from his head. He stared into her face and saw jagged teeth gaping out of her mouth. Once more she reached for him, and this time her mouth missed his lips as he was turning away, and she ended up biting his chin.

He struck her blindly in the face.

"Beto! Beto!" the woman shrieked, falling backward on the ground.

As she lay there, Samuel touched his chin—he wasn't bleeding, but he could still feel her teeth marks. Still, he went over to help her up. When he pulled her up by the arms, she began laughing hysterically with the same force and brusqueness of Mr. Price.

He let go of her and she fell again, tossing her head backward in laughter. "Just my luck! Going after a fag!"

"Please, you're drunk. You don't know what you're saying." Samuel tried to shush her by putting a hand over her mouth.

"Don't touch me, you queer!" she screamed, standing back up. "Beto, Ricardo, Joaquín, I've got a queer here!"

She lunged at him, wrapping her arms around his waist to hold him.

Samuel heard chairs shifting and footsteps approaching. He wrenched himself free and tucked his hat under his arm. He started running back in the direction from which he had come, but changed his mind because the revelers from the Palace Hotel bar had come out to the doorway, laughing and drinking.

He continued running down the narrowing road. He refused to slacken his pace till he was in the brush and his body had melted into the darkness. He stopped to listen and faintly heard voices bellowing behind him. He glanced back and saw the outline of trees against the road and the moon in the sky hovering above them like a huge spotlight. He dashed through a small settlement of houses with palm leaves for roofs and fences made from bound reeds. He could smell the aroma of food cooking, he wanted to enter a hut—any hut—and share the simple meal he would be offered.

He was so hungry. His legs ached and his lungs felt nearly on fire. He wanted to rest on the side of the road, but each time he slowed down, a dog's bark or a hooting owl changed his mind. It was only when he was immersed in the chorus of frogs and insects, and there were no more lights to be seen, that he slowed to a trot and finally stopped.

He took off his coat and folded it over his arm. It, like his shirt, was soaked through with sweat. His legs shimmied, almost buckled under his weight, as if he had been galloping for days through a forest. He limped over to an uprooted trunk just off the gravel road and sat down.

Samuel felt humiliated—never had he been so crudely slurred, especially by a woman. He was disgusted at himself for having, well, nibbled at her bait and not seen what was coming.

Lena would have found this whole seduction scene tawdry. But who was Lena to approve or disapprove? Samuel shook his head: why was he allowing a memory of love to have a say in his present life? Maybe this state of exhaustion was finally allowing him to admit that Lena's departure had been more painful than he had previously wanted to acknowledge. He had become a kind of self-contained vagabond, unable and unwilling to become emotionally engaged in anything.

Taking deep breaths, his tension began to ease. He tried orienting himself with what little light the moon supplied through the dense foliage, but he had no idea how he had ended up where he was. He blinked a few times trying to dislodge the image of the prostitute seducing him. Then he saw a streetlight down the road—was that even possible in Puerto Barrios?

Samuel pushed himself up from the trunk and started walking stiffly. The uphill climb out of the dip in the jungle made his legs ache again. He threw his coat over his shoulder and bent down to massage his calves. What a warm bubble bath would do! He then stood up and continued walking as the road flattened out. In some strange way, he had circled back around and was again entering Puerto Barrios.

Below the streetlight was a concrete building with a red hand-scribbled sign nailed above the doorway: *Comedor Pekyn*. An old black Packard was parked in front under a jocote tree.

Samuel lingered at the doorway, letting the pungent odors blowing out of the restaurant tickle his throat. His mouth filled with saliva—what he would give for a delicious meal and an ice-cold pilsner.

He put his coat back on, pressed his hat down on his head, and walked in through a red-beaded curtain.

CHAPTER NINETEEN

S amuel stood still, widening his eyes for a second till they adjusted to the bright lights. Across the dining room he saw a barrel-shaped Chinese woman in a full-body white apron sliding pots on a stove. At almost the same moment, the cook glanced at Samuel and waved him in.

Three men sat hunched at one end of a large table that took up almost half the restaurant. Away from them, toward the table's center, there were empty rum bottles, several plates piled with leftover noodles, a mix of glasses. It was only when he sat down at a table near the entrance that he saw a Chinese family of four sitting across the dining room toward the back.

Because of the steady hum of a generator, no one else had noticed Samuel come in. He laid his arms across the table, making it creak. The conversation of the men stopped and one of them looked toward him. Samuel flashed a polite smile and raised his hat to wave. The men looked impassively at him, till one of them nudged the others and they all turned toward him. The man was slender and wore a pencil mustache. He whispered something to the man next to him, who then laughed and nodded.

This man walked over to him. He looked vaguely familiar to Samuel. "Señor, won't you join us for a drink at our table?" he asked in Spanish.

"Thank you, but I only came to see what this place was," Samuel stammered, getting up.

The man stretched out an arm and stopped him. "Very few foreigners make it to these parts of town, and even fewer to our table. It's my birthday. I would be honored if you would join us for the celebration."

Samuel stared at the man. He appeared to be in his early thirties, with large slow eyes. Though he smiled, Samuel could tell that it wasn't easy for him—it was a false smile. His breath reeked of alcohol and tobacco. At first, Samuel ransacked his mind for some ploy to get out of this invitation, but ended up giving in—what could he possibly have to lose?

"Yes, of course." He took off his hat and placed it on a nearby chair.

The two other men clapped and whistled when Samuel sat down at the head of the table; he couldn't tell if they were welcoming him or congratulating the thin man with the mustache for having gotten him to join them. One of them looked a lot like the thin man—probably his brother—though taller, with less hair and eyes a bit too small for such a long head. The third man was fat and had large glasses perched on his nose, which hid much of his otherwise bland face. While the two brothers were casually dressed, this man wore green overalls.

Samuel grew nervous. The man who had fetched him raised a bottle high in the air, letting a stream of yellow liquid splash into his glass. His two friends applauded vigorously.

"Thank you, thank you. One of my humblest tricks." He filled a clean glass in the same manner and slid it in front of Samuel. "Your name, my elegant friend?"

Samuel hesitated.

"Well," said the fat man, turning to his friends, "maybe our friend doesn't really speak Spanish. Or perhaps he's forgotten his own name."

"No to both questions. I speak Spanish perfectly. I'm Rodolfo, Rodolfo Fuchs . . ."

The thin man extended his right hand. "I'm Hugo Alvarez—the Puerto Barrios taxi driver." He flicked a finger toward his car parked outside. "And this guy who has spent ten years trying to grow a mustache is my big brother Menino. And this scholarly fat boy over here is Guayo Ortiz, a good friend, a brother. Once a year, on my birthday, they come back to the town of our birth for a reunion. Tonight, my dear Mr. Fuchs, is the night."

Samuel shook their hands. The cook in the white apron drew up to take his order. Apparently he had been watching them from afar, waiting for a break in the conversation to approach.

Menino grabbed the cook's arm. "Mr. Fuchs, have you met Chino yet? Chino, say hello to Mr. Fuchs."

"Hello, Mr. Fuchs."

Menino slapped the cook's back. "I never feel quite at home here in Puerto Barrios till I've seen Chino. I'm a gentleman compared to a parrot like him. Chino, you'd eat my shit if I asked you to, wouldn't you?"

The cook—obviously not understanding—rocked on the balls of his feet. "Eat shit, eat shit," he repeated happily.

"Nod!" Menino ordered.

The cook bobbed his head up and down, wiping his hands on his apron.

"Good, Chino, good boy. I wish I had a bone for you. Now tell our guest what's on the menu."

The cook recited four or five incomprehensible items and stopped. Samuel glanced around at the half-finished dishes piled high with suey and noodles. "Do you have soup?"

"Chicken."

"Good. And some bread, if you have it."

"No bread, no bread," replied the cook.

"Bring him some johnnycakes," Guayo suggested.

"No johnnycakes. Woman try bring cakes with no coco. I say no coco, no cake. Want tortilla?"

"Yes, that'll be fine," Samuel answered.

"And make it quick," Menino added. "The man's hungry. Can't you see it on his face?"

The cook nodded quickly three or four times and went back to the kitchen.

Hugo turned to Samuel. "Your face looks familiar to me. I've seen you before."

Samuel pulled out a handkerchief and dabbed his sweating face. He half-looked at the taxi driver—*For the love of God, I hope he wasn't on the boat to Livingston*—and shook his head. "You must be mistaken."

"No, I don't make mistakes." Hugo smiled. "I forget many things, but not faces. I have lots of time to watch things and so I am a good observer of life . . . Aha! I know where I saw you! Last night—you came off the pier with that stupid dwarf, no?"

"Just after sundown," Samuel volunteered.

"You passed by my car and I asked you if you needed a ride into town. Remember? Price was carrying your bag."

"I remember passing a car." What Samuel recalled was the swastika on the back window. He suddenly felt weak.

"Do you work for the Company?" Guayo asked.

"No," Samuel answered, clasping his glass. He had lied about his name, good, that had been a smart move. But he had to be careful how he constructed his other lies. "I came to Panama on the Hamburg-Amerika line a few days ago. Fortunately, a cargo ship was heading to Guatemala. I hope to stay in Puerto Barrios another day or two and then go to Guatemala City. I have a job waiting for me there."

"Well, in that case, I propose a toast to our new friend. Are you German?"

"Yes."

"I have great respect for Germany. Salud to Mr. Fuchs. Long live the new Germany!"

"Salud!"

"Salud!"

"Long live the Third Reich!"

Samuel touched all their glasses faking a smile. "¡Salud, amor, y pesetas—y el tiempo para gozarlos!"

The three friends smiled. Menino leaned over and slapped Samuel on the back. "Bravo! Spoken like a true poet!"

"It's just a toast I learned while visiting Spain."

"You know," Guayo began, "I can give you a ride to the capital day after tomorrow. I came here to see my father and pick up some engine parts for my boss's truck. Maybe you'd like to visit Quirigua with Hugo tomorrow. He's not only a taxi driver, but also a tourist guide. He knows his stuff." Guayo's cheeks filled with color and he glanced at his childhood friend, proud to have made a plug for him.

"Sure," said Hugo. "I'm free tomorrow—as I am most days now! Quirigua has just been discovered. There are these huge carved stones that weigh at least five thousand kilos each. Imagine our ancestors moving those gigantic stones! With their bare hands!"

"We shall see," Samuel said cautiously. "I need to send a few more telegrams tomorrow. I'm quite anxious to take up my new position in Guatemala City."

"You'll like the capital," Menino said. "Full of prospectors and investors, most of them foreigners. Quite a few of your German countrymen. New roads being paved, new buildings going up every day. And President Ubico has begun building the biggest central park in the Americas—"

"With the biggest palace," Guayo chuckled.

"Yes, Ubico is building the National Palace across from the Cathedral, which will be the largest in all Central America. It will be made of green marble, each stone weighing a kilo, and he is importing tiles from Morocco and Tunisia. And then he's going to build a thirty-room house—"

"Just for him and his wife. A private residence! And, of course, another resting place for all his ex-girlfriends."

All three friends laughed together. Samuel laughed with them.

"Did you find that funny, Rodolfo?" Menino asked, challenging him to refute what he observed.

"A little," Samuel confessed.

"You laughed."

Samuel reddened. "I laugh when others laugh."

Menino arched his brow. "Laughter is an expression of solidarity. I like that, Fuchs! Well, you look like a man with a sense of humor. But you explain it, Hugo. You're a better storyteller than me."

Hugo shook his head. "I pass to our historian friend at my left."

Guayo's red cheeks lit up. He scanned the room, shrugging his shoulders at the Chinese family, then inched closer to Samuel. He pushed up his glasses, which made him appear less baby-faced. "Well, he did build a new residence on the Avenida Reforma. Then we heard that our President Ubico was constructing a new structure inside the Municipal Cemetery for all his old friends—they would be transported in pickup trucks. But no one could figure out why trucks full of bricks were going to the Municipal Cemetery, dumping their load, and coming out empty. Ubico loves big buildings, so maybe he was planning to build a bank or a hospital in the cemetery. But now we know that he was building Guatemala's first mausoleum to be called the Recently Dead Apartments. Once you move in, you can stay for life. It's a private complex, so you can only move in by invitation. Priority is given to his old girlfriends, Communists, lawyers, and unionists, but also students—they're all dying to get in!"

The three friends sprawled open-armed on the table, laughing hysterically. An ashtray and a glass fell to the floor and broke. The cook shuffled out of the kitchen and began cursing under his breath in Chinese. Samuel bent down to pick up the broken pieces of glass and ceramic, but Menino stopped him.

"Let Chino do it." He knocked several of the plates on the floor, shattering them. When the cook cursed some more, louder now, Menino grabbed an empty rum bottle by the neck and threatened him with it.

"A la chingada!" Menino shouted.

The cook threw up his arms and went into the kitchen. Everyone was laughing, except Samuel.

Guayo caught his horrified expression. "Relax, Fuchs, you shouldn't look so worried. Seriously." He gently touched Samuel on the hand. "Menino and Chino have been going at it like this for years. Chino is used to the breaking of dishes. We end up paying for them."

"What about the police?"

Guayo shook his head. "The old saying is that walls have ears. It's true, but in Puerto Barrios they don't understand Chinese!"

"Now you're talking, cousin!" Menino winked, poured himself another shot of rum, and passed the bottle around. "Do you like our president, Rodolfo?"

"I know nothing about him." Samuel took a drink from the rum, and winced.

"The best thing about him is that he is sympathetic to your country, Germany, and to General Franco. The problem is that he loves money and himself more than his values and ideas. I propose a toast—to his death!"

"To his death," his brother repeated.

"To his death," Guayo said softly.

The three friends lifted their glasses. "We're waiting for our German friend to join us."

"But I don't know anything about him."

"We rise and fall together. That is our motto. To his death, Rodolfo!"

"To his death," Samuel whispered.

The four men clinked glasses and drank. Then the three friends locked arms across the table as if making a secret pact and drank again. Samuel, for his part, tried to appear disinterested, though he worried about having joined in the toast. What did he know about Guatemalan politics? He hungered to be in a country where no one bothered you if you went about your business, whether you were a gentile or a Jew. He hadn't come to Guatemala to be enmeshed in more political messes.

How was he going to leave?

He recalled that Alfred Lewis had several times condemned union agitators and hailed Ubico for knowing how to handle troublemakers, once his hands were greased. But what did Samuel care about politics? Let a man work and eat in peace.

Samuel was afraid to say this aloud. As it was, he had already compromised his impartiality by toasting Ubico's death. If anyone else had heard him, this pledge could be held against him.

Menino poured the dregs of the rum bottle into each of their glasses. "Chino!" he yelled. "Where's this man's soup? Are you plucking the goddamn chicken? Bring us another bottle of rum—and may the Chinese devil get you if you don't hurry up."

The cook shuffled around in the kitchen for a few seconds and then trotted to their table clutching a bottle without a label.

"What the hell is this, Chino? I asked you for a bottle of rum, not pisswater."

"That all I got. Commissary say no more ron. All ron go to Guatemala City."

Menino thumped his fist on the table. "Chino, how can you be so stupid to believe that?"

Guayo touched his friend's arm. "Easy, Mino. This is a celebration, remember. Let's not spoil it arguing with Chino. You know that his head's thicker than a brick." He looked at the cook. "You sure you don't have any more Botrán hidden away? Menino can get very, very angry, you know!"

Samuel offered him his glass. "You can have the rest of mine."

Menino nodded his head. "Chino, don't trick me."

The cook shook his head. "No ron. No ron. I try for three days now. Just aguardiente. No more ron!"

Menino pulled on his mustache. He was tired, and the whites of his eyes had yellowed like the skin of a papaya. He snatched the bottle of aguardiente from the cook and uncorked it with his teeth.

The cook bowed to Samuel. "I bring you soup now."

As Chino went back into the kitchen, Menino filled the glasses. "Hugo, for the life of me, I don't understand why you continue to stay in this shitty town. There's nothing left here but trash. You should come back with me and stay on my farm. And you can drive your taxi in Huehuetenango. Clean air, brother, clean mountain air, not this gooey lard that sticks to your lungs! No gringos and no bananas. You can hunt wildcat or boars in the Cuchumatanes. A life of your own—you aren't obliged to serve anyone, not even your big brother.

"My garlic farm is thriving. And I grow all the food I need. Huge heads of lettuce, tomatoes like soccer balls, avocados that drop at your feet. Artichokes. Why stay here, brother? Frankly, I don't understand it."

"Maybe he stays here for the negras," Guayo broke in, laughing, pushing up his glasses.

Hugo brought his glass to his sad mouth, hung his upper lip over it, and slurped a drink. "Things will get better, you'll see. Like before, when we all lived here. Alfred Lewis says the Company is about to build a new factory here to make high-quality vinegar from the overripe bananas—"

"And you believe that hypocrite who hates you and every drop of Indian blood in your body?"

Hugo swallowed another mouthful of his drink, puckered his face, and coughed. Despair, like a sleepy moth, hovered in his eyes. He stared into space, focusing on nothing, tapping his glass with his silver ring.

"You have to believe in something," Guayo offered, in defense of his friend.

"Guayo, you know nothing about life. Stick to your books!"

"But cousin—"

"Don't cousin me, you fat ape! You know nothing of nothing. You're like Hugo, always bolstering your dead dreams. Open your eyes, Guayo. Look around you. What do you see? Do I have to remind you what happened?"

"There's enough hot air in here tonight, Mino," his brother said.

Menino glared at Hugo. "You never want to hear about it, do you?"

"And you never get tired of repeating it. I've heard the same lousy story a thousand times!"

"But you forget—you forget everything!" Menino slurred. "You, you forget how rich the soil was here. You forget how big and strong the trees were in the nearby hills, how the lumberjacks came and cut down all the mahogany and dried up all the rain. How each year the harvest of our fruit trees and cacao plants shrank and the leaves turned brown and spindly, so that the farmers cried with joy when they got enough fruit to survive for the next season. Then the Company came and told the farmers they would do better to plant banana trees and that they would set up a system of irrigation. But after five years, the nutrients in the soil were gone and the farmers could barely get two bunches growing on a stem. The Company knew that would happen because they sold us poisoned fertilizer. It was people like your friend Alfred Lewis—"

"He's not my friend."

"Like hell he's not. Gringos like him advised farmers like our father to stop planting cacao and fruit trees because bananas were as good as gold, and then when the bananas stopped producing, father was forced to sell his land—"

"That was his decision. No one forced him to plant bananas. And certainly no one told him to sell the land. The Fruit Company had already moved its offices to Bananera."

"All lies!" Menino shouted, snapping his fingers in the air. He grabbed the bottle of aguardiente by the neck and sloughed down another gulp. "I don't know why I bother trying to explain these things to you. Either you don't want to know or you're too stupid to understand."

The cook brought Samuel's soup and a pile of tortillas wrapped in a cloth napkin. The soup had an oily surface, under which floated chicken feet, lumpy carrots, and potatoes. Samuel took up his spoon, stirred his soup, and swallowed two mouthfuls of the liquid. It tasted good. He picked up a fork and attacked the carrots, potatoes, and the few strands of chicken. He kept eating as if that would buffer him from the argument between the two brothers. He stole glances up at the three men, hoping they had forgotten about him and that he would be able to escape without further problems.

"It was his fault."

"He had no choice, you idiot!"

Hugo slammed his glass down. "Mino, I don't know why you always dredge up the same old stories. Maybe you shouldn't come back here. It's always like this on my birthday—we begin celebrating, then you get skunk drunk, and we all end up depressed. We never have anything new to talk about! If your garlic farm were more successful, you wouldn't go on and on about things here. I'm happy," he said, sticking out his chest. "What about you?"

Menino gave a dismissive laugh. "You are happy to let everyone here trample all over you. Taxi driver? Tourist guide? What crap."

"Don't make this personal."

"Sorry, but they lead you around here on a leash."

"Brothers, let's not fight," Guayo said.

"Oh shut up, fat boy."

Hugo rolled his hands into fists. "I'm not blind to the crimes of the Fruit Company, but they brought jobs and money when Puerto Barrios was only a muddy swamp, a breeding ground for malaria and yellow fever. They drained the swamps and built—"

"Nothing."

"Brother, let me finish—"

"Nothing! Nothing!" Menino's copper face bulged red.

Suddenly the restaurant fell silent. The Chinese family had at some point left. The only sounds were scraping noises from the kitchen.

"They brought the telegraph and the radio," offered Hugo, trying to lighten the mood.

Menino turned to him. "How can you be so stupid? They brought the telegraph and their radio, that's true, but for their own use. They built roads and warehouses, for their own use. They built swimming pools and tennis courts, for their own use. They brought whores who spoke several languages, for their own use." He paused. "Open your eyes, Hugo. They bought all of us, for their own use. They gave us flush toilets and sinks that they imported illegally and for which they never paid duties—"

"Your brother was just making a joke," Guayo said.

"Let me finish! So now people here feel superior because they don't have to shit in the jungle like those people living in Petén. Here you can invite your friends over to your rotten shack that floods whenever it rains, and you can drink infected water from the faucet and watch that lousy toilet flush over and over again. Isn't that it?"

Hugo lowered his eyes. With his fork, he stabbed at a piece meat on the plate of cold noodles in the center of the table.

Samuel ate a piece of tortilla, cold now, and it dropped in his stomach like a stone into a well. The soup had nourished him, but now all that was left were the chicken feet staring up at him with nails still intact. He swallowed hard to hold in his vomit.

"If you'll excuse me . . ."

Menino got up and stood over Samuel. "Fuchs, do you know how our father died? It's important for you to hear how your kind treated the proud people that used to own all this—"

"Leave him alone, Mino. He had nothing to do with it—"

"Brother, I'm still talking. People around here think that the only time there was trouble was when those three men got killed. They whisper *Kingston* and shake their heads. And it's good for Guayo to hear this story because one day he wants to study law—"

"Mino, you've already told me what happened to your father."

Menino ignored him, as if somehow enthralled by his own telling of the story. "When our father came to Puerto Barrios from Coban, he and my mother bought two hectares along the shore where the dock now stands. It was flat land, rich and cleared, but most importantly, several feet above the flood tide. They worked day and night carting off limestone rocks and planting fruit trees. But when the Fruit Company wanted to build their pier, they told my father: 'Bananas, Mr. Alvarez, bananas. We will buy your land and give you another plot. Forget your cacao and papayas and plant bananas. We will even show you how to grow them.' But our father didn't want to sell his land until they greeted him with this." Menino picked up a knife from the table and waved it menacingly in the air.

"He should've gotten a lawyer," said Guayo, looking at Hugo who was sinking deeper and deeper into his seat and closing his eyes.

"No, cousin. A lawyer is no help when you have a knife to your throat backed up by the Guatemalan army! He unhappily traded in his land for jungle and ten gallons of gasoline to help him burn off vegetation that grew thicker than a beard. The Company drew him a map showing that they were going to put railroad tracks right through his land—he would become a rich man overnight! So he cleared the jungle alone—mother was pregnant with you—hoping that a little train would run through his tract of land. But the map wasn't worth the paper it was drawn on. The tracks were never laid there because the Fruit Company had already bought another piece of land for that—as you know, they bought off the judges, the newspapers, the Congress, the army, even our own goose-stepping president!"

"We know all that, brother."

"But you don't know that when Father finally harvested his first crop, he towed his bananas to the pier in a cart it had taken him three weeks to build. The Company had promised to buy his bananas. But it wouldn't because it had been decided that all the independent banana farmers were to be driven out of business. Supply was high and they offered him five cents a bunch. Father spent two days on the pier, wondering what to do. When he finally agreed to sell at their price, they offered him three cents because they knew he had to sell or throw out his crop. But Father was stubborn. He waited, hoping that another company's ship would come the following day. And it did come, but his bananas were already turning yellow."

"I know all that," Hugo said. "And he died of malaria. End of story."

Menino laughed. "You believe everything."

"That's what Aunt Nico told us."

"And you actually believed her?"

"Of course. Why should she lie?"

"Oh, brother," Menino shook his head, "maybe you'll leave this place once you learn the truth." He took a drink straight from the bottle and offered it to Samuel.

"I'm not thirsty."

"Are you afraid to drink from the same bottle as me? Drink!"

"Mino, please," pleaded Guayo. "Forgive him, Señor Fuchs, he's had too much to drink. We all have. Come on, Mino. Let's go home."

"*Forgive him, Señor Fuchs, he's had too much to drink,*" Menino mimicked his friend, raising his voice in pitch. "And Guayo's a frightened little piece of chicken shit."

Hugo clasped his brother's arm from across the table. "You're only hurting yourself, Mino, by attacking one of us."

Menino shucked off his brother's hand. "Cowards!" he shouted. Suddenly he stiffened and clambered up on his chair. It wobbled as he stood, but it didn't tip over. Menino cleared his throat, and like a soldier saluting, he placed his right hand next to his head: "And Pac Alvarez spent the night next to his banana cart because he couldn't pay for a hotel room. Each day he asked the Company foreman if he would buy his bananas and he was told no. When he asked for something to eat, the man laughed in his face and said, 'Eat your bananas, Mr. Alvarez. They'll harden your shit.'

"When his bananas rotted, the Company threw them into the harbor because he was interfering with the loading of the cargo ship." Menino closed his eyes and tears started coming down his cheeks. "I was with him. He gave me his cross, a garlic clove, and a string of dried beans. He told me to go home to Mother. What was I to do—walk home? Father thought I had left, but I hid behind a tree. I saw him walk to the end of the pier, unstrap his knife, and drive it straight into his chest."

"You saw him kill himself?"

"By the time I reached him he was almost dead. He lived another two hours."

Hugo got up to help his brother down from the chair. "I didn't know."

"You weren't supposed to ever find out."

"And our mother?"

"When she found out that Father was dead, she began convulsing and going into premature labor. She should have gone to a hospital but we were too far away—and too poor. Nico was there—thank God—otherwise you would have died with Mother. You know the rest of the story."

"Your poor father," whispered Guayo. "And your poor, heartbroken mother."

CHAPTER TWENTY

Throughout Menino's monologue, the question of how to excuse himself lurked in Samuel's mind. What had been three friends celebrating, drinking a bit too much, had reached such a highly charged pitch that simple parting words would not do. Of the three men, Menino seemed the most insightful and this gave him power over the others. And Samuel could see that this made him dangerous, very dangerous.

When Menino sat back down, he glanced at Samuel and began pulling his thumb along the serrated edge of his knife. Samuel paled, smiling back weakly. He reached for his hat on the chair behind him and placed it on his lap.

"You're right, brother," Hugo finally said. "I need a change. You and Guayo left, but I always felt like I had to stay here."

Menino tapped the knife against his palm and laid it down on the table. "For whose sake?"

"I don't know." Hugo slumped down in his chair. "I'm more sentimental than you, Mino. Maybe I'm stuck on the good things in the past or I have this dream that Puerto Barrios will one day turn around. If you ask me, I'd tell you it still just might happen!"

Taking up the bottle of aguardiente, Menino poured an overflowing drink in his brother's glass and pushed it in front of him. When Hugo made no effort to take it, his brother forced it into his webbed fingers. "Quit sulking, little brother. Drink this and your mood will change. We've had enough sad talk for one night, wouldn't you say? I propose that we move our celebration to the only other thing—besides seeing you, Hugo—that Puerto Barrios has to offer. What do you say?"

Guayo pushed up his glasses. "You want to go to the Palace Hotel?"

Menino picked up his knife and tapped the table. "Guayo, you are always two steps behind me. It must be the years you spent as an altar boy tied to Father Cabezón's skirt—"

"That's not fair, Mino."

Menino tapped the table again and slurred, "Guayito, don't tell me that my words have offended you."

"Does that surprise you? You're always challenging my manhood."

"To be honest, I've never seen your manhood!"

"What do you expect me to do," Guayo asked, "pull down my pants in front of Rodolfo and Chino? You're sick, you know that."

"You're acting like children," Hugo said, "getting into stupid arguments. You're both drunk!"

Menino guffawed. "For once you're right, brother. I am drunk. I say we go to the Palace and visit the new Negrita you've been bragging about, Hugo. Let's show Rodolfo what's meant by true Guatemalan hospitality. What do you say, Mr. Fuchs, to a little fun at our expense?"

Guayo giggled, somehow justifying Menino's way of treating him.

Samuel realized that this was what the evening's drinking was all about—finding the courage to go to a whorehouse. He pushed back in his chair as if he were about to get up.

"Thank you for the kind offer, but I can't join you. I have many things to do tomorrow and if I am going to visit Quirigua with Hugo, I better get some rest." He tried standing, but Menino's foot anchored his chair.

"To refuse an offer to celebrate—especially on someone's birthday—is a grave insult among our people."

"I don't mean to insult you, Mr. Alvarez, but I am quite tired. You see, I am still not used to the climate here."

"I don't give a damn about the climate, Mr. Fuchs. You've insulted us."

"That wasn't my intent."

Guayo shifted uneasily in his chair. "Let him go, Mino. We can have plenty of fun just among ourselves."

"Shut up, Guayito. I didn't ask for your opinion." Menino put down his knife and tried to caress Samuel's cheek with the back of his hand. Samuel turned his face away.

Angered, Menino grabbed him by the lapels of his coat and yanked his stiffening body toward him. "Look at me when I'm talking. Do you think your fancy clothes and your foreign languages will protect you out here? You are deeply mistaken—"

"Brother, please," Hugo said, grabbing one of Menino's arms. "We don't need to make trouble to have fun . . ."

Without loosening his grip on Samuel, Menino turned to his brother, his eyes merely black gashes against a brown face. "You are such a coward, a marica, afraid of what you feel inside."

"What I feel inside? What do you know about that? I'm telling you to let go of the man."

"Or what? What are you going to do?" Menino said sarcastically. "I'll tell you something. You hate this man and everything he represents as much as I do. The difference is that you're afraid to do something about it."

"You're not drunk. You're crazy."

"What are you so afraid of? He's only a Jew!"

"What does his being a Jew have to do with anything?"

The cook slithered out of the kitchen. "No fight, no fight. Restaurant closed!"

Menino let go of one of Samuel's lapels, picked up the knife, and lunged toward the cook. "I'm going to cut your heart out, you yellow scum."

The cook backed off and hurried to the kitchen, screaming in Chinese.

Samuel's body shook. He tried to dry his forehead, but now Menino pressed the knife against his chest. "Stand up, Jew." He flashed the knife at Guayo and his brother. "I don't want any interference from either one of you. This is between the Jew and myself."

"You're making a big mistake," Samuel muttered.

Menino shook his head. "No, I don't think so. From the minute I saw you coming in, I marked you for a Jew. That nose of yours doesn't help. But let's make sure. Stand up! Pull down those fancy pants and we'll have a look—"

"Please . . ."

Menino lowered the knife and pointed it to Samuel's silver belt buckle. "Let's open up! Let's see what you've been hiding in there. And then we'll go to the Palace and see how well you can perform."

Guayo stood up. "What's the matter with you? Do you want to get us killed?"

"He's not one of us. He's a Jew."

Hugo snapped his fingers. "Ah, I get it. Those boring meetings you took me to, that stupid seal you insisted I put on the back window of my taxi. My god! To think of all the time you wasted listening to Cuero, that moocher friend of yours, and all his excuses for being a sixty-year-old fat do-nothing!"

Menino kept his knife on Samuel's midriff and answered: "The Jews leave us nothing! Who do you think owns the Fruit Company? Zemurray, a Jew—and it was because of him that our father and our mother died."

Hugo kept shaking his head and started laughing, as if he hadn't heard a single word his brother had said. "That stupid, drunken oaf! Still making excuses for why no one wanted to pay to hear him sing. What a lousy voice. He couldn't sing his way out of a garbage can! I can see him now, standing in front of a club, closing his eyes under the lights, puckering his thick lips—and farting!"

"He's a fine singer. He could have been great, but the Jews in New York wouldn't let him record!"

"Cuero!" Hugo drummed on the table. "Just his name makes me laugh. A fat drunk with a wormy liver! Marching around his house in that silly Nazi uniform and a bottle of cheap rum stuck to his mouth. Is that who you admire, big brother? And you have the nerve to tell me how I should live my life and what I should do!" Hugo fell to the floor, laughing hysterically, holding his stomach.

Menino moved the knife toward his brother. "Brother, stop laughing. You don't know what you're saying."

Hugo was pedaling his legs, turning around in a circle on the floor. "And you follow Cuero around like an organ grinder's monkey. You should put on a red coat and get yourself a little tin cup! Give Cuero a red cap and a black cane. The only Jew that did him any harm was the poor one who paid for his trip to New York and got nothing in return!" He got on his hands and knees and began crawling on the floor, making monkey noises.

"Brother, I'm warning you. Stop laughing at me. I'll take care of you after I take care of Fuchs."

All the while Samuel's head was spinning, as if someone had punched him in the face. Was he imagining things? He looked at Guayo sitting at the table and saw that his face was red and his thin mustache was slipping off his face—his ears had become pig ears and his prominent brow was coated in sweat.

"He! He!" Samuel heard, and he turned to look at Menino. Instead he saw Mr. Price holding him off with a knife, laughing in his face, swiveling his squat hips.

Hey, how about a little company tonight? A girl or maybe a young boy if you prefer, to while away the hours? What do you say to a bit of fun after such a long voyage?

Samuel blinked again, and saw that Lena was standing behind the dwarf, egging him on, lovingly rubbing his thick neck. Her long, black fingernails with little stars on the ends were caressing his Adam's apple. Her face was talcum white, and a coral cigarette holder rested lightly between her lips. Then her hands moved down the dwarf's throat and unbuttoned the top button of his shirt—her fingers began curling the few hairs on his chest. The dwarf suddenly shuddered and he twisted an arm toward her blouse and touched her breasts. The cigarette holder fell from her mouth to the floor, making no noise. Lena, moaning softly, dropped her head into the dwarf's neck and began kissing him.

Revolted, Samuel picked up the bottle of aguardiente from the table and crashed it down with all his strength on Menino's neck. The bottle exploded, sending glass and liquid flying across the room. Menino made a vague effort to turn his head before slumping to the floor, pulling Guayo down with him, on top of Hugo. The three of them were snarled in a heap of food, shattered glass, and now blood.

Samuel straightened up, shaking, still holding the jagged neck of the bottle in his hand. For a brief second, he stayed riveted, gaping open-mouthed at the mess he had made. He heard a scream from the kitchen. He thought he heard a siren.

The three men on the floor stirred and groaned. Guayo lifted his head, as if signaling for Samuel to leave. Samuel threw down the glass in his hand and hurried out.

Chapter Twenty-One

Samuel parted the beaded curtain of the restaurant and ran outside. He paused for a second and looked down at his right hand, splashed with blood. He went over to the Packard parked on the side of the road and wiped his hand on the car's hood.

What had he done? He thought he had seen the dwarf's face loom up and Lena had been there as well. What could she possibly be doing at the Comedor Pekyn? Hadn't she gone back to Capetown? Other images floated through his mind like the vanishing pieces of some grisly, unsolvable puzzle.

A cry billowed out of the restaurant. One thing was certain—he had either killed or badly injured Menino. Samuel realized that if he didn't get moving, it would be all over for him. He had to race back to his hotel, pick up his valise, and remove all traces of his true identity from the room. Any more bungling on his part and he would be lost.

Samuel walked quickly, retracing his steps back toward the Palace and then to his hotel. The going was heavy, even though the full moon lit his way, revealing the wide ruts and cracks on the road.

He could not stop—he had probably killed Menino.

No battle, no open confrontation, and yet Samuel had slain a man. He saw a lopped head lying sideways in a pool of blood. What other choice did he have? A drunkard, a badgering Nazi, was threatening to castrate him and that might have been only the beginning. Had it been an idle threat? Menino was diabolical and Guayo and Hugo were only making lame gestures to stop him.

Samuel had acted in self-defense, but who, in a court of law—they'd probably lynch him first—would believe him? The cook had vanished, and the three friends would buttress one another's alibis like pigs trapped in the same stinking mud. Other witnesses—the dwarf, the railway clerk— would all testify against him and claim that he was crazy and capable of such crimes. Would there even be a court of law in this putrid place?

Samuel pulled a coat sleeve across his forehead; they would string him up by his belt from an almond tree.

He walked quietly by a few huts; the lights were out and the people inside were already bedded down for the night. Ah, what he would give to lie down now. His legs and arms ached; the palms of both his hands itched. When a band of howler monkeys shrieked overhead from their hideout in the ramon trees, Samuel started to run again, for their cries were like police sirens bearing down on his trail. And where the brush thickened, he ran into lianas, whose sticky vines threatened to envelope him. He escaped them by using the full thrust of his body and ripping through them as if they were badly rusted chains.

As Samuel approached the Palace Hotel, he slowed down to a trot. The jungle noises had disappeared, but he heard crunching sounds growing louder behind him. He stopped and perked up his ears—a motor car was coming. He turned around and saw, far down the road, the bobbing of weak headlights. In one motion, he leaped off the road and found cover in some bushes. He saw the road lightening in front of him. A few moments later, the black Packard swiggled by, its underside bouncing and scraping on the rocky road. He parted some brambles so that he could see who was in the car, but all he glimpsed was a mass of shadows. The car passed him and, at the crossroads, swept sharply to the right.

Samuel rubbed his face, grateful that the vehicle had turned away from the harbor, for this would give him a few extra minutes to escape. Either Menino was dying in that car and going to a hospital or he was already dead and Hugo and Guayo were hightailing it to the police station. No matter which it was, soon they would be hunting him all over town.

When he felt it was safe, Samuel popped back on the road. He was breathing hard and extremely hot; his heavy arms hung limply down his sides. He took off his coat, dried his face on the inside lining, then balled it up and threw it deep into the bush.

The passing car had drawn three or four people to the door of the Palace bar. Squinting, Samuel saw the prostitute who had tried to seduce him earlier in the evening. All of them were talking and gesticulating, and seemed to be in no rush to go back into the bar.

Samuel had no choice but to walk by and pretend he had nothing to do with the passing car.

Though he was filthy, the prostitute recognized him and began cursing. The men with her stepped back and laughed and applauded. Samuel kept on walking, looking straight ahead. As he passed the entrance, little rocks started raining down on him. He flinched whenever he was hit, but otherwise did not react. The jeering seemed to grow louder as he walked further away—he gulped down his desire to answer back. At the crossroads, he turned left and very casually began to pick up speed.

When he was sure he was out of their eyesight, he began to run. The muscles in his legs ached and were beginning to clam up. Samuel closed his eyes as if the darkness could somehow bleed out the pain. Instead, he was beset by images: his father waxing his mustache; his mother polishing and buffing her fingernails; Heinrich slumped in a corner chair, fuming about something; Lena in brown riding pants; a dwarf tackling him and laughing uproariously.

Samuel fell backward before fainting against an outcropping of rocks.

When he opened his eyes, he was lying on his back and looking up at Joshua, who had a frown on his face and hands on his hips.

"What's happened to you, Mr. Berkow? I can barely recognize you. Your clothes are ripped and filthy. Let me help you up," he said, extending his arms down.

Samuel turned away. He wouldn't let his eyes settle on the man towering above him. He glanced at his own hands, scuffed and scratched, but failed to recognize them. He wiped them on his trousers.

"Were you in a fight, mon? Speak up!"

Samuel coughed. "I just slipped in the mud."

"Well, it looks like a car has been dragging you down the road."

"I slipped, I'm telling you." Samuel touched the back of his head and felt a bump the size of a walnut. He turned to his side and tried pushing himself up. His legs wavered, but he managed to stand on his own. "Nothing happened."

"That's hard to believe." Joshua clutched Samuel's arms tightly.

"I told you I fell. You have no right to hold me. I've done nothing. If you'll let me by, I must get to my room!"

"I don't believe you, Mr. Berkow. You're covered in blood. Something terrible must have happened. You can trust me."

"I don't trust anyone." Samuel peered off in the distance.

Joshua grabbed him by the head. Samuel tried turning away, but Joshua wouldn't let go. "I told you this morning that you were alone here. You can't survive in this world by yourself. You might not want to believe me, but you do need me."

Samuel wiped his nose with the back of his hand. He didn't know what to do. The realization that he had no one to turn to hit him hard. "Do you remember our talk this afternoon?"

"We talked about many things."

"Yes, we did. But at one point I asked you if you had ever killed a man."

"I remember."

Samuel stared down at his hands. "I've always been so afraid to stand out, to have people make a fuss over me. My father said my mother pampered me. Maybe that's why I enlisted in the army . . . I thought I would do well in a group, no one would even notice me. I could slip by . . . And then tonight . . . it happened so fast . . . all the drinking . . . the screaming . . ."

Joshua stepped back. "What did you do?"

Samuel leveled his gaze. "I think I killed a man."

Joshua widened his eyes. He made a vague motion to leave, wash his hands of this mess, but then he stopped. "Are you sure you killed him? Couldn't you have knocked him down? Who are we talking about anyway?"

Samuel shook his head, scrunching his face.

"Where's the body?"

Samuel pointed behind him with the thumb of his right hand. "Back there. I can't tell you how far. A Chinese restaurant with a generator, electric lights—"

"Comedor Pekyn," Joshua said. "Chino's?"

"Yes. That's the place."

"And who did you kill? Certainly not Chino!"

"I seem to remember this dwarf laughing at me," he said while rubbing his head.

"Mr. Price. The dwarf who does odd jobs and spies for the police?"

Samuel shook his head. "He was there, but he wasn't there. And Lena, my first wife, was there, but that's impossible . . . She lives in South Africa . . . It was so confusing . . . There were three friends . . . two of them were brothers . . . one taunted me with a knife . . . he had a mustache . . . he's the taxi driver's brother."

"Menino!" said Joshua, tightening his lips against his teeth. "I know who he is. He left Puerto Barrios about seven years ago. He had some trouble with Alfred Lewis. A bully, if you ask me . . . And you think you killed him?"

"I broke a bottle over his neck," Samuel said, raising his right arm into the air and swooshing it down. "He fell down bleeding on top of his brother. I ran away. A few minutes ago I saw the taxi passing by the Palace Hotel . . ."

Joshua pulled down on his goatee. "And which way did the car go?"

"It turned right at the crossroad . . . Who cares where the car went? I'm sure Menino is dead."

"Maybe not. If they were going to the police station, they would have continued straight ahead. A right turn means that perhaps they were going to Doctor Heriberto's house, in which case Menino may still be alive."

Wrapped up in his gloom, Samuel did not respond.

"Mr. Berkow, he may not be dead."

"No, he's dead. And I am finished."

Joshua pressed his shoulders. "Get ahold of yourself. You can't just roll over and die like a sick calf—"

"It's hopeless. Everything's hopeless. I can't even get my own cousin to help me."

"Forget your cousin. We are talking about your life here. Listen to me— go back to the hotel and pack your things. But be very quiet. Don't wake up a single chicken. I'll go to the restaurant and see if I can find out what happened. You can't wait for me at the hotel—it's too dangerous—so wait for me in the band shell. I'll whistle twice so you'll know it's me. We'll find somewhere safe for you to spend the night. And in the morning, you must leave Puerto Barrios by boat or by truck. I doubt that there's a train leaving till tomorrow night—"

"There is," Samuel interrupted. He felt that the blood coursing through his veins was cold; he began shaking a bit. "At six in the morning. The station clerk told me a few hours ago. The train is already being loaded up."

"The station may be full of soldiers and police, but it's actually your best escape route."

"I told Menino I would be leaving Puerto Barrios the day after tomorrow."

"That means nothing. You have little time. You know what you have to do now?"

Samuel nodded.

"Get going. We have no time to lose," said Joshua, turning around.

Samuel clasped his arm. "Wait!"

"What is it now?"

"I left my hat in the restaurant," he said despondently.

Joshua looked at him in surprise. "A hat's a hat. You can buy another one."

"At the restaurant I gave Menino a false name—Rodolfo Fuchs. I was afraid something like this might happen. I thought I was being so clever.

Well, what difference does it make now? My real name is sewn inside the band of my homburg."

Joshua groaned. "I'll see if I can get it somehow."

"You must, or else all this hiding around is useless. I left my hat on the chair."

"I don't think anyone will be looking for your name inside a hat, mon." Joshua started walking off.

Samuel stood still for a moment, staring at the spot in the darkness where Joshua had disappeared. It was completely black now that the moon had set, except for the occasional flare of a firefly darting about.

CHAPTER TWENTY-TWO

As Samuel turned onto the walkway leading up to the hotel, a bony dog crept out of a hibiscus bush where he had been sleeping and yapped. It was a tired, half-hearted yap but it still rung out in the quiet night. Samuel tried shushing the dog by putting his hand out to him. The dog rolled his sleepy eyes, snarled mopishly, and curled up right on the walkway. Samuel had to step over the animal to get by.

The hotel lights were out, except for those in the lobby and bar. Samuel clambered up the steps and pulled back on the veranda doors. The hinges creaked, but the marimba music playing late into the night from some distant bar checked the noise.

He moved slowly across the lobby. As he passed the front desk, he heard garbled conversation coming from the bar. He approached it softly and saw George and Willie huddled together at the far end. The iguana stretched languidly on its towel on the countertop. Samuel turned on his heels and went back to the front desk. Glancing left and right, he stepped behind it and pulled out the hotel register from a drawer. He placed it on the counter and thumbed through the pages. He found his name on the last page and ripped it out. Hearing footsteps above him, he slammed the register closed and returned it to its drawer.

He headed up to the second floor, walking softly. At the end of the corridor, the breeze blew through the screens and Samuel could see the pier lights flickering between the trees. His room was just above the bar; he knew he had to be quiet.

As he approached his room, he saw that the door was open and the light on. He stopped dead in his tracks, made a vague gesture to turn around and leave. Were the police already in his room waiting for him? He inched closer, but before he had a chance to see who was in his room, the person spoke to him.

"I thought you'd never come. You're as unpredictable as the Messiah. What took you so long?"

Father Cabezón was lying flat on Samuel's bed, his hands behind his head. He wore his black robe, and his dirty feet were flat against the bed-sheets. He seemed quite comfortable, almost audaciously so. Tall candles were burning on the bureau, and the wax had dripped down the sides of the furniture and crusted on the floor.

"You have no right to be here."

The priest sat up. His gold-capped incisors shone through his crooked smile.

"But you invited me. Just this morning."

Samuel entered his room and latched the door shut. He was certain that George and Willie had heard him come in. "I did no such thing," he said through his teeth. "I barely know you. Why would I allow you to come into my room and lie down on my bed? How absurd!"

Father Cabezón held up a finger. "Shush, keep your voice down. You, of all people, should know that the devil is a light sleeper. Saint Augustine said that." He threw Samuel a towel and wrinkled his forehead. "You're a frightful mess. Why don't you clean up."

Samuel caught the towel, but the priest's intrusion so surprised him that he was paralyzed and didn't know what to do next. He shook his head and went over to the basin and washed his face. The warm water felt good, refreshing. Now he had to find a way to get the priest out of his room and make his secret retreat.

"Father—can't we talk in the morning?"

The man looked at him with great surprise. "I don't understand. Didn't you invite me down to confess you?"

"Confess me? I did no such thing. Why, I'm not even a Catholic. This is ridiculous!"

Samuel got a sudden whiff of cheap whiskey.

Father Cabezón shrugged his bony shoulders, then stood up. "Neither are the Indians or the Caribs living here, yet I confess several dozen every day at the marketplace or on the piers. Some of them come bearing gifts of beads and silver. They call me Kinich Ahau because several years ago I brought trick candles that had been given to me by a magician from a circus troop passing through Guatemala City. You know the kind—you light them, you blow them out, and on their own they relight . . . I don't know how I will impress them once I run out . . . oh well . . . Sprechen sie Deutsch?"

"Natürlich," Samuel answered.

"Ich auch nicht!" the priest said. "And if I did, I certainly wouldn't know how to confess you in another language. So let's pretend that I brought my confessional with me—let's put it here." He pointed to a space between the bed and the candle-lit bureau. "I will go in this make-believe door and you can either get down on your knees or sit on the edge of your bed." He pushed down on Samuel's shoulders. "I think you would be better off with your knees on the towel. I can just put my hand on your head—this is all a bit unorthodox, but no one will see us—and you just tell me all about your sins."

"But I've done nothing," Samuel resisted. The smoke of the burning candles dizzied him. He found himself genuflecting.

The priest rubbed a hand over Samuel's head. He felt grateful for the human touch, the warmth, the gentleness. "This lump on your head—how did you get it?"

Samuel touched his scalp. "It must have happened when I fell."

"Oh yes," said the priest, pushing down on Samuel's head, and closing his eyes. "In a fight, of course. That's how people settle things around here."

"I wasn't in a fight," Samuel responded, agitated.

"Please, please, no lies," the priest said sternly. "You are here with me because you want to be forgiven. Men, being what they are—weak and depraved and with little willpower—are always falling into error. Only by confessing your sins to God, in the presence of one of His earthly delegates—in this instance, me—and together with your resolve not to sin again, will you be cleansed and forgiven. Even if you repeat the same sin in a few minutes, all is forgiven . . . So where were we? Ah yes, the lump on your head."

"I know nothing about it."

"If the candle smoke is bothering you, I would be more than happy to blow them out!" The priest laughed. "Oh, I forgot, they'll light up again." He rubbed his chin. "But I don't think these long tapers are trick candles . . ."

"What is this nonsense?" Samuel asked, fidgety.

"Close your eyes and tell me what is in your heart."

"I won't," he said, growing increasingly agitated.

The priest leaned down, whiskey breath and all, and closed his eyes. "You will feel better."

There was silence, a huge overspreading silence. Without wanting to, certainly without thinking, Samuel closed his own eyes and heard himself say, "I think I may have killed a man, Father."

The priest inhaled and exhaled through the forest of hairs in his nose. "Well, this certainly is serious. Very serious." He opened his eyes and scratched a tuft of hair on his throat. "But I am not here to judge your crimes. In fact, for a priest to be caught selling rum to his congregants is a very serious offense, and the bishop of Guatemala, with all his mercy, forgave me. And God must be the most forgiving, for He didn't strike dead those monks in Antigua who built secret tunnels to visit the nuns at night in the convent—this after having sworn abstinence. And truly, we know that the archbishop confesses the bishop; the cardinals confess the bishops; the pope confesses the archbishops; and last of all, God grants absolution to the pope, unless He directs another priest to do so. But who confesses God? Can you answer me that question? Who can confess God for all the misery He has caused us, or allowed us to cause to ourselves without divine intervention?"

"I don't know what you are talking about," Samuel said.

"Hmmm, I think it would be better if we dealt with simple earthly matters. So—you say you killed a man. I cannot ask you if the man deserved to die. I can only ask you if you repent or you would avenge again."

"I had no choice. He would've killed me."

"Kill or be killed. I swore never to sell rum again, though from time to time, I do drink it. So would you kill again?"

Samuel shook his head. "I didn't mean to kill him, I just wanted to knock him out, I suppose. I only meant to escape, not commit murder."

The priest put thumb and forefinger into his left nostril. He fooled around with a hair, yanked at it, and snorted. "But would you promise—in a general sense because we never know what scenario might present itself—would you promise me and, therefore, our Creator, never to kill again?"

"I am not a murderer!"

The priest nodded his head. "In that case, all is forgiven. *You* are forgiven, my good man. So I forgive you in the name of the Father, the Son, and the Holy Ghost." He put his two hands on Samuel's face. "That wasn't so difficult, was it? You can stand up now." The priest walked over to the candles, wet his fingertips, and with a click of his tongue, touched the lighted wicks of all but one of them. A cloud of smoke fell over the room. Father Cabezón walked back to Samuel and pulled him up, shaking his hand vigorously. "Viel Glück! Or as my German teacher used to say in Quetzaltenango: Wahrheit gegen freund und feind. Do I need to translate that for you?"

"No," Samuel said. *Truth toward friend and foe.*

"Very well. Auf wiedersehen." The priest put his candles in his robe pocket and walked out of Samuel's room, holding up the skirt with his hand. When Samuel was sure that the priest was gone, gone for sure, he went over and latched the door shut again. He lay down wearily on his bed and nestled his head, which buzzed and thrummed, in the crook of his clasped hands.

He planned to doze for just a few seconds. As his lids closed, he felt a large insect land on his chest. He swatted at it and jumped to his feet—on his bed he saw a huge roach stirring its legs in the air, trying to right itself. He tied the ends of the sheet together, trapping the roach, and threw it into a corner. Then he settled back down on the straw mattress. He couldn't fall asleep again because his body itched terribly—he imagined that roaches were invading the room through the walls, the floorboards, the holes in his mattress.

His mind was racing. All of a sudden he had a novel thought—because he had killed someone, perhaps that act had freed him from his old feeling of being and doing nothing. Never again would he be like flotsam floating on the waves or a balloon drifting in the wind. For the first time in his life, he had acted and acted decisively. He would gladly face the repercussions.

"Murder is salvation, murder is salvation," he heard himself saying aloud. He seemed not to care if anyone heard him. For too miserably long he had lived in the thrust and backwash of his own uncertainty. Like a roach.

Why should he, at his age, still suck in his stomach to appear fit, fret over what others might think of him? Why should he be so concerned about appearing polished, when in truth he was just a pair of old, scuffed shoes?

Why should he shave every single day and take cold showers just because this is what he had been forced to do at home and then later in the army? Why continue the charade or masquerade of courtesy and polite discretion with the meager hope that no one would whisper about him, say he was a pompous fool or an ass, as soon as he left the room? Let them say what they want, to his face, if need be. He'd break the chains he had placed on himself that called for—actually demanded—his affected grace. He had stood paralyzed for too long, watching himself sink deeper and deeper into a swamp he had created. He had finally fought back and now realized that he could not rely on anyone else to help or save him . . .

As he finally drifted into sleep, Samuel saw the drawing room in his parents' Hamburg apartment. His father had gone out with his friends and his mother was playing Chopin polonaises in the darkening afternoon. He was seven or eight, lying on a rug listening to the music. It was such a peaceful setting. Wood was burning in the fireplace and the recently polished and-irons sent flashes of light toward the breakfront that held his mother's precious Wedgwood and Dresden china. A crystal carafe with cognac and six crystal goblets stood on a tray on the butler's table. On the fireplace mantle sat three pieces of Capodimonte porcelain that his father had brought back from Florence.

Samuel had never felt so peaceful as he had then.

Now he struggled to open his eyes. The candle Father Cabezón had left on the bureau had burned all the way down to a stump and gone out. He pushed himself up. He was sapped of strength, yet calm and serene. His soul was at peace.

The priest had confessed him and he was somehow ready to move on.

He had no idea how long he'd slept. He tiptoed, knock-kneed, out of his room and peered down the corridor. Nothing. He walked down the corridor and looked toward the band shell—there was Joshua waving his arms frantically at him. Samuel squinted, but couldn't see his hat in his hands. This made him feel more annoyed than troubled. Back into his room he went, stuffing all his clothes, rumpled or not, into his suitcase except for a pair of dark trousers and a matching cotton shirt.

Shoehorn, comb, cologne, shaving brush, toothbrush, and paste were all tossed in his suitcase and he was ready to go. One last look around the room before he left forever—

Something caught his eye, something he hadn't seen before. A wooden crucifix had been nailed on the wall over his bed.

He stepped closer to examine it. Christ's arms and legs dangled shapeless from a red cross. The strange thing was that His face looked straight ahead, almost defiantly, at the onlookers, not down and to the side. The face had been painted by hand and the eyes were made of kernels of white rice.

At the top of the cross was a Fanta bottle cap—was this His crown of thorns?

Samuel wondered if the crucifix had always been in the room and he just hadn't noticed it. Or had the priest placed it there? If he had, was this some kind of a joke or did the priest have special powers of discernment that allowed him to communicate symbolically? What was the hidden meaning?

Just then Samuel heard two shrill whistles. Joshua was calling up to him. Without thinking, he yanked the crucifix from the wall and stuffed it into his suitcase.

He walked out of his room, leaving the door ajar, and moved down the stairs. The bar doors were closed, the lights off, and the lobby was quiet. As he passed the front desk, Samuel realized that he still owed George another four dollars for the room. While this would have normally troubled him, this time he didn't think twice. Pushing open the double screen doors, hopefully for the last time, he saw Joshua motioning for him to hurry it up.

Samuel slapped a mosquito buzzing in his ears as he crossed the park. When he reached Joshua, he opened his mouth to speak, but the black man put a hand over his mouth, took his suitcase, and gestured with his head that they should go up into the band shell.

"Let's talk here a minute."

Samuel couldn't keep quiet any longer. "What were you able to find out?"

Joshua dragged Samuel next to him and sat him down on his suitcase. He squatted on the floor. "I spoke to Chino," he breathed in. "He stayed in the restaurant the whole night, even when the fight happened. Yes, your bottle hit Menino on the back of the head. But after you left, he sat up and said a few delirious words before closing his eyes and passing out. It could have been from all the drinking. Chino said that they had a whole bottle of rum and a half a dozen beers before you even got there. God knows how much they drank afterward."

"I drank nothing," Samuel said.

"Guayo and Hugo drove Menino over to Doctor Heriberto—just as I had hoped. Chino was mopping the blood off the floor."

"He'll die," Samuel said softly.

"Chino said he was breathing—"

"Joshua, it doesn't matter if he is dead or alive, what matters is what I did." Samuel shook his head. "You didn't find my hat, did you?"

Joshua clenched his teeth. "Hugo took it with him, so Chino said, but I think it's just as likely that he took it himself. Chino is a sly one. When I accused him of stealing the hat, he denied it loudly. Almost too loudly. Then he told me that a policeman had come and taken the hat as evidence."

"I see," said Samuel, stretching his legs on the band shell floor.

"He's probably lying, Mr. Berkow."

He felt the old war sensation of snow falling, the clods of it burying him under a tree, layer after layer of snow and ice. "The hat doesn't matter," he said. "Everyone but those three know my name anyway. That dwarf, Mr. Price, would be more than happy to help in the investigation and see me thrown in jail."

"Let's get out of here now, Mr. Berkow. The police will come by soon."

"Maybe I should just surrender. I can't spend my life running away."

"Listen, you can't turn over and play dead because you struck someone in the head and you lost your hat. Forget what's happened. We have to think about escaping, getting you out of here as quickly as possible."

"I suppose you're right," Samuel said. "But I have to recognize that I have nothing, no one—except you, of course—to help me. I believe you read my cousin Heinrich's telegram: in so many words, he told me to go to hell. I don't even know who I am or where I should be going." Samuel tucked his head in his arms. "I've killed a man, fine. I can accept that. I feel no guilt; I had to protect myself. That Menino was crazy. His own brother and friend will admit to that."

Seconds ticked by. Joshua remained on his haunches as if too tired to move. Suddenly footsteps were drawing near. Samuel was about to say something, when Joshua clamped a hand over his mouth—if it were the police, both of them would be in lots of trouble.

A man was walking briskly but unevenly toward the hotel; every few steps he strayed off from the walkway. Then he stopped abruptly and turned to face the shrubbery at the front of the hotel. The man hummed the same six notes over and over again while urinating.

Joshua removed his hand from Samuel's mouth and edged closer to the band shell steps. The man buttoned his fly and jingled coins in his pocket. He proceeded up the steps of the hotel, not noticing them. A flurry of soft voices was heard from inside, but it soon stopped and the lights went out.

"Who was that?" Samuel asked.

"Kingston, thank the Lord. I thought we were finished."

"Kingston? That's impossible," said Samuel. "He's a mute."

Joshua smiled showing his girdle of white teeth. "That's what you're supposed to think. He can talk all right. If anything, it's hard getting him to shut up."

"But even George thinks he can't talk!"

Joshua shook his head. "Who do you think he was just talking to, mon? George! When Kingston was hospitalized after the picker's strike, Lewis came and threatened him. Kingston never answered and he hasn't spoken in public since. It's strange, though, to see him back here at the hotel. He's got his own little house. Maybe he came here to either warn you or try to capture you."

A jeep pulled up, interrupting Joshua. Two Guatemalan soldiers jumped out. One of them pulled a lantern from the backseat and lit it. They approached the hotel, talking loudly. They made no effort to keep the screen door from slamming.

After a few seconds of commotion, the lobby lights went back on. A man laughed.

"That's George. I would know his voice from miles away."

"How can you be sure?"

"I am as sure as I am of anything. The soldiers weren't looking for you. Your identity is still safe. Let's go now." Joshua tugged on Samuel's sleeve. "While there's a chance." He grabbed the suitcase.

"But where will I go? The train's not leaving till six in the morning, if then," he despaired.

"Yes, but you're not safe here. If anything serious happened to Menino, the first place the police would search is the hotels—and there aren't that many left in Puerto Barrios. But if they come here and don't find you in your room, the next place they will look for you is around here. I know where you can stay. Follow me—quietly."

Joshua led the way down the steps. He circled the band shell so no one could see them, then walked swiftly across the park toward the bay.

Chapter Twenty-Three

Joshua took Samuel to the shack by the shore where he had lost his passport so many hours earlier. Without the moonlight overhead, the outlines of the huge wheels and sprockets on the ground were barely visible in the darkness. Samuel could hear the bay water licking the rocks, smell the putrid stench of salt, seaweed, and feces fusing with the thick odor of grease. He sat down on a wooden box while Joshua used a crowbar to jimmy open the shack's lock. Seconds later, he returned with a blanket.

"I think it would be better if you slept outside," he said, spreading the blanket down in a sandy area behind the shack. "If you hear any noises, it'll only be the wind or the water or some passing bird. You have nothing to fear."

"The police?"

"They'll never look for you here . . . The police don't know this shack exists. You're going to be okay. It was smart of you to give a false name—that may have saved your life. If Menino is badly hurt, no one will really care. Everyone knows he's a troublemaker. If he dies, that's more serious. Let's see what happens. Mr. Berkow, you must get on that train tomorrow—what am I saying?—in four hours. You will be far from Barrios when they come looking for you. Did you tell them at Chino's where you were going?"

"To Guatemala City."

"It's too dangerous for you to go there now."

"Even if Menino survives?"

"It's just not worth the risk," Joshua said, pulling on his goatee.

"That's not so good!"

Joshua appeared lost in thought. "But wait! That's it. You can get off the train before it reaches the capital. It makes several stops along the way."

"I see." Samuel felt somewhat relieved. He could imagine the train chuffing slowly, and him stepping off. "But where?"

"I wouldn't suggest in Bananera. It's only a village, and the Company headquarters are there. Quirigua is also no good—there are only Mayan ruins and banana plantations there. El Progreso is a small desert town. Zacapa is a little bigger. Either would be fine, if you're careful. You can start a new life there, settle down. Who knows, you might even end up getting married and raising a family."

"Yes," said Samuel, feeling the same old hopelessness that he had struggled with all his life. All well and good—a fantasy fairy tale, the part about getting married and having children. But just maybe once it would happen. And then he remembered something and a stony expression filled his face.

"What's wrong now?"

"I didn't tell you. I lost my passport—it fell into the water somewhere near here."

"You lost it?"

"It was during the rainstorm. It must have sunk to the bottom. I have no identification papers."

"Hmmm. With your passport, you could have proven you were Samuel Berkow, not this Rodolfo Fuchs. On the other hand, it might be better if you simply aren't either—you have the opportunity to be a new man. I wouldn't mind not being Joshua. Think of it this way, Mr. Berkow, you can be anyone you want."

"But the police will want proof."

Joshua considered this. "If a soldier or policeman asks you to identify yourself on the train, I think you have two choices: you can either become indignant and refuse to cooperate, or you can pull him aside and bribe him. Either way, he will surely leave you alone. You are lucky not to be a poor black man."

"And if he doesn't? If he wants to make trouble? I'm telling you, I have no passport."

Joshua peered out at the still dark bay. He noticed the tiniest of ripples dancing on the surface of the water like silver worms. "Then you're in trouble . . ."

Samuel dropped his head. He trudged over to the blanket and sat down. He felt the dew creeping into the seat of his pants, but what did it matter? He looked further out in the bay where a huge white ship was moored snugly against the pier, peaceful and calm.

"I must be going," Joshua said. There was nothing else he could do.

"Yes," said Samuel, stroking his bruised palms. He slapped at a mosquito that hovered near his left ear. "You've done so much for me. How can I repay you?"

Joshua patted his shoulder. "I wish I could do more, but I'm too tired to think. You should get some rest. You'll need it tomorrow."

"I will. You've been a good friend, Joshua. You've saved my life and risked yours. What more can a man do? If I survive this, if I somehow manage to escape this nightmare, I'll—" But he was too choked up to finish. He stood up and embraced Joshua.

"Good luck, mon," the black man said, somewhat embarrassed. He pushed away from Samuel's body and walked briskly into the darkness and disappeared.

Samuel sat down and plunked his back against the shack wall. He tucked the suitcase under his legs and spread the thin blanket over him. Before long he was slumbering. He dreamed he was attending a military funeral in a small town in the desert highlands. Six blond-haired soldiers dressed in khaki and knee socks were hefting a wooden coffin on their shoulders. When they drew near to him, they lowered the coffin for him to look inside. The wooden box had a red velvet interior and resting on top was his own body, impeccably dressed in a dark suit and striped tie. Teary-eyed, Samuel stroked the face of his own corpse, still warm to his touch. He noticed that the eyes were open and that the mouth pulled up at the corners and smiled ever so slightly. One of the pallbearers was an attractive young blond; she whispered in his ear that the dead man had been executed that very morning for sharing military secrets with the enemy. When Samuel told her that the dead man was an imposter and that he was still alive and would never reveal military secrets—all the woman had to do was to look at both of them to see they were the same man—she winked, took a cigarette out of her mouth, and gave him a kiss on the cheek as if to say that it hardly mattered.

Samuel was furious. He placed his ear on the dead man's chest and heard a low, prolonged whistle. He looked again at the dead man who continued smiling. He closed his eyes and moved his hands down to the dead man's crotch. He unbuckled the belt, pulled down the trousers, and found a stuffed canary where his penis should have been—

Samuel awoke in a frightful state. He had tipped over onto the ground during the few hours of sleep. It was nearly daybreak. He rubbed his face with his sweaty palms, wishing he could erase all his features.

What a strange dream, to be attending one's own burial. He sat up, his back against the shack, trying to understand what the dream might have meant. He had died, but where had it been? In Africa! South Africa, to be sure. The men carrying him were Afrikaaners. Lena, of course, was from Capetown. That had something to do with it. The pallbearer who had spoken to him looked a lot like her brother Max, but actually it was Lena.

So that was it! Lena had set it all up! Why couldn't she just leave him alone after all these years? Hadn't he allowed her to go home to South Africa when their marriage was beginning to fail, without any sort of encumbrance? He had let her divorce him. Why continue the torture?

Oh, Lena. She had been so disappointed, he could see it in her eyes every day after their wedding.

They had only been married for five months, living in Berlin where Samuel was completing the last few months of a commercial apprenticeship. Lena was terribly unhappy. She would wake up early every morning, bathe, paint her face, and do up her hair to have breakfast with Samuel before he headed out for work. After he left, she would spend the rest of the day tromping through their dark apartment wearing a tan silk robe, eating chocolates, opening then closing books without reading a single page. Sometimes she would play his 78 opera recordings on the gramophone.

Samuel knew, when he got home from work with groceries in his arms, that she had done absolutely nothing all day. The apartment was in chaos, with her dresses thrown down everywhere. He should have said something to her about it, as he cooked dinner for both of them, suggested that she join some sort of club, uncover some hobby, volunteer at the South African embassy—anything to keep her entertained. He knew he couldn't stay home and, well, pamper her, keep her entertained, and still earn a living. Even Klingman, who felt no particular affection for Lena—he believed she was just a silly girl, flighty and capricious—warned him that he needed to pay more attention to his wife. But Samuel—like a juggler already balancing ten balls in the air—felt incapable of discussing this with her. What did he know of depression? Whenever Lena mentioned that she felt bored and useless, he clammed up, for he felt immediately accused of having instigated her boredom.

Samuel knew nothing about sharing his life with a woman.

And then Lena started drinking, which culminated in a sorrowful incident.

One night when the South African ambassador had sailed to Capetown on home leave, the chargé d'affaires threw a party at the embassy. It was a wild evening: a hot buffet, two jazz bands, hundreds of guests, the nonstop popping of champagne. Samuel wore a dinner jacket and Lena a long, almost transparent chiffon gown that had certainly cost her—and him—more marks than he cared to know. As soon as they arrived, she went off on her own to the "powder room" and proceeded to get drunk. By nine she was chortling like a chorus girl, gliding back and forth from the dance floor to the trays of champagne while Samuel stayed seated, glumly watching her. She did the Charleston, the fandango, and the rumba with different partners, kicking off her shoes to be in stocking feet, while Samuel grew hopelessly dispirited. Half a dozen times he got up to take hold of her hand or elbow, to escort her outside for a breath of air, but Lena defiantly pulled away. When he told her that he would be departing even if it meant leaving her there alone, she stamped her feet, lifted the hem of her dress in one hand, and turned and grabbed a young Frenchman's arm.

She didn't come home that night.

Even when she went to the store after lunch and apologized in tears for her behavior, he remained cold and distant. She begged for forgiveness, but her pleading went unheard, not because he wanted to punish her or wanted to rebuke her but because he couldn't look at her without feeling bruised. Her hand on his arm made him shiver.

Samuel's reaction was to simply close down.

That night, and for the nights to come, they slept in separate rooms. After a few days, they began to talk again, in polite terms. She began to shop and cook for him, she would even tousle his hair from time to time, but he couldn't let the matter drop. Samuel kept seeing Lena naked in the arms of a Frenchman whose features remained blank.

Klingman told him he was being unfair, but Samuel was in an arctic freeze, lost under blankets of snow, unable to listen, not allowing her back into his bed.

Now that he could look clearly at the situation, twelve years later, he had to admit that he had been wrong to blame her. Samuel had forced Lena to behave childishly because he was incapable of expressing his hurt to her, and he had been blaming her for his failings, his coldness, his emotional deadness ever since.

He had been an unfeeling bastard.

Samuel shuddered, trying to shake off that image of himself—the statuelike moral rectitude that he had aspired toward. He hated himself: the shrugging wanderer who went from city to city, unwilling to drop anchor, settle down, face whatever crisis or difficulty might erupt. There were so many instances of his peripatetic nature.

And then there was the issue of his inflexibility. For example, that night at Spielberg's in Amsterdam: why had he congratulated himself all those years for standing up to a Nazi-courting Jew when, in fact, he had merely slapped his host and retreated? Another meaningless defiance! Over and over he had chosen to live in a bottled-up, protected world, where nothing could really touch him.

What was he to do now?

If he couldn't go to Guatemala City, he would have to root elsewhere, not as a skulking outcast, but as someone who like the first Zionists in Palestine had to build new lives and new identities in an altogether new landscape.

So what would the new Berkow be like?

In his new home, he would teach himself not to curb his feelings. He would be more expressive and learn to open his heart.

There was so much he could do. He would begin to dress in a more subdued manner, throw off his fancy clothes, the raiment of a Viennese dandy who sips tea twice a day and spends all his time on leisure activities like reading the newspaper and attending concerts. He would stop preening over himself.

Samuel was in a new world, and he was finally realizing he might want to be a part of it. The lies, the excuses, the rationalizations he had so readily accepted, he would have to forego, come what may. It was time to open his eyes, to live in the moment, to stop seeking shelter in poses and attitudes which, in fact, meant nothing to anyone in Guatemala.

A stray rooster crowed and two parrots cut across the lip of the bay, flying inland across the pink sky.

Samuel's chest ached. He searched around in his shirt and fished out the crucifix that had been nailed over his hotel bed. He stood up rather stiffly, held the blanket tight around his shoulder, and hooked the cross onto a nail sticking out of the shack wall. Christ's iron arms dangled tiredly from the horizontal beam; his face seemed dull and cheerless now, resigned to his fate.

Samuel heard a generator turning on somewhere along the pier, setting off a ruckus of cawing in the air. He rubbed his face again, and sat further back against the shack wall with his buttocks against his heels.

Almost without thinking, he brought the corners of his blanket to his lips and kissed them as if they were the fringes of a tallis. He dropped his head and prayed for the soul of his dead father and for the strength to go on living. He prayed for Joshua's well being and for his old friend Klingman who had surely been picked up by the Nazis. He wondered how well his Uncle Jacob had fared in getting his mother out of Germany. He even prayed for Lena, for having borne his grudges unjustly over all these years.

For his coldness and his betrayals.

For his stony hardness.

For denying her his forgiveness.

Samuel threw the cowllike blanket over his head.

And in as much as he was in a mood of compassion and forgiveness, he couldn't keep his lips from wishing for Heinrich's death—he begged God to spew an invisible acid onto his flesh so that his skin would burn ever so slowly. He imagined him scoured by his own malice and cruelty for the rest of his life. And after all this, Samuel closed his eyes and recited the only Hebrew words that he remembered from his Bar Mitzvah in Hamburg twenty-five-odd years ago:

Barechu et adonai hamevorach
Baruch adonai hamevorach le'olam va ed.

Let us praise God, to Whom our praise is due
Blessed is Adonai, the source of blessing.

Saying these words, Samuel felt chills running up and down his body. He wiped his nose, then looked up at the shack wall. The crucifix had fallen onto the ground. He picked it up, kissed it, and wrapped his hand around it.

A deep orange mist festooned the horizon. Samuel stood up, stretched, and yawned as if he had spent the last three days cramped in a trunk. He folded the blanket Joshua had given him and placed it back inside the shack in case some other troubled soul might need it in the future.

When he stretched again, several bones cracked. He placed the crucifix back on the nail. He urinated on the ground next to the shack, then walked over to the water. Shafts of yellow light raced across the surface of the bay, turning the white freighter resting against the pier into a glowing gas lamp.

Samuel looked down toward his feet where the gurgling water lapped the lichen-covered rocks. On a flat stone, just inches above the water, lay his passport. He picked it up and gently patted the pages one by one against his pants. He noticed that the ink had run a bit and blurred his name, but that most of the other information about him—his age, his place of birth, the color of his hair and eyes—remained legible.

He placed the passport in his pants pocket, feeling strangely elated at this apparent miracle. Was his luck finally changing?

He bent back down, got on his hands and knees, and dampened his face in the bay. He could see the minnows scurrying away from his fingers each time he dipped them into the water. Everything felt fresh and cool and damp in the morning light.

He let the water drip from his face, setting off circular waves in the bay. He felt so welled up with emotion that his heart was almost in his mouth. He smiled foolishly and looked back out across the bay. The sun was inches above the horizon now, no longer in his eyes, and Samuel could see the boats anchored in the deep water. He heard more cawing sounds and saw several egrets wading in a marshlike estuary, pecking into the water with their beaks, trying to slurp small fish.

Samuel turned to glance at the pier and saw a man in the distance throwing a fishing line into the harbor.

Two loud train whistles rang out. Samuel picked up his suitcase and began moving again.

CHAPTER TWENTY-FOUR

Samuel rounded the corner of the station and saw the train flush against the single platform. Several workmen were down on the tracks, tapping the rail car wheels and tightening bolts with giant wrenches. Every once in a while, there was a loud whoosh from the front of the train and the cars and the workers would be temporarily obscured by steam.

The platform bustled with the sort of activity that Samuel had only seen in Puerto Barrios on the ferry to Livingston. He saw a group of Indian women wearing colorfully patterned white blouses, ankle-length wraparound skirts, a blend of silver, obsidian, and coral around their necks. Next to them were baskets heaped with strange tropical fruits and vegetables, gourds spilling over with spices, rope hammocks, large sacks of rice and several colored beans, straw hats, painted clay jars, burning incense, plump chickens, squealing piglets.

Samuel felt excited. It was like the Saturday market on Hamburg's Lutterothstrasse, only here it was more colorful!

He was so thrilled by the women jabbering to one another in a strange dialect that for a moment he forgot all the fears that had tormented him throughout the night. He knew he should be more cautious, yet he paraded the length of the platform—suitcase in hand—smiling at the women lounging beside their wares. They giggled and smiled back, hiding their faces from him.

By the ticket booth Samuel saw a teenage Indian girl picking lice out of a child's head and behind her, a woman nursing a baby by a large basket of yellow mangoes. As Samuel passed her, she took the child off her breast and it began to cry. The mother jammed her other nipple into its gulping mouth and the baby immediately began smacking its lips and wiggling its fingers in the air. The mother hummed evenly. When she caught Samuel eyeing her, she merely pulled the infant closer to her chest, picked up a mango, and offered it to him. He shook his head, dropped a few coins in her lap, and walked on.

Seeing the woman breast-feeding unsettled Samuel, but in a good way. He realized he was weary of being alone, packing and unpacking his suitcase in strange rooms. The child and mother made him imagine a house filled with color and sunlight, and inside, a man much like himself, sitting on a sofa reading a book. His wife would be sitting with him, and a flock of children, three or four of them, playing happily at their feet.

If he met the right woman, he believed, he would remarry and things would work out differently. He wouldn't worry so much about how he should comport himself, but rather devote himself to keeping his young wife and family happy—

Another train whistle shot up, longer and louder than the previous one, and more steam flooded the platform. There was a scurrying and pattering of feet—the train was about to leave.

When the steam cleared, Samuel walked to where people were being escorted on board by a porter who simply shoved them into the three passenger cars. He saw Father Cabezón sitting cross-legged on a straw mat down a ways demonstrating to a group of Indian men how his magic candles worked. The priest's face lit up when he saw Samuel. "Guten tag, guten tag!" he called out.

"Hello, Father, I have a train to catch."

Cabezón waved him over. "It's just for a minute. Let me show you something."

"You've already shown me your tricks," Samuel said spunkily.

"I have? Well, never mind then." He looked at Samuel's suitcase and said: "I was wondering if you could do me a favor."

"Perhaps I can."

"If you come back to Puerto Barrios, would you bring me some more candles? There's a store near the Parque Centenario in Guatemala City that sells boxes of these."

Samuel smiled. "I may not be going to Guatemala City."

The priest pointed to his robe. "And I was hoping you could go to the cathedral and get me a new cassock. As you can see, this one is in shreds."

"I certainly won't be coming back here."

Father Cabezón said something back, but three sharp whistles drowned out his words. The train lurched forward a foot and stopped. There were final hugs on the platform, and passengers hurried onto the train with their bags and sacks and baskets of wares.

Across from Samuel a uniformed inspector leaned out of a compartment and shouted that the train would be leaving in two minutes and there were plenty of empty seats in the first class car immediately behind the coal bin and locomotive.

Samuel said goodbye to the priest and walked down the platform toward the front of the train. He passed some Indians with bloodshot eyes and unsteady feet embracing one another. He saw three soldiers by a post talking, sharing the same cigarette. Samuel sauntered up to them and asked for the correct time.

Anyone else would have known the soldiers didn't own watches, but Samuel was in a state of near reverie, as if tempting fate. The thinnest soldier, the one with a bullet belt around his waist, looked him up and down and said through his teeth that it was nearly seven and if he were leaving, he'd better get on the train.

Samuel was about to tip his hat when he remembered he had lost it. He smiled awkwardly and walked ahead past the first passenger compartment and the coal car, toward the locomotive. He greeted the engineer who was running through the final tests of his instrument panel. The man waved and went back to work.

Then a railway official grabbed Samuel's arm. "The train's leaving. Do you have your ticket?"

"No, I haven't bought it—"

"You can purchase one from the conductor on the train." He pointed to the carriage, gesturing for him to go on up now.

Samuel took back his suitcase and climbed slowly up the car's metal steps—scurrying to a seat would have seemed unbecoming. He went into the car and almost laughed aloud when he saw wooden seats—what could possibly make this a first-class car? Ten years ago these seats had had cloth and straw batting cushioning.

Samuel placed his suitcase on the seat facing his and sat down. At least the car was nearly empty.

The train soon lurched forward. Samuel was sitting backward since he preferred to see the landscape once the train had passed it. He lowered his window and noticed several policemen on the platform talking and motioning to one another. A man in a blue uniform came up to them and began talking animatedly. There was a clanking of chains, a series of flat, short whistles, and the train actually rolled backward ten feet.

Samuel shook his head. What was happening? Was the train about to drive itself straight into the harbor?

Then he saw Mr. Price running down the platform frantically looking up into the windows, followed by a soldier with an amused smile. At each carriage, the dwarf jumped into the air, trying to peer inside. Seconds later, Samuel saw that Mr. Price had the homburg gripped tightly in his left hand, almost as if it were a warrant for his arrest.

Samuel jerked back, flattening his head against his seat, as the train shifted forward. The dwarf was coming closer to his carriage. When he jumped up at Samuel's window, his eyes widened in recognition. Samuel simply leaned out of the carriage and snatched the homburg away from him.

"Damn you, you murdering bastard!"

Mr. Price's hand was obscured as billowing smoke filled the compartment. When the smoke had cleared, the train was beyond the platform and skirting past a gang of workers drinking out of ceramic cups near a shed. A flock of barn swallows rose like potshot into the air.

Samuel put the hat back on his head. Had Mr. Price been inside the restaurant, after all?

The train picked up speed and Samuel's eyes absorbed the passing landscape. Each chug of the engine, each turn of the wheels, marked another day of life, another mile away from captivity. It bore slowly through some thick banana groves, which darkened the inside of the compartment; after passing a few shacks, the train began winding out of the jungle.

As the train climbed, the edges and colors of the trees and shrubs sharpened in the distance. Soon it was riding the crest of a plateau that balanced precariously between a pocket of fog and a fluffy green valley below.

Samuel took deep, even breaths. This is what he needed, to be in a landscape where he could see things in the distance, not feel walled in by brush and vines. He was happy while the train continued in a straight ascent, but when it plunged into the valley the locomotive seemed to groan. The train slowed down, and appeared to be swallowed up again by thick walls of fronds, vines, and leaves similar to the Puerto Barrios landscape.

Was the train circling back to the port? Samuel considered changing sides, so he could see the landscape as it approached, but what difference would it make?

He wanted the open spaces again. A tapestry of images of Puerto Barrios flared in his mind and just as quickly slaked and disappeared. He was restless once more and began shifting around in his seat. His stomach tightened.

Two other passengers had strolled into the first-class carriage and were trying to sleep. They seemed so calm, terribly undisturbed. And here he was, with his sureness petering out and his chest beginning to pound.

If only the train would once and for all rise out of the tangled mire.

To make matters worse, a soldier entered the compartment. Samuel followed his steps on the wooden floor as he waddled guardedly down the aisle, scratching his green uniform with the tip of a pen. A sense of helplessness gripped Samuel's throat. He shut his eyes, as if that would erase the soldier's presence. When he opened them again, the soldier stood blandly by his seat.

"Your name, please?"

Samuel tried to remember Joshua's advice.

The soldier repeated the question.

"Berkow. Samuel Berkow."

The soldier wet the pen in his mouth and slowly wrote the name in his pad. He wasn't an ugly man, but his eyes, nose, mouth, and ears didn't add up to a normal face. Samuel realized this was the same soldier he had asked for the time on the platform awhile back.

When he was done writing, he showed the pad to Samuel. "Is this correct?"

"Yes. Except there is a *w* after the *o*."

The soldier nodded, made the correction, then put the pen back in his mouth. "Can I see your passport?"

Samuel dug into his pants and pulled it out. He felt his cheek twitching just above the right corner of his mouth.

"It's wet, señor."

"Yes, I know," Samuel said. "Yesterday during the storm, well, I dropped it in a puddle."

The soldier thumbed through the moist pages, from back to front, as if he were looking for something. When he reached the name and photo page, he glanced at Samuel and squinted. "I can't read your name. I'm not even sure this is a passport."

"Of course it's a passport. Can't you see the German seal on the cover?"

"An official German seal?"

"Yes, yes, of course. Let's not be foolish. "

"No one is being foolish, sir. I'm going to have to ask you to get off with me at Bananera," said the soldier, running his fingers over the passport cover.

"But my papers are in order!"

The soldier shrugged and slipped the passport into his own shirt pocket. "A man was attacked last night in Puerto Barrios. He died a little over an hour ago, just before the train was about to leave. There are witnesses.

We're under orders to detain anyone who happens to be German. The killer may be on this train on his way to—" The soldier stopped short, realizing he was saying too much. "For all I know, you could be the murderer!"

"I had nothing to do with it," Samuel said, trying to keep his voice from cracking. "Absolutely nothing. You're making a big mistake, which will get you in a lot of trouble. I hope you know that."

"I have my orders."

"Very well," said Samuel, settling his head against his seat. He glanced out the window and saw that the train was on a trestle crossing a river. He half imagined himself climbing out the window and diving into the water. It was at this moment that he remembered what Joshua had said about offering a bribe.

"We have witnesses," the soldier repeated, sitting down on the seat across the aisle.

"Very good."

"Reliable witnesses."

Samuel simply closed his eyes. He could imagine the Puerto Barrios courtroom with a long line of expert witnesses—Hugo, Guayo, Mr. Price, the cook, the Palace Hotel prostitute, the little girl on the boat to Livingston, even Joshua—ready to testify against him. A photo of Menino's fly-infested corpse would be shown to the jury. There would be no denying the crime, but perhaps he could make an argument for self-defense. He would tell the judge that several Guatemalan Nazis were planning to lynch him in the restaurant.

If he were found guilty, he'd beg the judge for mercy. Deportation, even if it meant going back to Germany, would be a godsend. He put his hand in his pocket and began to pull out his remaining bills.

Suddenly a familiar voice rang out. "Berky boy, where've you been hiding? I thought I might see you on this train."

Alfred Lewis was walking down the aisle with his signature alligator bag looped over his shoulder. He had a raccoon cap on his head and he seemed to be wearing the same clothes as the day they'd met on the *Chicacao*.

The soldier stood up, blocking Lewis's way. "Do you know this man?"

"Of course. He's an associate. He's my buddy!"

The soldier wouldn't let Lewis pass.

"Do you mind?" he asked angrily.

"This man is my prisoner."

Lewis lifted his cap and scratched his head. "Say, do you know who you're talking to, soldier?"

"I have my orders to bring this man to Bananera."

Lewis eyed him in disbelief. "This is absurd. Totally and absolutely absurd. Do you know who I am? I'm Alfred Lewis, in charge of port operations for the United Fruit Company. For your information, I could have *you* shot!"

The soldier hesitated. "Who is this man?"

"Samuel Berkow."

"Last night someone killed Menino Alvarez, the taxi driver's brother, in Puerto Barrios. This man fits the description of the attacker, Rodolfo Fuchs."

Lewis glanced down at Samuel, then rubbed his neck and brought his face up to the soldier's. "Rodolfo Fuchs? What kind of a cockamamie name is that? I already told you this is Samuel Berkow. I gave him a ride on my boat from Panama to Puerto Barrios. He is an associate of the Frutera."

"How do I know you weren't in on the murder?" the soldier asked, beginning to lose his air of assurance.

Lewis pushed a finger into the soldier's chest. "Are you trying to get yourself killed, soldier? Listen to me! This person is a very important German businessman. Look how he's dressed! And he's also a personal friend of the president. You do know who Jorge Ubico is, don't you?"

"Yes," the soldier replied, less steadily.

"I'm telling you, this man's my associate. We had dinner together last night at my house and we stayed up late discussing the building of a new vinegar distillery in Puerto Barrios. It got so late that I invited him to spend the night with me. We were both planning to be on this train, but my colleague had to go pick up his luggage, which you see here, at the Hotel International, where he was staying. We agreed to meet on the train because we still have some business to discuss before I reach Bananera."

The soldier seemed increasingly confused.

"I heard about the murder," Lewis said, "just as I was about to board the train. If you ask me, this sounds like a barroom scuffle, nothing more, among *your* people."

"What you say may be true, Mr. Lewis. But the tourist guide, Mr. Price, confirmed the description of the murderer."

Lewis laughed dismissively. "You can't be serious! Why that half-pint, that poor excuse for a human being, is no tourist guide. At best, he's a liar and a thief!"

"That may be."

"The guy's a crook! He would sell his own mother down the river for a measly buck. *Capiche?*"

"And then there's the description of the taxi driver."

"Look, I would hate to see you lose your job over this mistake." Lewis took two twenty-quetzal bills out of his wallet and stuffed them into the soldier's hand. "This will ease your doubts, I'm sure. Buy yourself something. A house for your mother. Just tell your people that no one on this train fit the description. By the time you get back, you'll have another crime to solve. Now, if you'll move along, this man and I have some important business to discuss."

The soldier peered about the compartment; the couple at the front weren't paying any attention. He folded the bills and slipped them into the side of his right boot.

"Sorry to have bothered you and your friend."

"No problem."

"I can't afford to make a mistake," the soldier said, handing Samuel back his passport. "By the way, señor," the soldier said loudly, for the other passengers to hear, "where are you going?"

Lewis tapped Samuel's shoulder and blew air into his hands.

"Quirigua," Samuel answered. "I plan to visit the ruins. Then a driver will pick me up later this afternoon and take me to Zacapa."

"I see," the soldier said, tipping his hat. "The murderer was heading for Guatemala City. Enjoy your visit, señor."

"Thank you," Samuel breathed out, feeling a rope slacking around his throat.

When the soldier had left the car, Samuel moved his suitcase so that Lewis could sit down. "I thought you had left town."

"A storm blew in and I had to change my plans," Lewis said, taking the seat across from him.

"You've saved my life again."

Lewis leaned over and put his hand on Samuel's knee. "Nonsense! I admit the thought crossed my mind that maybe you were involved in that drunken brawl. If I were a good patriotic Guatemalan citizen, I would have to turn you in. Everyone was yapping at the station house about some German being involved in a scrap with the locals. I had a hunch it might be you."

"Fuchs is the name I used last night."

"Well, that kinda confused me, Berkow. Jeez. I didn't know you had the balls for something like that. You're pretty nifty. Why'd you kill the bastard?"

There was no point in holding back. "We were together in the restaurant. I don't even remember how I got there. I wanted to leave, but he and his friends were threatening me and wouldn't let me go. So to escape, I broke a bottle over his neck. I didn't mean to kill him."

"Mean to or not, kill him you did. It's a fact." Lewis opened his alligator bag and pulled out a cigar. He lit it, and began puffing happily. "And you needn't feel so darned ashamed of it either."

"It was horrible. The insults, the blood . . ."

Lewis slapped his knees. "Hey, Berkow, you aren't going to spend the rest of your days bemoaning what you did. Take it from someone who's been through the same mill. Or do I have to remind you of what happened to me?"

"No, I remember."

"Of course you do. I killed a bum in Ohio and now you killed a bum in Puerto Barrios. Boy, those dead bums add up. That Menino Alvarez was always stirring up people with his lies and accusations. I'll bet he was some damned Nazi too, on the dole from Hitler. He tried to shake me down for a few bucks after Kingston got hurt. Told him that I would run him into the ground if he ever started up with that crap again." Lewis eyed Samuel proudly. "But you took care of that, my boy." He stuck out his thumb and forefinger. "Pow! Pow! Why, you'll be the toast of Bananera. You've done the Company a service . . . You should get some commendation! Damn, I can't believe it."

"I had no choice."

"Of course you didn't. Sometimes you find yourself going down a par-ticular road—a dangerous road, mind you—but you got to keep on wiggling your butt till you come to the end. I'm telling you that you got rid of some real garbage and there isn't any point in hashing and rehashing what you've done. I told you that when I first met you on the *Chicacao*—Germany's be-hind you, buddy. And now this killing's behind you too. No one will bother you about it, believe you me."

Samuel gazed out the window. "Well, maybe you're right."

"Damn straight."

The landscape had broadened considerably. Flat ochre fields now stretched out toward the foothills of an impressive blue mountain range. Young, knee-high fruit saplings grew in straight, orderly rows parallel to the train tracks. Every once in a while hired hands, under the cover of straw hats, turned over the soil with hoes and pitchforks.

Samuel realized he should just shut up. Lewis saw things differently—it was like discussing Schiller with someone barely able to read. Why discuss issues of remorse or contrition? Lewis wasn't a bad man, at least to him, but what would be the point to going on? And in truth, the man had just saved his life.

The train blew its whistle and began slowing down. It crawled, snake-like, across a wobbly bridge spanning a dry creek. On the other side a few thatched huts appeared. Bony mongrels approached the tracks, giving out half-hearted barks. The train entered a kind of freight yard, crowded with banana cars and flatbeds, where a work crew was building up an embankment with rocks and stones and laying down new tracks.

The braking train—metal grinding against metal—deafened all sounds. After the squealing subsided, the whistle blew again. Steam rushed by the windows and the train ground to a halt. A conductor in an ill-fitting uniform hurried over to them to check their tickets.

Lewis paid for both of them and got up.

"This is my stop, Berky," he said, tossing his lit cigar out the window, not looking where it might land. He grabbed his alligator bag. "Well, I've just entered the foyer to heaven. Also known as Bananera. Got a meeting with Dexter McKinley and some of the other bigwigs. They're pretty happy with how things are going on the docks down the coast. Maybe this'll be my chance to make a good presentation, come here permanently, get out of Barrios, that shithole."

Samuel tried standing up.

"Nah, don't even bother," Lewis coughed, as smoke curled into the compartment through the open windows. "I think they put the first-class car behind the furnace so that we could all die from the coal fumes . . . Anyway, I'm glad I saw you again, Berkow. Didn't even get a chance to ask you where you got the balls to kill the bum, eh? Well, you'll tell me about it next time."

"One day I'll pay you back, Mr. Lewis, for all you've done."

"Forget about it, Berkow. The forty quetzales are not my money—I'll write it off as one of my business expenses," Lewis chuckled. "Anyway, we now know something about each other that nobody else knows. That somehow makes us brothers, don't it?"

Samuel gave the expected response: "Yes, it does."

The whistle blew again.

"Gotta go, Sammy. That soldier's going to get off here, and my advice is to delay your trip to Guatemala City. Stop off in Zacapa or El Progreso, and spend a couple of days there resting up . . . And you know how to look me up if you come back by these parts. Remember—keep your chin down, you little devil." Lewis playfully slapped Samuel in the face, then hurried down the aisle, pushing and shoving the few oncoming passengers out of his way.

CHAPTER TWENTY-FIVE

Women and children were gathered on the platform selling tortillas and
hot sausages through the open windows. Samuel saw Lewis and the
soldier who had interrogated him walking together. Lewis seemed to be
joking with him and at one point put his arm around the soldier's waist and
tickled his stomach.

Samuel fell back against his seat. He was safe.

A few seconds later, the train gave off three strong whistle blasts and
jolted forward. Half a dozen workers came through the doors of the first-
class compartment and took up seats, two or three on a bench, near the
coal car and furnace. Then the car door opened again and a man wearing
khaki shorts and a white linen shirt entered. He had binoculars and a box
camera around his neck; sketchpads and boxes of crayons stuck out of his
open shoulder bag. As he passed Samuel, he smiled and the wealth of freck-
les on his face lit up.

"Say, do you mind if I hunker down next to you?"

"Not at all," Samuel said, reluctantly squeezing himself closer to the
window. He had wanted to be alone with his thoughts, but maybe some
company would keep him from worrying too much.

"The name's Eddie Blassingame. I'm from Little Compton, Rhode
Island."

"Samuel Berkow. Pleased to meet you."

"I arrived in Guatemala five days ago on one of the White Fleet ships
from Boston. I've spent the last two days in a guesthouse, compliments of

the Fruit Company. I'm an artist," he said proudly, pointing to the paraphernalia that he had dropped on the seat across the aisle. What about you?"

"I'm heading to the capital."

"I'll get there too." He told Samuel that he was planning to spend the next six months painting the highland Indians in their natural settings and visiting his various retired American friends who had bought fincas dirt-cheap all around the country. His wife would be joining him next month. Had Samuel read Sylvanus Morley's articles in the *Geographic* about his Mayan ruins discoveries?

"The one about Quirigua was amazing. That's my next stop. I'll be sketching the Mayan stele and zoomorphic stones—as big as a house, they say—and visiting my friend Dr. Clifford who runs the area hospital near there."

There was no pressure on Samuel to respond beyond an amiable yes or no, or an agreeing nod: loquacious Eddie Blassingame clearly loved to talk and delighted in the sound of his own voice. As the train poked along, he described his first days in Guatemala—whom he met, what he saw, what he did—in such a glowing way that Samuel wondered if they had been in the same country.

While Samuel had been in a maze of dead ends, Blassingame had yachted up the Rio Dulce to sketch Castillo San Felipe, and had gone game fishing outside of Amatique Bay. He had caught an eighty-pound grouper, hooked a small sand shark, and reeled in a couple of feisty barracudas. He had seen a hammerhead shark and plenty of dolphin. After a balmy two days of sketching seabirds and the Carib deckhands, he had been driven to Bananera. There he had played tennis in the morning, read books in the afternoon heat, and painted at twilight when the temperature dropped. He feasted and drank mint juleps late into the night with the encargados at the Company canteen.

"I'm really sorry I didn't bring my drawings. I did some wonderful watercolors of toucans and macaws and a drawing of Indians cutting down banana stems in the field."

Samuel listened in quiet astonishment, not recognizing a single scene that Blassingame described. After his tongue had galloped for twenty minutes straight, he asked Samuel about his own experiences, to which he mumbled that he had rested in his air-conditioned hotel in Puerto Barrios.

What else could he do? Tell him about the Nazis in Germany; the dwarf Mr. Price; the aborted trip to Livingston; his cousin Heinrich? Should he tell Blassingame about how he had crawled like a slithering worm until he had salvaged his self-respect, if not his life, by killing someone?

How would this tireless chatterbox understand? Samuel wasn't even sure he could explain the last forty-eight hours to his old friend Klingman, a man who knew him inside and out. He realized that he had been through something so unique that he would never ever be able to explain it to anyone.

The locomotive whistled loudly, and the train began slowing down again. Nearly an hour had gone by. It was none too soon for Samuel, whose legs had fallen asleep in his cramped position and whose brain couldn't absorb any more of Blassingame's optimistic chitchat.

When the train stopped, the American struggled up to gather his trappings. "I've enjoyed your company and I'm sorry we haven't gotten to know one another better."

When Samuel gave him his hand, Blassingame pumped it up and down nearly a dozen times and then hurried out of the compartment. He was met by a gray-haired man in a white poplin suit who was probably Dr. Clifford, and a barefoot servant who relieved him of his belongings.

There was no station in Quirigua, but a handful of Indians zoomed to the side of the train to sell food. A minute later, the train pulled out of the station. The green shoulders of bananas gave way to brown savannas and eventually to desert and cactus. The air grew hotter, drier. Samuel could finally breathe again without feeling his lungs clotted with moisture.

Orange dirt extended for miles till it met up with a blue wall of mountains. Samuel saw a rapidly flowing river, the Motagua, where oarsmen struggled to keep their cayucas from banking on sandbars and running aground.

The desert fascinated Samuel. The cacti were so proud and unyielding, dark olive sculptures whose many arms opened supplicatively to the sky or angled sideways and down for no apparent reason. Though locked into a barren and dusty landscape, they managed to not only survive, but also to flower and bear pink fruit.

Samuel glanced up at the sky. Not a shred of cloud marred the blue umbrella over which the sun blazed—it wasn't simply a mass of burning gases, but a holy stone, a ball of fire that could force people down on their hands and knees to pray for its strength and power . . .

What were desert nights like? Samuel saw a bone-white moon against a sheet of black velvet. He felt the cool of evening spreading over him and watched numberless stars coming into view. He saw constellations sliding across the sky like slow-moving desert caravans. He would learn to identify and trace the Great Bear, Aries, the Twins, the giant hunter Orion, the Pleiades, the archer Sagittarius. He would be able to recognize Scorpio, his own zodiac sign, with its curved stinger poised tensely in the sky.

At some point along the way, the train stopped abruptly. It was stuck in the desert, halfway to Zacapa. Dazed and dreamy-eyed, Samuel stuck his head out the window. He saw the trouble. Two boys were frantically herding dozens of goats across the tracks. The engineer hooted impatiently, but the procession of hooves and ringing bells continued at its own pace.

The children in the compartment began racing down the aisles, while their parents called to them in laughter. There was nothing to celebrate— after all, the train was being delayed—but the passengers didn't care. Their travel had no sense of urgency. They were free to enjoy the moment.

The gaiety around Samuel infected him, and soon he too was yelling good-humored insults and baaing sounds to the goats.

Fifteen minutes went by. The goats crossed the tracks only to suddenly buck and go back the way they had come. The hooting and howling and dancing kept up in the car. Finally, a shot rang out and the goat herd stampeded. The train lurched forward and the passengers settled back down into their seats.

Samuel soon fell asleep.

An hour later, around midday, the train pulled into the Zacapa station. Samuel didn't know if he should disembark. He had momentarily escaped capture, but he was still being sought. Lewis had suggested that he spend a few days in Zacapa until all the excitement had waned.

The train wheels locked. The conductor opened the compartment door and shouted that the train would be making a half-hour stop for repairs; the passengers could leave their belongings on their seats—there was enough time to get off and eat lunch.

The children squealed and rushed past the conductor, and the parents hurried after them. When the car was completely empty, Samuel grabbed his suitcase, paid the conductor for the latest segment of his trip, and went down the metal steps to the platform.

The bright sun stung his face—it felt so good. Chills ran up and down his body as if the heat were drawing the mustiness out of his joints and sockets. He put his suitcase down on the platform and stretched back till every bone in his body seemed to crack.

A young girl of nine or ten approached. "Tacos, señor, with beans or goat meat. Cheap." She was barefoot and clothed in a simple cotton sack. She was squinting even though she had a straw hat to shade her eyes.

"Do you have any bread and cheese?" Samuel asked.

The girl giggled. "Bread? We don't have bread in Zacapa."

"No bread? How's that possible?"

The girl tossed her head back and shouted to a woman with gray hair tied in a bun who was peddling tacos to other passengers from a shaded spot on the floor.

"Isn't it true, Mamá, that there's no bread in Zacapa?"

Without slowing her deft hands, she answered: "You know that the nearest bakery is in El Progreso."

"See?" the girl answered.

Samuel smiled.

What he had missed these last two weeks, first on the liner from Hamburg and then in Puerto Barrios, was a sense of usefulness, a purpose to his life. Too much free time. He needed to work!

He fished out a few coins and bought two bean-filled corn tortillas from the girl. He wolfed them down without chewing and bought two more.

His appetite had returned. *Bread*, he kept thinking giddily, *that's a good idea*. He didn't know how he could do it, but he was convinced that without knowing anything about Zacapa or bread making, he could open a bakery here! Not baking fancy rye or date-nut bread, but something simple and wholesome—flour, yeast, salt, and water.

Samuel sat down on his suitcase to think. A couple of young whelps came up to him and stuck out their hands for money. He obliged by dropping pennies in their hands. They seemed so pleased. Next to the mother selling tacos, an old hag argued with a cripple over who had permission to sell roasted cashews from this spot—they seemed on the verge of hitting each other.

Then a boy came up to Samuel, flashed him a stained card, and offered to carry his bag to the very best hotel in Zacapa. Samuel shook his head, but the boy wouldn't leave.

He looked out to the town and stared at a leafless ceiba. What did he know about baking? It would be foolish. He couldn't stay in Zacapa. He was on a mission. Whether Heinrich wanted to see him or not, Samuel had promised his Uncle Jacob to bring him his personal regards.

He finally asked the young boy to carry his suitcase and follow him into the train station. They headed over to the telegraph office and he asked the clerk for a message form, which he filled out.

Heinrich. Am arriving later today on the train from Puerto Barrios. Work or no work I must see you. We have much to discuss.

The train whistled and Samuel paid for the telegram. He asked the boy to follow him to the same compartment he had been in before. Fortunately, no one had claimed his bench. He gave the boy some coins and snuggled into his seat, trying to fall back asleep.

* * *

As the train continued on its way, Samuel began thinking about what precisely he wanted to "discuss" with Heinrich. Certainly he wanted to talk about "the incident," the one that had driven them apart when they were boys. It was time for Samuel to face the truth and admit he had failed his cousin.

They had been such good friends, inseparable, playing together and going on common escapades. With so many girls in the family, they were almost like siblings. Once, when Samuel was spending the weekend at his uncle's apartment, Heinrich confessed that he looked upon him not just as his cousin, but as his brother and very best friend. *We are like twins*, Heinrich had said, *milk brothers*.

Lying in the single bed next to his cousin so many years earlier, Samuel had wondered what he had meant. Instead of saying something—*You are my best friend too*—he had felt smothered by Heinrich's confession. He had been unable to speak.

"Samuel, did you hear what I said?"

Samuel feigned sleep, actually letting out a false snore.

Heinrich had rolled over, confident that they were best of friends.

Summer was almost half over. The next day, Heinrich, his sisters, and his parents went away to a spa in Interlaken, Switzerland.

Toward the end of August, the families got together again at his Uncle Jacob and Aunt Gertie's apartment. Heinrich had been bored spending so much time with his sisters. He beamed when he saw Samuel and gave him a big hug. Again, Samuel had been disturbed by the show of emotion and he gravitated toward his girl cousins who were only too happy to have another male companion.

After lunch that first day, Samuel's mother and aunt took the girls shopping to the center of Hamburg and the boys were left alone while the uncles talked. Heinrich asked his cousin if he wanted to go swimming with him in a nearby lake. After some hesitation, Samuel nodded and the boys went off, walking in the shadows to avoid the hot sun, picking blackberries along the way, acting as if everything were normal between them. But something was different.

The lakeshore was crowded with summer picnickers. After splashing around and tossing a ball with some boys Heinrich knew from synagogue, the two cousins decide to swim across the lake to their favorite spot—a forested island in the middle where they could swing on a rope from a tree and jump into the water.

It was a half mile to the island, but they were both good swimmers. Once they got there, they climbed up the steep banks and lay on a flat rock just below the rope to catch their breath. After a few minutes of lying there together, Heinrich asked Samuel if he was angry at him for something.

Samuel had shaken his head, but a minute later he confessed that his parents were constantly fighting. He was worried that they would be divorcing.

"You seem so quiet," Heinrich said, his already high voice cracking.

Samuel looked across the lake. "I don't know, Heinrich, but lately I've really enjoyed being alone. It gives me a chance to think. I want to be a friend to myself."

Heinrich sat up. "What do you mean by that?"

"I need to find out what it is that I want to do."

"But Samuel, aren't I your best friend?"

Before Samuel could answer with some sort of pat, innocuous lie, Martin Gibbel, a gentile a few years older than the cousins, came out of the woods. Heinrich knew him from gymnasium, and he and his classmates considered the boy a bully. He told Heinrich and Samuel to leave, for this rock was his. He was a brawny-shouldered boy, already sprouting fuzz on his upper lip. His eyes were a deep blue, like cobalt, and very cold.

Samuel was no fighter and he got up to leave. Heinrich, on the other hand, felt that in principle the rock belonged to no one and said so.

Martin pushed Heinrich hard. He fell on the rock and started screaming in pain. A huge gash had opened up on his back. Martin fell on top of Heinrich and the boys started fighting. They rolled and tumbled, arms locked, onto a bed of pine needles. Heinrich was shouting out for Samuel, as the stronger boy pummeled him.

It would have been a simple thing for Samuel to go over and help his cousin.

Instead—without knowing why—he simply rushed over and grabbed the rope, pushed off the rock, and plunged into the lake. He let himself go down in the water till his toes touched the squishy bottom. Then he pushed himself slowly up. He felt his lungs were about to explode from the pressure, but he was not about to rush his ascent. When he broke the surface of the lake, he coughed and gasped for oxygen. He exaggerated his effort, as if to say to any witness that he had not come to his cousin's aid because he had slipped off a rock and nearly drowned.

Samuel swam slowly back to the rock, keeping his head just under the surface so that he could not hear any sound. When he reached the island, Heinrich was standing on the rock holding his left elbow. His right eye was black and closing, and his bottom lip had swollen to double its size.

"You did nothing to help me," he wailed.

Samuel was panting. "When I got up to help you, I slipped off the rock and nearly drowned. Didn't you notice?"

"You didn't slip," Heinrich cried. "When Martin attacked me, you dove—to get away."

"Liar. You don't care a thing about me. I almost drowned. I thought Martin was your friend from school and you were just horsing around!"

"Horsing around? Look at me!" Heinrich screamed, pulling on his bottom lip so more blood oozed out. "Does this look like a game to you?"

Samuel pushed his cousin away. "So who told you to start a fight with that big lug? Anyone could have seen that he could whip us both. It was stupid of you."

"You betrayed me."

"You're nothing but a big baby," Samuel shot back.

Heinrich glared at his cousin and spit blood to the ground. "I will never forgive you for that."

"Good. I'm tired of you," Samuel said before jumping in the water and swimming back.

The two cousins never discussed the incident again. That was all they said to each other that afternoon, and for many afternoons to come.

Months later, they started talking to each other again, but it was in a completely different framework, almost like relatives forced to be civil to one another. Their friendship was never the same again.

Samuel sat on the bench with his eyes closed as the train wound up a mountain. He kept seeing Heinrich's bloody face. He realized that not only had he failed to help his cousin, he had refused to take any responsibility for his cowardice. In fact, he had secretly taken pleasure in Heinrich's thrashing, as punishment for having tried to make their bond more intimate earlier in the summer.

All these years, Samuel had refused to accept blame for what had happened. He had seen so much brutality and carnage on the battlefield, and had become an expert at picking up injured comrades and dead bodies after an onslaught.

He had felt no responsibility for what had been, for Heinrich, perhaps his most terrifying afternoon. He had abandoned his cousin.

And was Samuel so stupid, so self-absorbed to think that his cousin had ever forgotten that incident?

The train stopped briefly in El Progreso, a small town known for its cashews, before beginning its rise out of the country's central plains. Three hours later, the train pulled into the station house in Guatemala City. Dozens of passengers disembarked rapidly.

Samuel was among the last to leave his compartment. The sun was going down and the gas lamps had already been lit. The air was crisp and cool, almost like a September evening in Hamburg, when it seemed as if the day was pivoting between returning to summer or beginning the slow descent toward winter.

On the platform, he let one of the countless shoeless urchins carry his suitcase. The boy seemed to know exactly where to take him. They moved down recently cobblestoned streets until the boy stopped at a small hotel on Séptima Avenida with the unlikely name of La Casita. While the boy waited just inside the hotel gate, Samuel crossed under the wooden lintel and filled out the registry forms at a small table in the lobby. As soon as the clerk gave Samuel a key to a room on the second floor, the boy came into the hotel carrying his bag.

Samuel opened the door to his room and the boy placed the suitcase on the bed. Samuel tipped him generously and awaited a response. The boy pointed to his throat, indicating that he was a mute. Samuel smiled and shook his head in thanks.

The room had heavy wooden furniture and a woolen Indian blanket on the bed. Samuel closed the door, opened his suitcase, and put his few shirts, pants, and undergarments in their proper places in a closet that smelled of mothballs. He glanced around the room; a moth was frantically trying to free one of its wings from a crack in the window.

Samuel went back downstairs and entered the first restaurant he saw. After eating a simple meal of steak, potatoes, and squash, he walked along the stores in El Portal. He enjoyed the chilly evening air and sat down on a stone bench under a rubber tree in the Parque Central. Bootblacks approached him and pointed to his dusty shoes, but Samuel shook his head no. He wanted to sit quietly alone. He was enthralled by the façade of the Metropolitan Cathedral, austere with its orange stones, directly in front of him; and, to his left, the blocks of green stone set in piles behind barbed wire that would become the National Palace.

Tradition and renovation.

Soon he returned to his room to bed down for the night. Would he sleep soundly? He sensed that this kind of respite was still months away.

He took off his clothes and slipped into the cold sheets of his bed. He was exhausted, but wide awake. In quick succession he saw the faces of Lena, Alfred Lewis, Mr. Price, Joshua, and finally the bloodied head of Menino. But he had escaped and was glad to finally be in Guatemala City, even if he still felt somewhat ill at ease.

Tomorrow would be a significant day. Could he make amends with his cousin by simply apologizing for what had happened decades ago? It might not make a difference, but in the morning he would go to his cousin's store, La Preciosa, and say hello. He would look into his eyes and apologize.

What Heinrich would say or do was another matter.

RUINS
a novel by Achy Obejas
208 pages, trade paperback original, $15.95
*A selection of the Barnes & Noble Discover Great New Writers program

"Usnavy, a man of tender resolve who wants only to do his part as a good revolutionary . . . is nimbly drawn, with genuine depth . . . endearing, sad and funny."
—*New York Times Book Review*

"Obejas evinces a new, focused lyricism as she penetrates to the very heart of the Cuban paradox in a story as pared down and intense as its narrator's life."
—*Booklist* (*starred review*)

BLACK ORCHID BLUES
a novel by Persia Walker
272 pages, trade paperback original, $15.95

"The best kind of historical mystery: great history, great mystery, all wrapped up in a voice so authentic you feel it has come out of the past to whisper in your ear."
—Lee Child, author of *Worth Dying For*

"A remarkable achievement; imagine the richly provocative atmosphere of Walter Mosley or James Ellroy's best period work, and a savvy, truly likable heroine, and you have *Black Orchid Blues*. Persia Walker is a rising superstar in the mystery genre."
—Jason Starr, best-selling author of *The Pack*

THE DEWEY DECIMAL SYSTEM
a novel by Nathan Larson
256 pages, trade paperback original, $15.95

"Like *Motherless Brooklyn* dosed with Charlie Huston, Nathan Larson's delirious and haunting *The Dewey Decimal System* tips its hat, smartly, to everything from Philip K. Dick's dystopias to Chester Himes's grand guignol Harlem novels, while also managing to be utterly fresh, inventive, and affecting all on its own."
—Megan Abbott, Edgar-winning author of *The End of Everything*

"The perfect blend of dystopia and the hard-boiled shamus. It's great to know that there are still debut novels coming through the pipe that can knock me on my ass. With *The Dewey Decimal System* Nathan Larson has announced his arrival with style and clarity. I'll be first in line for his second novel, and his twentieth."
—Victor Gischler, author of *The Pistol Poets*

AMERICAN VISA
a novel by Juan de Recacoechea
260 pages, trade paperback original, $14.95

"Dark and quirky, a revealing excursion to a place over which 'the gringos' to the north always loom."
—*New York Times Book Review*

"Beautifully written, atmospheric, and stylish in the manner of Chandler . . . a smart, exotic crime fiction offering."
—George Pelecanos, author of The *Turnaround*

THE UNCOMFORTABLE DEAD
(WHAT'S MISSING IS MISSING)
a novel of four hands by Paco I. Taibo II & Subcomandante Marcos
304 pages, trade paperback , $15.95
*Expanded edition with bonus materials, including an interview with Subcomandante Marcos by Gabriel García Márquez

"Great writers by definition are outriders, raiders of a sort, sweeping down from wilderness territories to disturb the peace, overrun the status quo and throw into question everything we know to be true . . . On its face, the novel is a murder mystery, and at the book's heart, always, is a deep love of Mexico and its people."
—*Los Angeles Times Book Review*

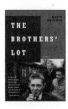

THE BROTHERS' LOT
a novel by Kevin Holohan
320 pages, trade paperback original, $15.95

"Kevin Holohan's strange yet disconcertingly recognizable world has echoes of Flann O'Brien's and Monty Python's, but there is rage as well as absurdist comedy. *The Brother's Lot* is a memorable, skillfully wrought, and evocative satire of an Ireland that has collapsed under the weight of its contradictions."
—Joseph O'Connor, author of *Star of the Sea*